40 Days 40 Nights

Wendy Cartmell

Costa Press

DEDICATION

To Mum and Dad, for their love, patience and
understanding.

Day 1

They found the body at 04:00 hours. As he drove to the scene Sergeant Major Crane's hands gripped the steering wheel, his vision sharpened and his breathing rapid. Excitement that he had something to investigate overlaid, as always, with guilt. For his good fortune was at the expense of another man's life. He parked his car in front of the Aldershot Garrison Sports Centre, a squat grey lump surrounded by green and rushed to the scene. It was 04:45 hours.

He slowly walked around the remains, wearing protective clothing over his dark suit and white shirt, keeping well clear of the corpse, whilst he waited for the pathologist, Major Martin. As Crane crouched down to get a clearer view of the dead man, voices overhead interrupted his study.

Rising, he called, "We're down here, Major. The body's at the bottom of the steps." Crane's words echoed around the large underground cavern that was the underbelly of the huge Olympic sized swimming pool. The Major emerged, ducking his head under large grey pipes as he picked his way to the bottom of the stairs, encumbered by his medical case and the protective overalls he was wearing.

"I thought I recognised your voice, Crane. Right, what have we got?" The Major placed his case some way from the body and turned to look at it.

Crane called Sergeant Billy Williams from out of the shadows.

"Well, sir," Billy said, "as members of Team GB are on the garrison as part of their preparations for the Olympic Games, routine security patrols are made of the swimming pool every hour during the night. The soldiers keep in touch by radio whilst they are separated. Corporal Simms failed to meet the others at the front door of the complex and didn't answer urgent calls on his radio. So," Billy consulted his notes, "Lance Corporal Fielding went to find him. He saw Simmons crumpled at the bottom of the stairs here, that lead underneath the swimming pool. Unable to find a pulse, he swept the area, which he found to be empty and retreated. He then called the Royal Military Police as per procedure."

"So, the question is," Crane took over from Billy, "did the lad fall or was he killed?"

"For God's sake, Crane, at the moment I have no idea." Major Martin rose from his examination. "His neck appears to have been broken. It could be from a fall, possibly accidental, or he could have had some help. Another option is that someone surprised him and broke his neck here at the bottom of the stairs. I won't know anything until I get him on the table." The Major snapped off his gloves.

"Which would be?"

"Later this morning."

"I don't need to remind you…"

"No, Sergeant Major, you do not," the Major's voice

was as taut as the latex he had just peeled from his hands. "I am well aware of the sensitivity of the situation at the moment, as no doubt Captain Edwards will also be happy to make clear to me. Including the Commanding Officer and anyone else who feels they have a right to put in their two pennies worth." Glancing at his watch, he continued. "It's nearly 05:30 hours. I'll do the post mortem at 10:00 hours. You can come if you want."

"I will… sir." Crane eventually finishing with the acknowledgement that Major Martin was an ex-officer. Even though Crane was a Sergeant Major, his position within the Special Investigations Branch of the Military Police, enabled him to cut across the rank system when on an active investigation. Making the Branch as feared as it was respected. But officers, even ex-ones such as Major Martin, who was an accredited Home Office Pathologist whilst in the army, still expected the deference their rank deserved.

Crane decided to attend the post mortem later that morning, meeting the Major in the morgue at Frimley Park Hospital. Not out of ghoulish curiosity, nor because he enjoyed seeing corpses reduced to a pile of organs and empty cavities, but simply because it was the quickest way to find out how Corporal Simms died. Actually, Crane hated everything about the morgue. The sterility, the smell, the noises. An incongruous operating theatre, where instead of opening up a living human being to heal them, doctors cut open a dead body to find out what had gone wrong. Once he was suitably kitted out and standing beside the metal trolley that held Corporal Simms in its icy embrace, Crane asked Major Martin to start on the neck first.

"I hope you aren't trying to tell me how to do my job, Crane?" the Major shouted over the noise of the grinding electric saw he was holding in his hand, which loomed perilously close to Crane's head instead of the corpse's.

"Not at all," said Crane, only just managing to duck out of the way in time. "It's the quickest way to get me out of your hair." A bizarre comment as the Major was practically bald under his protective headgear. "Figuratively speaking, of course," Crane finished lamely, adding, "sir."

"Very well, Crane." The Major turned off and put down the saw, then manipulated the young Corporal's neck. "Definitely broken. Feels like the spinal cord is ripped as well." Turning the head backwards and forwards, and peering at the face, he continued, "No obvious sign of trauma."

"Any sign of trauma to the neck itself? Bruising from fingers, or a garrotte of some kind?"

"No nothing. Here give me a hand to flip him over," the diminutive Major asked Crane. Crane helped to turn Corporal Simms over onto his front. A young man reduced to an ignominious naked body. Even through latex gloves the grey flesh felt rubbery and unyielding, reminding Crane of the texture of squid he once ate and hated. He waited whilst the Major cut through and then peeled back the defensive skin covering the young soldier's neck, exposing the bones and spinal cord.

"There!" the Major exclaimed with some satisfaction. "Broken between C3 and C4 and here are the loose ends of the spinal cord, see?"

Crane didn't want to, but glanced at the neck anyway, seeing mangled flesh and bones that meant nothing to him. Straightening up he said, "So now we definitely know what killed him."

"Certainly. Broken neck and spinal cord."

"But not how it happened."

"No evidence to suggest foul play at this stage. I would say it was most likely an accident."

"Most likely or definitely?" Crane wanted the distinction clarified.

"Most likely," confirmed the Major turning back to get on with the rest of the Post Mortem. "Now get out of my hair, Crane!"

By 11:00 hours Crane was reporting the findings to Captain Edwards.

"Excellent news," was Captain Edward's verdict as he smiled at Crane.

"Excellent sir? A soldier s dead!" Crane looked at Edwards, unable to mask the horror that must be etched on his face. Not wanting to believe what he had just heard.

"Oh for goodness sake, Crane. You know what I mean. Excellent news that it was an accident." Edwards went on, "I'll draw up a press release immediately to say that there has been an unfortunate accident, that has resulted in the death of a soldier on the garrison and, of course, confirm that to the family." Edwards gathered up his papers. A clear indication the meeting was over.

"But, sir, are you sure you shouldn't err on the side of caution and treat it as murder? There could be a potential threat to the athletes here. Someone could have been staking out the swimming pool and been surprised by Corporal Simms." Crane leaned forwards, his elbows on his knees.

"Crane, as I see it I am 'erring on the side of caution' as you put it. I am not about to spread panic throughout the Olympic community and the local community, by calling an accident a murder. Imagine the implications." Captain Edwards shuddered. "No. Sorry, Crane, accidental death it is."

"But -"

"No buts, Sergeant Major." Edwards rose from behind his desk, as was his habit, showing Crane that he was not only superior in rank, but superior in height.

Crane stood, but didn't leave the office. "Major Martin said 'most likely' not 'definitely'. I specifically queried that point."

"Crane, that's enough. I really think you are splitting hairs. I'm going with accidental death." Edwards moved from behind the desk and opened the door. "That will be all."

"Sir," Crane moved towards the open door. Then stopped. "You don't think?"

"I don't think anything, Crane!" Edward's voice rang out, causing a passing soldier to stop and look round. "And neither should you. Dismissed."

As Crane stalked off he tried to rein in his temper by reminding himself his special assignment was only for just over a month. As of today he was responsible for security on the garrison for forty days and forty nights whilst Team GB and then the Paralympians were on the garrison - so he better get on with it.

Night 1

The cold seeped into his bones, making him shiver. From his position under the trees, Padam Gurung could just make out the sports centre, ethereal in the dim light, as if the hopes and dreams of all the athletes that practiced there surrounded it. He prayed their hopes and dreams would not be shattered as his had been, for he knew how important hope was. Without hope there was nothing.

Shifting his small frame slightly to avoid a sharp branch from the tree he was leaning against, Padam wrapped the army great coat given to him by the Gurkha Welfare Society more tightly around him. His friends back in Aldershot town centre couldn't understand why he spent night after night outside like this, keeping silent watch over the garrison in general and now the sports centre in particular. But Padam loved to be in the open. After spending a lifetime outdoors, firstly in the British Army and then working his small farm in Nepal, he found the dirty, small flat he shared with five other men, claustrophobic.

Plus, he needed a purpose and what better purpose than being close to his beloved army? Serving it as best he could, even in old age, by standing guard in the cold early hours of the morning. He chose the sports centre tonight as he felt it was most vulnerable to terrorist attack. After all, what could you do to an athletic track? Plant track side bombs that would be found by the regular checks? So a building, particularly one containing an Olympic sized swimming pool, squash courts, gymnasium and badminton courts, needed his protection.

He couldn't get inside, of course, to patrol the actual building, nor could he openly patrol the parameter, so he did what Gurkhas do best. Lie patiently, hidden. Watching. Waiting.

Needing to move, as his old joints were stiffening, he carefully lay face down in the long grass. He wished for a pair binoculars, although he knew they were of little use at night. But even so they would be better than just his rheumy old eyes. Buying a pair was out of the question, though. He had no possessions to speak of and no money to buy anything with. Lured by the promise that 'England will look after you', after the Gurkha Re-settlement Agreement in 2009, championed by Johanna Lumley, he had sold everything he owned in Nepal to pay for his visa and flight. His family were now marooned back in Nepal and he was stranded in Aldershot. His hope for a glorious future in the land he had once fought for, shattered by the reality of life in England.

Glancing up at the sky, he saw the slight lighting that heralded the coming dawn, still about an hour away. He had to be gone at first light. With part of Team GB on the garrison in preparation for the start of the Olympic Games he knew he couldn't be found, even though his presence was benign. Who would believe him? And anyway how would he be able to explain, with his English limited to basic words such as 'hello' 'goodbye' and 'thank you'.

Lifting his head, as he prepared to crawl back under cover of the trees, he saw a flicker of a shadow out of the corner of his eye. Was it something, or just his old eyes playing tricks? Temporary night blindness, after looking at the lighter dawn sky? From his vantage point he had an uninterrupted view of the front of the building and part of the left hand side. But could see nothing beyond the right corner. Taking great care not to move his body and rustle the long grass, his eyes swept from left to right along the length of the sports centre. Nothing. Slowly peering back along the grey frontage he still saw nothing untoward, until he reached the left side of the building.

A black smudge. Low against the wall. Padam waited. The smudge waited. The rising dawn called to Padam, urging him to move so he could return to the town centre safely. But Padam knew he must stay where he was. His arthritic knees locked tight and his thigh muscles went into spasm, but Padam still refused to move. Ignoring the cries of pain that were turning into screams. Until his vigilance was at last rewarded. The smudge left the shelter of the wall and ran low and fast towards a clump of trees about 100 yards distant.

Crawling backwards, stiff legged, into the shelter of the trees, Padam rolled over and began to massage his limbs, slowly coaxing his knees to bend. As he hobbled away in the early light of dawn through the trees towards Queens Avenue, he pondered on who he should speak to about what he had seen.

Night 2

Here I stand among you, the mischief makers. Those who attack Islam. I am mired in your society, the modernity and the western influence that is also perverting my country. I am engulfed by your media - television, radio, newspapers and magazines. It sickens me how they try to subvert people, especially the young, with song, dance, fashion, alcohol, drugs, sex and freedom.

In your towns I see citizens gorging themselves on un-necessary trinkets. Electronic nick-knacks they insist they cannot live without. Bigger, better televisions, radios, mobile phones and computers. All the while worshiping their God - money. This way of life is abhorrent to me.

I am disgusted by your young people. Boys who think they are men, who have no respect for themselves, their elders or their leaders. They don't work, just stand around on street corners openly drinking alcohol. And don't get me started on your women. I have never seen such sights. Acres of female flesh on show. Women degrading themselves, by allowing men to ogle parts of their body that should only be seen by their husband. Jezebels taunting every man who walks past them in the street. At least on the garrison, I am shielded somewhat from their adulterous provocations.

But even here I cannot escape their tantalising ways. Look here comes one now. A woman serving in your army. A woman who should be at home looking after her husband, children or parents. See how she marches along head proudly held high. The sight is repulsive to me. She should be modestly veiled when in public. By not doing so, she spits in the eye of Muhammad, the Prophet, who is the epitome of all virtue and honour.

But in truth some of the men I have met are no better than their blasphemous women. Yesterday I happened to meet one of the padres on the garrison. A Christian leader, looking after the spiritual wellbeing of the men and women who serve here. He wanted to engage us in ideological and theological discussion, but I found I couldn't speak to him. Watching him, a man of religion, quaff alcohol - I tell you it made me feel ill. So I made my excuses and walked away. I couldn't stand it that you evil infidels in the West think that you can pick and choose which parts of your religion to adhere to. Separating out the bits you don't want and discarding them. Thinking that it's enough to turn up to church once a week and go through the motions.

For a Muslim this practice is unthinkable. The Muslim world view does not compartmentalise and dichotomise the various areas of life. It is holistic. Our beliefs are incorporated into every area of our daily lives. Our religion tells us how to dress, bathe, eat and pray. No part of a devout Muslim's life is separate from his Islamic beliefs.

And so it has become our cause to expel the

crusaders from our homelands and re-establish Sharia law. This cause is not without reason. We are following the command of the Qur'an. Look, this is the place. Let me share with you for a moment the words from our Holy Book:

Fight those who believe not
In good nor the Last Day,
Nor hold that forbidden
Which hath been forbidden
By God and His Apostle,
Nor acknowledge the Religion
Of Truth. (Qur'an 9:29)

How can you argue with that? You Westerners don't acknowledge the religion of truth, the Muslim religion. So, for this reason my men and I take part in the struggle. In the jihad. An external struggle against the forces of evil and non-believers. That's why I am here in your country. In England.

For the time being I am forced to wear a mask. No one must know what lies behind it. My real thoughts and feelings. I will play my part. All the while looking for an opportunity to strike, to teach you, the infidels, a lesson you will never forget.

Day 3

Crane imagined he saw the face of Captain Edwards reflected back at him in the mirror and his curled fists itched to smash it to smithereens.

"Bloody Edwards," he turned and said to his wife, "this is his way of getting back at me, because he doesn't like my methods when it comes to investigating. Tosser. He likes the solutions though."

Crane's fingers fumbled with the mess of his tie, so he gave up and tried to rip it off.

"Come here, Tom, and let me do that for you."

Moving over to the bed, he sat next to his wife, Tina, and allowed her to put right the chaos he had created, calming slightly under her slow languid movements.

"I'm sure you're over reacting," she said, her dark eyebrows arching.

Crane felt the pressure of her hands on him, an attempt to stop him rising from the bed.

"Captain Edwards has great respect for you, Tom, and anyway, what could be more important than protecting Team GB as they prepare for the Olympic Games on Aldershot Garrison?"

"Solving crimes, not babysitting. For fuck's sake, Tina, Special Investigations Branch doesn't do babysitting, especially not warrant officers. This is a job for the Royal Military Police."

Crane jumped up and began to comb his short dark hair, that didn't in fact need any combing. He carefully inspected his face in the mirror, checking to see that his beard, that he'd had to get special permission to grow, covered most of the scar that ran across his cheek. A souvenir from shrapnel in Afghanistan. Chucking the comb back on the dressing table, he returned to the bed and couldn't help smiling at Tina lying there looking like a beached whale. Albeit a glowing one.

"Anyway, enough of that." Crane pushed his anger and frustration to the back of his mind and continued, "How are you and the little man doing this morning?"

"Fine, I think, although he's a bit stuck at the moment, see?"

As Tina pulled back the duvet to expose her swollen stomach, he saw a large bump close to her extended belly button. Reaching over, Crane massaged his son's extremity until the baby shifted slightly and the lump disappeared. It worked every time and every time it amazed him.

"Are you staying in bed?"

"No, I think I'll get up if you'll just give me a hand and I'll come downstairs for a cup of tea."

After helping Tina, Crane ran downstairs, collected his briefcase from just inside the front door and slipped his suit jacket over his white shirt. As Branch Investigators don't wear army uniform whilst on normal duties, Crane had found a uniform of his own. Dark suit, white shirt and dark tie. The white shirt close fitting to emphasis his stocky muscular build. Placing the case on the large pine table in the kitchen, he checked through the files to make sure he had everything he needed. He was looking through the Strategic Security Review as Tina joined him.

"Are those the security arrangements?" she asked, peering over his shoulder as she tied back her long dark hair.

"Yes, Staff Sergeant Jones seems to have done a good job. I've really no idea why I need to oversee it. God knows what Edwards was thinking of."

"For goodness sake, stop grumbling, Tom. It's not for ever. It's just a temporary arrangement."

"I know, but it's still over a month." Glancing down at the calendar stapled to the inside cover, he said, "Thirty-seven days to be precise."

"And nights, don't forget, if you're going to be that pedantic," Tina replied.

Those phrases rattled around in his head as he drove from his semi-detached Victorian house in Ash, towards the Royal Military Police Barracks on Aldershot Garrison. Forty days and forty nights. His own personal wilderness. Until he could get back to his real job.

Whichever way he looked at it, he couldn't get away from the feeling that this was part of his punishment after the last big case he investigated. A few days ago, Captain Edwards explained it was just a way of easing Crane back into active duty after nearly four months of sick leave after being shot twice. He was also careful to stress that it was an important role that needed an experienced man. What a knob, Crane thought, shaking his head. If I believed that bullshit, then I'd believe anything.

As far as Crane was concerned he'd emerged from the whole ordeal fitter, lighter and raring to go. After spending the previous month on light duties, helping to shape the security plans, with a gradual return to full time hours, he had grown in confidence and frustration in equal measure. He should have been leading his investigating team by now, not overseeing security.

But still, it was an unusual situation on the garrison Crane had to admit. And with no major crime for him to investigate, as Edwards was insisting the young dead soldier hadn't been murdered…well he supposed it made some sort of weird sense. And even if it didn't, whatever his frustrations, he knew he had to obey orders.

Crane shouted ineffectually at a motorist in front of him, who was taking too long to turn right at the T junction. The man couldn't hear him, but must have been able to see the abusive gestures that accompanied the words. Ignoring Crane's outburst the man placidly remained stationary. Clearly waiting for what he considered to be the right moment, despite Crane's frantic bursts on the horn, before eventually crossing the road during a break in the flow of traffic. Crane took the opportunity to follow, his tyres squealing as he raced away, narrowly missing a car coming up the road on his right hand side.

Crane was on the back route today from Ash to Aldershot, so he entered the garrison via Government Road. A little way up on his left he could see the new St Omar Barracks that had risen from the debris of the demolished concrete tower block. A new complex of single soldier accommodation, constructed in just less than four months. Crane had watched the barracks take shape when the modular blocks were delivered to site complete and then fastened together. To Crane St Omar Barracks now looked more like student accommodation, or an office block, rather than a traditional army building. But he knew he had to move with the times, despite his fondness for army tradition, history and architectural heritage.

The new modular units were now the home of the Olympians, who arrived a couple of days ago to much local fanfare. Crane was unhappy about that as well. In his opinion the less people knew about the whereabouts of Team GB the better. But the army was keen to publicise their involvement with the athletes who were carrying the pride of the nation on their shoulders. Also the local mayor was panting for any conceivable opportunity to get his face on the front page of a newspaper - any newspaper local or national. Crane grimaced as he glanced at the front page of a tabloid newspaper on his car seat, showing the mayor's grinning face in its pock marked glory.

As he passed the barracks, Crane saw armed soldiers at the entrance, carefully checking each vehicle, oblivious to the long line of cars awaiting entrance to the complex. Soldiers were also patrolling the perimeter, some with guns, and others with dogs. He hoped it wasn't putting off the athletes. The last thing the army wanted was to make them feel like they were in prison. But it was better to be safe than sorry. Each athlete, coach, PR, liaison, dietician and myriad of hangers on, no doubt providing essential support, had been photographed, recorded and background checked. The army and Crane left nothing to chance.

As St Omar Barracks wasn't Crane's destination, he continued around the garrison to Provost Barracks, where Staff Sergeant Jones was in the operations room taking the morning briefing. Crane slipped into the room and leaned against the back wall, quietly observing the tall, bald headed man in his pristine uniform double checking that the security details were in position on each barracks and running through the order of the day for his RMP. As Aldershot Garrison was the main thoroughfare for civilians from Aldershot to North Camp along Queens Avenue, the decision was taken to provide extra security around each barracks, leaving the wider garrison open to civilians as far as possible. The hope was that the added traffic caused by the athletes and their entourages, not to mention the press, would create traffic jams which local people would rather avoid if possible and so stay away.

As the briefing finished, Crane looked at Jones and inclined his head towards the outside of the building. The resulting grin and nod of the head meant his message was received and understood.

Outside, the two men lounged against the mellow red brick wall of the barracks, basking in the early morning July sun. Although Crane was the higher ranking of the two, they were friends as well as colleagues and when alone didn't adhere to the formal use of titles.

"Good work, Jones."

"Thanks, Crane. Maybe now you can see I don't need you babysitting me," the accompanying grin taking some of the sting from his words.

Lighting his cigarette allowed Crane to think before he spoke. "Not my intention. I don't want this assignment, anymore than you want me watching over you."

"Okay, fair enough," was the slow reply. "So what is your intention then?"

"To follow orders, of course."

"Which are?" Jones dragged deeply on his own cigarette, squinting at Crane through the smoke.

"To oversee the whole security operation. Liaise with you lot, with the British Olympic Association, Aspire Defence and the Intelligence Operative."

"Isn't that what Captain Edwards should do?"

Crane couldn't resist a wry smile, but bit back a reply, instead concentrating on putting out his cigarette. Glancing at his watch, he said, "Got to go, Jones, I've a meeting with the BOA in 10 minutes. Call me on my mobile if you need me."

As Crane moved away, Jones called out, "Don't forget to tell them we've got the garrison sewn up. Nothing can possibly go wrong!"

Lifting his hand in acknowledgement, Crane continued to his car, unable to share Jones' attitude. Prior experience meant he always expected the worst.

Crane was listening to an altercation between a member of the Aspire Defence kitchen staff and the warrant officer brought into to oversee the feeding of the proverbial 5,000 in St Omar Barracks. The large, gleaming kitchen rang with the chimes of metal and porcelain. Above that could be heard the churning and gurgling of the industrial plate and glass washers and above that, the raised voices Crane was listening to. At the same time people weaved in and out, around and past each other, their movements a well choreographed ballet. The sharp clean whites of the kitchen staff contrasting starkly with the black uniform of the waiting staff.

"Watch what you're doing!" the Chef shouted.

"Don't you speak to me like that!" the recipient of

the Chef's anger retorted.

"Look, just get out of my way and get those bloody eggs out to the hotplate now," ordered the Chef, flapping his hand in the direction of the double doors leading from the kitchen to the dining room.

"Right, that's it, I've had enough. You could stick your fucking job. I'm off." The man undid his apron, snatched off his hat and threw them both at the Chef before disappearing into the staff room.

"It's going well then?" Crane called, failing to keep the mirth out of his voice.

Whirling round, the Chef nearly knocked off his tall white hat, precariously perched on top of his large round head. Seeing who the speaker was, he wiped flour off his hands onto his apron and held one of them out. A large meaty paw, seemingly incapable of the intricate delicate pastillage icing structures Crane knew the chef could produce.

"Bloody hell, Crane!" he said, lifting Crane's hand up and down as though it were the handle of an old fashioned water pump.

"Are they always this bad, Dunn?" Crane asked nodding towards the kitchen staff.

And that was all the invitation Sergeant Major Dunn needed. Retreating into the small head chef's office, he firstly gave Crane a cup of coffee and secondly chapter and verse on the problems of whipping civilian staff into shape, in order to feed the athletes whilst they were on the garrison.

"Basically we're running a rolling buffet," he concluded. "Because the athletes all have differing dietary needs and eat certain foods at certain times depending upon their training schedule, it seems as though we're working morning noon and night and some of the civvies can't keep up." Dunn shook his head in disgust making his hat wobble once again. "For me, it's no different than being in the field, having to feed men as they arrive back at all times of the day and night. I tell you, I don't know about progress, but personally I wish the Army Catering Corp was still in existence. Things have never been the same since the army disbanded the Corp and contracted catering out to civilian companies."

"I think that's a discussion best kept for over a pint in the Sergeants' Mess, don't you?" Crane looked around to make sure no one was standing at the door and listening to their conversation about army politics.

"I suppose so," agreed Dunn leaning back in his chair, which creaked in protest and folded his arms. "Anyway, what brings the Branch over here?" Dunn used the euphemism for the Special Investigations Branch.

Glad to leave the subject of the Army Catering Corp, Crane explained that as he was responsible for overseeing security on the garrison for the next month or so, he thought he would call in and see that everything was in order within St Omar Barracks itself, not just along the perimeter.

"Apart from discipline you mean?" Dunn laughed.

"Yes, Dunn, apart from discipline. Can I see the background checks on the staff?"

"Sure. There're in the top drawer of that filing cabinet. Can I leave you to it and get on?" Dunn asked rising.

"No problem," replied Crane. Then just as Dunn was heading out of the door he called, "Let me know if anything seems a bit off won't you?"

"Off?" Dunn's weather beaten face crinkled.

"Yes, out of kilter. Oh I don't know. Anything really. Just give me a ring."

"Whatever, Crane," Dunn said, as he tied his apron more tightly around his waist, rose to his full height and marched into the large luminous industrial kitchen.

Once satisfied that all the paperwork was in order, Crane left the kitchen by the back door and had a quick cigarette, sitting on top of boxes of supplies already delivered but not yet put away. The fresh air revived him, or was it the nicotine? Either way he now needed to find the equivalent to the mess manager.

On a normal barracks, the mess manager was responsible for liaising with the head chef about the kitchen and its staff, whilst being responsible for front of house – the waiting staff and cleaning staff. Things, however, were not normal and Crane knew that under the circumstances, Aspire Defence had appointed a housekeeper to solely look after the cleaning staff. Consulting his notes, he had to find Juliette Stone, by all accounts drafted in from their head office on a temporary basis.

After putting out his cigarette in an overflowing ashtray provided for the kitchen staff that disgusted even a hardened smoker like Crane, he went round to the living quarters.

As he entered the main lobby he saw a young woman, probably in her late 20's or early 30's striding towards the accommodation wing. She was dressed in a dark suit and white blouse, wearing sensible court shoes, with a clipboard in her hand. Her blond hair was pulled back in a pony tail. Her demeanour reminding Crane of the housekeeper of a large stately home at the turn of the 19th Century. If he were a betting man, which he wasn't, Crane would wager a reasonable sum of money that he was looking at Juliette Stone. The large Aspire Defence identity badge she was wearing clinched it and he approached her.

Standing directly in her path, he called, "Ms Stone I presume?"

Stopping and looking Crane up and down she retorted, "Sergeant Major Crane, I presume?"

"Am I that obvious?"

"Yes, Sergeant Major," she said pointing to the ID he had hanging around his neck and then pointing to hers, "As indeed I must be."

"Touché" Crane inclined his head. "May I just have a quick word?"

"Certainly, but on the move I'm afraid," she said as she swept off towards the living quarters. "I have to check on the staff," she called over her shoulder.

"That's precisely why I've come to see you." Crane matched her stride for stride, as they moved along the carpeted corridor, although the top of her blond head was slightly higher than his.

"Oh, really?"

"Yes, just keeping my eye on security inside St Omar Barracks as well as outside." And he went on to explain his current role, once again requesting to see the staff files.

"Very well, Sergeant Major, but I'm sure you'll find everything in order. Just because we're not the army, doesn't mean we do a bad job, you know. We at Aspire Defence appreciate how important security is at the moment. Heaven forbid something awful should happen to the athletes whilst they are on the garrison."

"Heaven forbid indeed," Crane echoed the sentiment, watching the cool blond woman walk away.

He wondered if she was always like that, or just at work. Crane got the feeling she was simply projecting an image, maybe something to do with being a woman in a man's world.

Having satisfied himself there was nothing untoward in the staff files, Crane looked at his watch. As it was nearly 19:00 hours, he decided to check on his young team in the office. Sergeant Billy Williams and Sergeant Kim Weston would be coming on duty to take over the night shift from him.

Arriving back at his barracks he found Billy and Kim updating themselves on the day's events and going over the athlete's schedules for the evening. As he entered the communal office, they stood to attention.

"Sir," they called in union.

"Billy, Kim," Crane nodded to each in turn and they settled into the hand over, pulling up chairs at the conference table in a corner of the large space.

Crane explained that for the moment things were running smoothly. There were no complaints to deal with, nor any special requests from the BOA.

"So, for tonight," he concluded, "it's just a matter of doing the rounds every now and again and being on hand should an emergency occur. Obviously any problems should be phoned through to me at home immediately."

"Okay, boss," said Billy, the only member of Crane's team who addressed him in such a casual way. Crane found it hard to be offended by the title Billy naturally gave him when they first started working together last year. A fine young soldier, Billy was well built and muscular, with a shock of blond hair constantly falling into his smiling eyes.

"You might want to read these, sir."

Kim handed Crane a few sheets of paper. Her pristine army uniform an outward reflection of her attitude to her work. Her blond hair tied back in a bun so severe, that Crane thought it must be giving her a headache.

"They're the latest intelligence reports. I thought you'd like them tonight before your regular meeting with Captain Edwards first thing in the morning."

"Thank you, Kim, as usual you've thought of everything." Kim preened under the praise but Crane didn't miss Billy's raised eyebrows.

"Anything else you need, boss?"

"No thanks, Billy, that's all for now. As everything's in order I'll push off home and see you both in the morning."

Happy with the growing tension between his two sergeants, Crane left them to it and went home. Earlier in the year Billy had been demoted from staff sergeant to sergeant due to his reckless behaviour that endangered the life of his nephew, and was nearly thrown out of the Branch. Only Crane's intervention saved him from being put back into uniform and pushed into a backwater for the next couple of years.

Kim on the other hand, provided a vital link in the case, consolidating her place and permanency in the Branch not as an investigator, but as office manager. Crane now had two sergeants determined to outdo each other. That's something he needed, as Crane had the uneasy feeling that things were going too well at the moment – and he still had thirty-seven days to go.

Day 4

The past few days had not been good for Padam, being filled with bureaucracy and hunger. He had spent interminable hours at Social Services, the Job Centre and the Gurkha Welfare Office and was still no nearer to getting any money or work. In the Aldershot Council building he was handed a plastic card by a scowling woman. He dutifully said "thank you" and left, puzzling over what it was for.

To find out, he walked several miles to the Gurkha Welfare Office in Farnborough and showed them the plastic card. It was a bus pass. He could now use the buses for free, a harassed man told him in Nepalese and waved vaguely in the direction of the street, before disappearing into a back room. The man actually said "bus free no pay" in Nepalese, being English and having a Nepalese vocabulary nearly as limited as Padam's English. However, Padam was greatly heartened by the news; it would save a lot of time and energy.

Back outside, he stood at the bus stop. Only then did he realise he didn't know which bus went where. Was he standing on the correct side of the road to go to

Aldershot? He wasn't sure. There was a plaque on the pole of the bus stop sign. He thought it was probably the timetable, which explained to passengers which bus went where and at what times. But peering at the jumble of names and numbers proved futile. They meant nothing to him. He wished he could understand it. But had to accept he couldn't. So Padam had no choice but to walk the long lonely miles back to Aldershot.

Once there Padam remembered he needed food, but with no money, the best he could do was to call in at the local Gurkha supermarket and hope that they would allow a little credit for some bread and dried fruit. But first he would try again to tell someone about the smudge he had seen near the sports centre on Aldershot Garrison. He tried to tell people at every official business he visited. But they neither understood nor cared. A friend had mentioned an official interpreter who was based in the newly formed Gurkha Liaison Office in Aldershot. But his friend didn't know when the office was open, or when the interpreter might be there.

Undeterred and before getting some food, Padam went to find the office. His friend had told him it was located in a building above a shop in the town centre. As he walked through the streets he realised most of the shops around him had large posters and notices in the windows. He had no idea what the notices said, but as he looked through the grimy windows, the shops were empty, so he guessed they had closed down. Failed. For every five shops he passed, two or three were like that. Rubbish bins were overflowing with debris from the fast food shops. Food that Padam couldn't afford. The only shops doing any business were those full of second hand clothes and furniture. The others were empty of customers, the staff hanging around outside the shop taking a cigarette break.

Padam finally saw a small brass plate screwed to the wall between two empty shops with a word he could understand on it, Gurkha. He climbed the steep stairway to a large brown doorway. The paint was peeling off and scuff marks decorated the bottom, but the large brass knob turned easily in his hand.

Opening the door, he peered around it before walking in, but found this office no different to others he had been in since arriving in England. The walls were light coloured, the desks brown and covered with papers and what he had learned were computers. He wasn't exactly sure what computers were used for, just knew that every office he went into had a lot of them and people spent an inordinate amount of time looking at them and playing with them. There were three people in the office. No one looked up, so he sat on a red plastic chair and waited. He was very good at waiting.

Eventually an older lady dressed in a tweed skirt, blouse and cardigan, with a kind face looked up, smiled at him and beckoned him forward. Padam shuffled over to her, for by now his feet were very sore indeed. He placed his plastic carrier bag on his lap and took out his two most precious possessions. His Lal Kitab (the official record of his British Army Service) and his bus pass. The lady studied each document carefully and then said, "Hello, Padam."

Unfortunately he couldn't understand what she said next. It must have been English, but the words she spoke meant nothing to him, not being part of his limited vocabulary. Rooting through his plastic bag once again, he found the piece of paper his friend had written one word on. Interpreter. He handed this over accompanied by a large smile.

Nodding, the lady reached for a calendar on her desk. She showed Padam a date on it. He didn't understand the writing, but knew his numbers, so understood the number four. Using her pencil she touched the desk with it, several times. Pointing to the number and then once again at her desk. Padam nodded in agreement. He understood today was day four. So he gave her the universal sign of thumbs up. She then pointed to the number ten and once again mimed 'here' by pointing her pencil to the desk and then by pointing to his piece of paper bearing the magic word 'interpreter'. She repeated this action several times. Padam put his thumb up again to indicate he understood. Today was day four; he could see the interpreter on day ten.

So he didn't forget he mimed to the kind lady to write it down on his piece of paper, under the word 'interpreter'. That done, Padam put his precious documents and the piece of paper back into his plastic carrier bag and hobbled out of the office. Day ten seemed a long way away, but there was nothing to be done about it. And anyway, at the moment, hunger was his most feared rival.

Day 5

The athletics track spread out before Crane, was a sea of blue and white. The dark sea of officials, trainers and physiotherapists in their blue tracksuits swelled and rolled around, topped by athletes in white running vests. Frothy white energy that suddenly raced away, before burning out and being consumed once again by the mass of blue. As Crane watched he was struck by the structure of it all. There were huddles of officials consulting clipboards. Athletes were spread over the grass having limbs attended to, whilst watching the front line - those waiting at the starting gate for their opportunity to race away.

In the centre of the track various factions had formed. Pole-vaulters in the middle, brandishing their unwieldy weapons, and at end, long jump and high jump respectively. Over in the far corner, shot putters, hammer and javelin throwers practiced at a safe distance from the main pack. Crane realised they were like an organised army. Each section possessed different skills. All were ready to fight for their right to be first on the world stage.

Crane walked around the perimeter, at a pace just

short of jogging, glad to be out in the warm but blustery July day. It was day five of his forty days and nights. The twelve hour shifts, which involved racing around the garrison at everyone's beck and call, were beginning to take their toll. Not because he was tired, just cramped and stiff from lack of exercise. And if the truth be told, a bit bored. As he walked he did some simple arm and shoulder exercises to loosen the muscles. He was an incongruous figure in his white shirt and dark trousers, amongst the blue, white and khaki.

Instead of just passing each soldier watching the outer limits of the area, he took time to have a quiet word with them. Making sure everything was in order and they hadn't seen anything suspicious. Happy that the track and surrounding areas had been swept for bombs earlier that morning, while the athletes were eating breakfast. Crane left the area with a backward glance; as he'd much rather stay out there in the open, than go to a meeting with Captain Edwards.

On his arrival at Provost Barracks, after yet another slow trip along Queens Avenue, following the ever increasing number of cars on the road, Crane found his Officer Commanding Captain Edwards ensconced in his small beige office with another soldier.

"Ah, Crane," Edwards said, looking and speaking down his long aquiline nose. "Come in and meet Lance Corporal Dudley-Jones from Military Intelligence."

Crane nodded his head in the direction of the young soldier, who jumped out of his chair, snapping off a salute.

"Please don't do that, Lance Corporal," Crane said. "I may be of superior rank, but I'm not in uniform."

"Yes, sir, sorry, sir."

Crane took a seat and watched the Lance Corporal's

pinched, pointed sallow face permeate with colour as he groped behind him for his own chair and sat down. Dear God, thought Crane, a boy in a man's uniform.

"Shall we get down to business?" said Captain Edwards, pushing back his hair to reveal his copious forehead and then reeling off a list of the Lance's Corporal's credentials. None of which Crane took any notice of. Especially the parts that extolled the man's exceptional analytical skills, first class communication and language abilities, coupled with an eagle eye for detail. Crane realised the corporate crap was straight out of the brochure for Military Intelligence recruitment and felt it had little to do with the Lance Corporal sitting next to him. As Crane tuned back in, Captain Edwards was reminding him the Intelligence Corps gathered all kinds of information from countless sources.

"Which are, sir?" Crane leaned back and crossed his legs, trying to get comfortable in the cheap visitor's chair.

"Which are what?" Edwards echoed, his brow creasing and his head darting from side to side like a sparrow looking for a worm.

"What kind of information and from what sources, sir?"

"Well, um, I think that's something you should discuss with the Lance Corporal after this meeting."

"You mean, have another meeting, after this one, sir?"

"Yes, Crane. Why, do you have a problem with that?"

"Only insomuch as it interferes with my job, sir. But if you'd rather I attend meetings, then I gladly will." Crane shrugged and began swinging his crossed leg as though in time to some music only he could hear.

Throughout this Dudley-Jones said nothing at all. Crane noticed him swivel his head as he followed the speakers, looking more and more perplexed. His eyes were wide and his mouth was pulled down on one side, reminiscent of a stroke sufferer.

"Interferes, Sergeant Major? Why would talking to the Intelligence Corp interfere with your job?" Edwards raised his hand as if to scratch his head and then looking at it, quickly placed it back down on the desk.

Uncrossing his legs Crane said, "Because meetings have to have a purpose, sir, and unless the Intelligence Operative here has something concrete for me to follow up on, then I feel sure you would prefer me to be on the ground."

Placing his arms on his legs and gazing at the Lance Corporal Crane asked, "Do you have anything?" Then answering his own question said, "No I thought not. In that case, sir," Crane turned his attention back to Edwards, "I'll get out and about on the garrison, personally checking security and dealing with any minor hiccups that may occur."

Crane stood, nodded to Captain Edwards and Lance Corporal Dudley-Jones and left the room before either man could react.

Night 5

Today we had instruction in military law. I could not believe it. Muslims given instructions in English military law. A law that you infidels are trying to make us adhere to. A military law that Westerners want to impose upon our Muslim army. A law that has nothing at all to do with Islam. I cannot believe the impudence of your military rulers, the effrontery they have, to think that we Muslims should bow to your laws and your ways. I do not live in England therefore I do not want English or any other law in my country, other than the one true law. Sharia law.

You seem not to understand that the Islamic religious control of government and society is an expected and necessary part of Muslim evangelism and discipleship. Sharia means path or road. And Muslims willingly follow this road, the road that governs every facet of Muslim life. The path along which the true believer has to tread.

Shall I tell you about Sharia law? It recognises specific crimes which have fixed punishments. For instance, theft is punished by cutting off the hand or fingers of the thief. Adultery is punishable by stoning.

Drinking alcohol means eighty lashes from a whip. In public mind you. Then highway robbery and apostasy, which includes blasphemy, are punishable by the death penalty.

But what you miserable excuses for men don't understand is that they are not just punishments but also deterrents. These limits imposed by God are not just penalties for a proven crime, but also act as a disincentive against further crime. This means that in my society there is little or no crime and the people feel safe. Safe in their way of life. Following the one true way, the Muslim way.

The Qur'an also demands swift justice against those who oppose Muhammad and Islam. This is how we know how to deal with you infidels, who try to take over our lands.

The Punishment of those
Who wage war against God
And His Apostle, and strive
With might and main
For mischief through the land
Is: execution, or crucifixion,
Or the cutting off of hands
And feet from opposite sides,
Or exile from the land.
(Qur'an 5:36)

You Western infidels just don't seem to understand that *you* are the terrorist in *our* midst. All you see is that we are terrorists in yours. So in that case I will live up to our reputation. At the moment you don't realise you have terrorists in your midst. But you will. Soon. I promise you that.

Day 6

Tina asked, "So can you make it?"

"Make what?" Crane stopped reading his file and went to the percolator to collect their early morning coffee.

"The scan. This morning. Frimley Park Hospital. 11 o'clock." His wife's punctuation made the words sound like punches rather than statements.

Crane took his time fiddling with the milk and sugar. He was used to having two sugars instead of three now and wanted to make sure he kept up the good habit. Perhaps he should bring it down to one? Maybe after the athletes had left would be a better idea?

"Tom, stop procrastinating."

Turning to face his wife, he handed her one of the two mugs he held in his hand.

"It's just that….."

"Bloody hell!" Tina's coffee spilled as she placed it on the kitchen table.

"Tina, it's not that I don't want to come. Here let me help you." Crane lowered his wife into a pine chair and mopped up the spill. "I'm sure you'll bring me back a picture."

"I knew this is how it would be. Once you were back on full duty after your sick leave." Tina grabbed handfuls of her hair, securing it with an elastic tie she pulled off her wrist.

"But, Tina, how can you expect me to be allowed to leave the garrison at a time like this?"

"That's the problem, Tom, isn't it? There'll always be 'a time like this' for one reason or another. How about our 'time like this'? The last opportunity to see our first baby during a scan before it's born. Doesn't that mean anything to you? Our family? What happens if they find anything wrong? Then I'll have to deal with it on my own, as usual."

Placing her hands on the table, Tina pushed her heavy body out of the pine chair brushing away Crane's helping hand.

"Just go to work will you," she snapped as she lumbered out of the room. Leaving him standing alone in the kitchen, an un-drunk cup of coffee in his hand. The word 'family' reverberating around the cheerfully decorated room.

That's what it comes down to Crane knew, as he packed his briefcase. Family. Which one to choose? The army family or the civilian family? He cleared the kitchen of the breakfast debris, collected his suit jacket and briefcase and went out into the chill of the early morning sunshine. Stopping at the car, his brow creased and his hand fingered his scar. Could he live without the army he wondered, unlocking the door. If he left would private security be enough of a challenge or too much like his current babysitting job? Driving down the road he remembered his pension. That was a major factor in any future financial planning. Waiting to turn right at the top of the garrison, it occurred to him that he would miss the camaraderie of the army. And what about the opportunities for travel, sport and adventure? Not to mention the safe(ish) secure(ish) future career the forces offered. Arriving at St Omar Barracks, to deal with his first problem of the day, he was no nearer an answer. But as his main priority was seeing Sergeant Major Dunn about a series of petty thefts, he pushed the confusion of thoughts to the back of his mind and got on with his job.

Crane found the Dunn by spotting the bobbing white hat, which kept appearing periodically between the boxes Crane was sitting on a few days ago.

"I don't bloody believe it, Crane," Dunn shouted and waved his hand seemingly in time with his wobbly hat. "There's loads of this shit missing!"

"Well, it's not surprising, Dunn, leaving the stuff lying around outside."

Crane considered lighting a cigarette, until he got a whiff of the volcanic ash tray.

"I know, but I'm so short of space in the kitchen stores. I suppose I'll have to get a few of the lads to try and find somewhere to squeeze it all in."

"Leave it for a bit will you?"

"Leave it? And get more stuff stolen? Are you out of your mind? God knows what Aspire will say about the increased cost as it is. I'm not about to make a bad situation worse."

This time the chef's hat did fall of his head. Dunn snatched at it and crumpled it in his hand.

"How about if I can guarantee no more stuff will be lost?" Crane asked.

"And how the hell were you going to do that?"

"Simple."

Crane decided to light a cigarette anyway and drew the Dunn away from the back door of the kitchen so no one could hear them.

"This is an opportunist crime. So you leave the stuff where it is, I'll get the lads on the gate to inspect cars going out as well as coming in and I guarantee you'll have your culprits and your stock back by the end of the day."

"This better bloody work, Crane," the Chef grumbled, trying to smooth out the creases he had put in his hat. "Are you sure?"

"Absolutely. So say nothing, do nothing and just leave it to me."

Grinding his cigarette out on the floor, Crane strode off to the entrance of the barracks to implement his plan.

The second problem Crane faced was not as easy to deal with. Juliette Stone. She kept calling his mobile demanding his presence in her office in St Omar Barracks. Immediately, if not sooner. So he supposed he better go and see her. Walking to her small office he wondered what trivia she wanted him to deal with. He found her sat behind her modern desk in a pristine office with no personal frills.

"Thank you for coming so quickly, Sergeant Major," she said, pushing a file across her desk at Crane as he sat opposite her. "It seems a couple of the athletes have noticed personal items missing. At first they thought they were mislaid, but after a careful search it seems they may have been stolen. Nothing of terribly high value, a gold watch and gold engagement ring, but as you can imagine, extremely embarrassing for us and upsetting for the athletes. No one likes to lose sentimental pieces of jewellery that can't be replaced."

"Indeed, Miss Stone," Crane agreed, flicking through the papers.

"So, I thought I would lay this one in your lap as you're responsible for security. What do you intend to do about it?" she tossed her head, her tied back ice cool blond hair flicking like a horse's tail.

"Well, Miss Stone," Crane closed the file, "It's true I'm responsible for security on the garrison at the moment, but really it's the security of the athletes against outside attack." Seeing the arched eyebrows, he quickly continued, "But, of course, I'll sort this out for you."

"Good. How?" Her pupil's contracted and the blue chips of iris harden.

"Well, strictly speaking your employees, who to be fair are the likely suspects, are civilian staff. However, as they are on army property they also fall under the jurisdiction of the army."

"Let me make it clear, Sergeant Major" she cut in, "I don't intend to have my staff interviewed and intimidated by gun toting soldiers!"

"Of course not." Crane briefly closed his eyes and tried not to sigh. "That's not my intention at all, Ms Stone. I was going to suggest that I call Aldershot Police and we do a low key joint operation. I don't want to cause any panic amongst the athletes, nor amongst your staff. But as you say, you want something done about it immediately."

"Very well, Sergeant Major. Please keep me informed." She sounded like Captain Edwards and dismissed him with a wave of her hand.

Crane left her office wondering how he was ever going to keep up this façade of diplomacy. If he'd wanted this sort of job he'd have joined the Diplomatic Corp. What had Captain Edwards called it? Oh yes, learning new skills. However, Crane was of the opinion that you can't teach old dogs new tricks. And anyway he didn't want to change. Saw no reason to. Added to that, Tina's scan appointment kept poking into his thoughts like a hot pin. So he was stuck in the middle of a maelstrom of emotions that included resentment and guilt by the time he arrived at Aldershot Police station fifteen minutes later. A journey that should had taken five, hindered by the increased traffic on the roads, pissing him off even more.

Crane tried to find a parking space outside the monolithic structure, a study in grey concrete, split into two halves. One half contained Aldershot Police Station and the other the Magistrates Court. Handy, Crane had always thought. Saved the police a lot of driving around taking offenders backwards and forwards to court. Crane eventually managed to squeeze his Ford Focus into a tight parking space, the only one available. Once Crane was upstairs, Detective Inspector Anderson greeted him as if his visit was the return of the prodigal son.

"Crane, good to see you," Anderson enthused, getting out of his office chair and coming round to pump Crane's hand, attempting to brush the crumbs and other detritus from his suit jacket before enveloping Crane in a hug.

"So you're back on duty then?" he continued as Crane searched for somewhere to sit in the cramped office, overflowing with books, papers and files. Crane often wondered if Anderson actually read all this shit, or just left it lying around to make himself look busy.

"How are you? God wasn't that awful. I was sure we were going to lose you at one point, Crane." Anderson's voice was gruff and he cleared his throat.

Crane didn't want to talk about the events of earlier in the year, when he was incarcerated in Frimley Park Hospital for far too long, so he steered the conversation back to the present.

"I'm fine, thanks, Derek. I just need to see you about a problem we've got in St Omar Barracks at the moment. Petty thefts from the athlete's living quarters and as they're civilian staff…"

"Oh, okay," But instead of looking at the file Crane handed him, he looked around the office. "Where's your shadow? Isn't Billy with you?"

"No. He and Kim are doing the night shift liaison."

"It's just that you look a little, um, lopsided on your own, Crane, without your sergeant. I'm more used to seeing the men in black, rather than the man in black." Anderson's wispy grey hair flew around his head as he laughed at his own joke.

Luckily cups of tea arrived before Anderson could move onto other famous partnerships so Crane was able to get down to business. They decided that a joint operation be set up, with Crane and Anderson overseeing the interviews as a courtesy to Aspire and the BOA, although neither man was entirely happy with having to get in involved in such low level crimes. As they put the flesh on the bones of their plan, Crane's hot pin poked his brain again and glancing at his watch, realised Tina would be at the hospital waiting for her appointment. But there was nothing he could do about it, apart from keep his fingers crossed that all was well with mother and son, so he turned his attention back to work.

Night 7

Padam was once again on sentry duty, surveying the sports centre. He'd changed location and now blended into a thicket of trees, looking directly at the side of the building where he saw the smudge a few nights ago. Aware that he was now where the smudge had probably begun and ended his recce of the building the other night, Padam was buried into a pile of leaves and branches at the foot of a tree. Being at one with the earth calmed him and gave him a peace he wasn't able to find during the day.

A stroke of luck had also added to his sense of wellbeing. Being part of the unseen and ignored section of society, those unfortunates that most people give no more thought to than the litter on the street, meant that the cast-outs tended to band together. It was through such an encounter that Padam and his friends had been introduced to Tesco. Being the largest and most popular supermarket in the area it meant there were opportunities for free food.

Two days ago, Padam was sat on the grassy knoll overlooking the supermarket's overflowing car park, waiting for his new homeless friends. Watching the greedy customers grab empty trolleys, snarling at people who got in their way. Once the customers had their plunder, barely contained by the groaning trolleys, it became a race against time. They rushed to stow away their booty, eager to be gone. To consume their spoils in private. Driving their cars at break neck speed out of the car park, leaving abandoned trolleys in their wake.

It was explained to Padam in a mixture of pigeon English and a great deal of pointing, that not all the fresh food in the food store was purchased each day. Anything out of date and unsold was thrown away each evening. At nightfall therefore, the Nepalese were persuaded to climb inside the high waste bins scattered around the back of the store. Being smaller and lighter it was an easy enough task for them to get in and root around in the rotting vegetables, to find packets of sandwiches, cakes, pies, pasties and other such gems.

Whilst being amazed by a society that could afford to throw away good food without a second thought, Padam was nevertheless grateful. Now he could focus his attention on his sentry duty, without the distraction of hunger.

Hearing a faint rustling of leaves behind him, Padam's breathing became slow and shallow. He was confident that even on close inspection he would be seen as a lump of rock, covered by fallen leaves and twigs. The human brain being programmed to see what it expected to find in any given location. Once again his army greatcoat had come in handy and was draped over his body to help with the camouflage. Moving just his eyes, he scanned the area directly in front of him.

He almost missed the smudge as it ran towards the side of the sports centre and settled into the shadow of the wall. Ignoring the tickle in his nose from the mouldy undergrowth, Padam concentrated on what he could see. The smudge. Edging slowly along the wall, away from the front of the building and stopping half way down. A leaf dislodged itself from the pile above Padam and came to rest on his eyelid, making him blink several times. When he once again focused on the wall, the smudge had disappeared. Mentally turning the area into a grid system, he slowly scanned it, but found nothing.

His inner clock estimated it was at least thirty minutes before he saw the smudge again. Appearing at exactly the same point it had disappeared from earlier. Seemingly morphing from a wall into a smudge. After another incessant wait, the smudge disengaged itself from the wall and ran towards Padam.

Day 8

Crane was reading, yet again, the file Kim had opened on the accidental death of Corporal Simms. She had also logged the initial details onto the REDCAPS computer system, filing away the detailed statements taken from all the soldiers on duty with him that night, the post mortem results and finally Captain Edward's press release. The only thing missing was any forensic evidence that would come in over the next couple of days. The various tests they had to undertake in the laboratories using materials gleaned from the scene of crime, or during the post mortem, took as long as they took. Not even Crane could persuade a machine to hurry up; although he always tried to make sure his evidence was first in the queue.

Closing the file, Crane got up and wandered across the office. He was studying a large map of the garrison that Kim had put up on one of the walls of their large communal office, showing the location of Corporal Simms' unfortunate demise, when she walked past to go off duty.

"Kim," he called. "Just a minute."

"Sir?"

"What are all these pins you've put on the map of the garrison?"

"Oh those," Kim moved to stand next to him. "I decided to plot the location of each battalion on the map. I don't know why really. I just thought it was interesting."

As Crane continued to study the map he scratched the scar beneath his short beard.

"Sorry, sir." Kim spoke into the silence.

"No, no, it's alright. It's just that..."

"What's up, boss? I told Kim that was a waste of time," Billy said appearing at Crane's side with alacrity.

Standing back and looking at them, Crane said, "No, Billy, I don't think it was a waste of time. Kim why are there two pins in New Mons Barracks? Is that an error?"

"No, sir." Kim strode to her desk her uniform skirt rustling and picked up a piece of paper. "Here," she held it out to Crane. "A routine memo came through last week, it was sent to the RMP though, not us. I got a copy of it last night when I was talking to one of them. It advises that a group of Afghan officers will be the guests of the 1st Battalion The Coldstream Guards for the next month. I didn't know how to classify them, but I thought they should be on the map. Especially as New Mons Barracks is directly opposite the sports centre, just on the other side of Princess Avenue."

Billy whistled.

"Exactly, Billy. Good work Kim. Yet again."

"I was just wondering when you were going to tell me about this..." Crane waited a beat before adding, "sir." The tone of Crane's voice more suited to finding something disgusting on his shoe, than addressing his

Officer Commanding.

A minute ago, anger had made him push past the soldier waiting outside the Captain's office and walk in uninvited.

"What now, Crane?" Edwards seemed to treat the implied insubordination with boredom rather than outrage, as he indicated Crane should sit. Wrong footed, Crane complied, some of his irritation dissipating.

"Purely through the good work of Sergeant Weston, I've found out that there are Afghan officers training on Aldershot Garrison." Crane said throwing the memo onto the Captain's desk, sitting back and crossing his arms.

"And?"

"And, don't you think this could have some bearing on Corporal Simm's death, sir?"

"No, Sergeant Major, I don't," Edwards sighed. "But I expect you were going to tell me why it should."

"You mean you don't see them as a potential threat?" Crane muttered several expletives under his breath.

"Potential threat? What on earth are you talking about, Crane? These are perfectly respectable Afghan officers, who are here at the invitation of the Coldstream Guards. After working with them in Afghanistan, their Commanding Officer thought it would be beneficial for the Afghans to come and see for themselves how our training works in situ."

As Edwards warmed to his political speech, he leaned forward across the desk.

"They will see firsthand what the attitude of our lads is. How they work together, trust each other and watch each other's backs. Moreover, they will learn from our own officers how to foster and achieve that attitude. And if the Commanding Officer of the Coldstream Guards thinks it's a good idea, then believe you me, Crane, it is."

Crane left his chair and paced the small space in front of Edward's desk. Feeling trapped, not only by the confines of the office but also by the small mindedness of his Officer Commanding.

"But don't you see the problem is timing," Crane said.

"Timing? What on earth has the timing of this got to do with anything?" The Captain pushed his lustrous black hair away from his sloping forehead.

"The Olympic athletes, sir." Crane closed his eyes and shook his head in frustration at the inability of the man in front of him to see his point of view. "They are an obvious target for the Taliban, Al Qaeda and any other loony terrorist on the planet."

"Sit down, Crane." A barked order. As Crane complied Edwards continued. "For God's sake, you're assuming that one or more of the Afghans are terrorists. If they hadn't been properly vetted they wouldn't be here."

"What about Corporal Simms?"

"Corporal Simms? Jesus, Crane you don't change. The death of Corporal Simms was an unfortunate accident. It had nothing to do with any Afghan officers or anyone else who may be on the garrison. Stop seeing things that aren't there and get back to the job in hand. Ensuring the security of the athletes on the garrison."

"That, sir, is precisely what I'm doing and will continue to do."

Crane walked out of the door, leaving Captain Edwards spluttering into the empty space.

After leaving Captain Edward's office, Crane went to see Derek Anderson at the station. As he drove he realised he was seeking refuge but was past caring. After an internal debate he decided to leave the matter of the Afghan officers stewing for a while, until the best course of action revealed itself to him. Which it usually did. So he concentrated on another problem that was irritating him. The petty thefts from the Athlete's living quarters. Nothing else had been stolen but something still needed to be done. Especially before anyone outside the garrison, namely the press or, heaven forbid, the mayor, found out.

As Crane drove, he opened the windows. The weather was holding and Aldershot didn't look as bleak in the sun. Even a Mediterranean beach, which looks inviting in the sunshine, isn't much of a paradise in the cold wind and rain. Aldershot was no different. Its mean streets were today brightened by sunlight and looked less threatening and desolate.

Driving along the dual carriageway, towards the police station, he glanced to his left at the Queens Theatre, where the civic reception was held to welcome the athletes to the town. It was deserted now, apart from a small cluster of men perched on the tiered steps. It seemed they huddled together for protection, rather than warmth, as it was over 20°C. A group of elderly Gurkhas, small and insignificant in the large wide space, drinking bottles of water and clutching plastic carrier bags.

After accepting a welcome cup of tea, but declining Anderson's invitation to share his cake, Crane asked what was happening with the investigation into the petty thefts.

"Nothing." Anderson choked on a piece of cake and had to be revived with a swig of tea. "No more thefts, but we're still no nearer to finding out who did it. Whoever it was probably thinks they've got away with it by now."

"Just what I thought. But that won't be acceptable to the Wicked Witch of the North."

"Wicked Witch of the North? Oh, you mean the ice cold Miss Stone," Anderson laughed and threatened to choke on his cake again. "Mind you she's a looker don't you think, Crane? If you can thaw that ice cool exterior that is. If only I was twenty years younger..."

"Sorry, Derek, not interested and neither should you be. Don't forget you're a happily married man. So if you don't mind, can we get back to work? I've come up with a plan."

"Why does it always worry me when you come up with a plan, Crane?"

"Don't worry, Derek, it's only a small spot of misdirection," and Crane leaned in to give Anderson the details.

By the end of their chat, it was decided that a young WPC would join the workforce as a temporary helping hand, subject to the witch's approval, of course. By posing as the kind of girl who couldn't care less about her job or the athletes, they hoped she could ingratiate herself with the person or persons who were interested in pilfering a few more trinkets.

It may take a few days for the undercover operation to work, but the WPC wouldn't be in any harm and the witch would prefer working with the police rather than the army. Crane's final trump card was that Anderson could take the credit if it worked.

"Just so long as it's your idea if it doesn't,"

Anderson called to Crane's retreating back as he left to return to the garrison.

Night 9

The plan about sending a WPC under cover, stuck in Crane's mind, so he phoned Tina to check she was alright and to let her know he'd be late – again. Making a second phone call he requested that Lance Corporal Dudley-Jones attend the SIB office that evening, bringing with him any background information he had on the Afghan officers.

The Lance Corporal's sallow complexion hadn't been improved by the good weather. Crane thought he was no doubt too busy pouring over his satellite images and computers, or whatever the hell he consulted, to spend any time outdoors. And God forbid he should do any exercise. The lad looked like he'd be blown over by a gust of wind, in sharp contrast to Billy, who stood all rippling muscles, blond hair and freckles.

"Um, Sergeant Major, um oh, Sergeant Williams," the Lance Corporal bumbled his way into the room, laden with files, which he nearly dropped as he caught sight of Billy.

"Lance Corporal, thank you so much for coming over and bringing your information to share with us. Shall we sit at the table?"

Crane led the way, giving a slight shake of his head at the puzzled look Billy had thrown him. Shrugging his shoulders Billy also sat as the Lance Corporal's precarious pile of papers slid out of his arms and onto the table's shiny surface.

"So, what have you brought us?" Crane continued to charm.

"Well, sir, I've got the files on the Afghan officers, as you requested and I've also taken the liberty of bringing the latest intelligence for you. I would, of course, be happy to decode anything that you may have trouble understanding. Is Captain Edwards joining us?" The Lance Corporal looks around the room, as if expecting to see the Captain materialise from under a desk and shout 'boo!'

"Not tonight no, Lance Corporal. He's tasked me with running the security operation for the garrison, remember?"

"Oh yes, of course, sir. Sorry, sir."

Taking pity on the Lance Corporal's flaming face, Crane and Billy turned their attention to the files. Unfortunately it didn't take very long. Each file was slimmer than a credit card. They also looked at the Intelligence Operative's 'intel' as he proudly called it. Crane had to admit he couldn't actually understand a word of it and that's when the young man came into his own, pulling out maps and charts, which indicated where each officer was from and where their units were deployed. Noted on the map were details of how many men they commanded and what their main area of operation was. Satellite photographs indicated the last known location of each unit, none of which had moved in any direction without their officers.

"Probably enjoying a bit of time off," Billy observed.

Ignoring the comment, Dudley-Jones then provided log sheets which monitored mobile phone calls the officers had made since being on the garrison. Most of them were to family, only a handful to their units.

"So, sir, the idea is to crack the code," he explained to Crane.

"The code Lance Corporal? What code?"

"The language used in the phone calls. Whether they actually mean what they are saying."

"Why wouldn't they?" Billy asked.

"Because they are trying to disguise what they really mean by using normal everyday language."

"Isn't that rather difficult to determine?" Crane wanted to know. "After all it's mostly conjecture, surely."

"Possibly, sir, but we have men trained and practiced in this and you'd be amazed what we find out. We've likened it to cracking the German codes in the Second World War."

"Well, it's all very impressive, Lance Corporal."

"Thank you, sir," Dudley-Jones puffed up with pride.

"But I was just wondering, how are you tracking them whilst they are on the garrison?"

"Tracking them?" Dudley-Jones looked at Crane and then Billy, whose stony face held no answer. "On the garrison?"

Crane nodded.

"Do you think we should be?" Dudley-Jones looked as if Crane had just pulled a gun on him.

"Yes, Lance Corporal." Crane stood and moved around the office. "What if they are planning something here on the garrison? Without outside help. How would we know?"

Dudley-Jones glanced down at his files, but the inert pieces of paper said nothing. He turned to Crane, tilting his head back to look at the man looming above him.

"We wouldn't," he whispered and his face began to tinge with pink.

"That's what I thought."

Crane made the Lance Corporal wait, while he strolled over to the coffee machine and helped himself.

Remaining standing he said, "So, if we're all agreed it's a problem," Billy and Dudley-Jones nodded, "then," Crane smiled, "I think I may have the solution."

The solution involved Lance Corporal Dudley-Jones attaching himself to the Commanding Officer of the Coldstream Guards, ostensibly as a part-time aide. He would then be able to come and go as he liked, staying in the shadows, observing and most importantly, listening to the Afghan officer's conversations. The Lance Corporal had admitted that whilst not being fluent, he had a fair working knowledge of Pashtu. The plan seemed perfect in its simplicity but Crane still sensed some reluctance on the part of Dudley-Jones.

"I'll certainly pass your plan along to my superiors, Sergeant Major Crane," Dudley-Jones sighed and collects his files.

"My plan? Is it my plan, Billy?" Crane tried and failed to keep the smile off his face as he looks at his young sergeant.

Taking his cue Billy said, "No, sir, I wasn't aware that it was. If I remember correctly it was the Lance Corporal here who came up with it."

Dudley-Jones' head shot up.

"A stroke of genius on his part, identifying a potential chink in the armour of intelligence surrounding the protection of the athletes, I'd say."

"Couldn't agree more, Billy. So, Lance Corporal, well done on your incisive over view of the situation. I'm sure your superiors will be impressed. I know Captain Edwards will be when I tell him all about it tomorrow."

"Oh I see, yes, sir. Thank you, sir." The young man stood and marched from the office as though anxious to get away before Crane changed his mind.

"That should do it." Crane didn't bother to keep the satisfaction out of his voice, as the office door swung shut on the retreating Dudley-Jones.

"Nice one, boss," Billy grinned. "A very incisive overview of the situation."

Day 10

Padam awoke to a cluster of black dots hovering in front of his eyes. As he blinked, he saw the mass was growing, advancing across the ceiling and down the walls. He was afraid of what the damp mould was doing to his lungs. Several of his friends appeared to have developed breathing problems, but weren't able to see a doctor as their paperwork hadn't come through yet. If only they had all understood the importance of birth certificates. Not having one made things very difficult indeed here in England. Nepal wasn't big on paperwork when he was born. You were just born. End of story. Or rather, the start of it, depending on which way you looked at things. Padam hoped his story wouldn't end before he was re-united with his family.

Fed up with staring at the ceiling, he climbed out of bed, picking his way around the still sleeping bodies of his friends on his way to the bathroom. More mould. The bathroom suite was old and decrepit but still sturdy under the grime. It was a shame they couldn't afford cleaning products. Shuffling into the kitchen Padam made himself a cup of hot water, wishing there was some tea to put in it. He was hungry but didn't bother to look in the cupboards for any breakfast. He knew they would be empty. But despite these problems Padam was feeling positive, as today he was going to see the interpreter at the Gurkha Welfare Office about the smudge. And it wasn't far to walk.

He was glad to see the kind lady was in the office when he arrived. She looked up and smiled at him, indicating he should once again sit on one of the red plastic chairs. It seemed a very long wait, but Padam amused himself by looking around the office. Brightly coloured posters were plastered on one of the walls. Perhaps conveying information? Padam wasn't sure. He checked through his plastic carrier bag to make sure he had his important documents with him. If in doubt produce them, he was always told. His eye was caught by a picture of his family. His wife, son and daughter. Their image caught forever on a small glossy square of paper. Waiving him goodbye as he left for England. Would he ever see them again? Somehow he doubted it. But had to keep hoping.

His introspection was interrupted by the sound of an old Nepalese man coming out of an office in the corner of the room. The kindly lady called to Padam. It was his turn.

"Welcome, Padam," the man greeted him speaking in Nepalese accompanied by a small bow, which Padam returned. "What can I do for you?"

It was such a relief to tell someone his important news. A fellow Nepalese, the interpreter was much younger than Padam. His name was Unman Bahadur and Padam learned that his father was currently a captain in the Gurkha Regiment. Glossy black hair topped the round happy face prevalent in his race. Padam noted the man was dressed smartly in a dark suit and didn't look hungry. Unman listened with respect, making notes along the way as Padam hesitantly told the story of the smudge.

Perhaps because the interpreter was from a family with military connections, he wasn't perturbed by the fact that Padam had been out on the garrison at night. He agreed that the authorities needed telling and promised to let them know at the earliest opportunity. But that wasn't good enough for Padam, who refused to move until Mr Bahadur contacted the Royal Military Police. This forced the interpreter to pick up the telephone and have a conversation, which he translated for Padam along the way.

- "Good morning, this is Unman Bahadur from the Aldershot Gurkha Welfare Office. Could I please speak to someone in charge? Yes I'll hold. Thank you." Mr Bahadur translated whilst he waited to be connected.

- "To whom am I speaking?"

- "Good morning, Staff Sergeant Jones. I wish to let you know of a suspicious sighting that has been reported to this office by a Gurkha, living in Aldershot."

- "Yes, I do think this matter should be taken seriously."

- "What's happened? Well, it appears that Padam Gurung was on the garrison on July 4th and again on July 7th between Midnight and four am, when he saw a suspicious shadow moving around in the vicinity of the sports centre."

- "Yes, on both nights, that's correct."

- "He has been unable to report it to anyone because of the language barrier, Staff Sergeant. He's had to wait until today, which was the earliest appointment with me."

- "Yes, Padam can be contacted through this office. I'm sure he would be happy to talk to you through me. We could do that now on the telephone if you like."

- "Oh, I see. Yes, please do call me at any time on Aldershot 774302. If I'm not here a member of staff will be able to contact me straight away."

- "Yes, thank you, goodbye."

Throughout the telephone conversation, Padam interrupted, telling the interpreter that he would go to the RMP that very minute to tell them what he had seen. But as the conversation went on, he became deflated, realising that wasn't going to happen.

After replacing the receiver, Mr Bahadur explained that Staff Sergeant Jones was very interested in what Padam had seen, but unfortunately had to go and deal with another equally pressing matter. But Padam could be sure the RMP would be in touch with him, through the Welfare Office, very shortly, and someone would take a statement from him. After taking Padam's address, the interpreter said that he himself must get on as he had other people to see this morning, but he was confident he would see Padam again quite soon.

Collecting his carrier bag Padam shuffled out of the office, smiled goodbye to the kind lady and went back to the wasteland of his life.

Night 10

You might ask what I'm doing here? How I came to be here? Well I am one of the lucky but small contingent of officers deemed to be 'brilliant'. The ones with the most potential. The ones with leadership qualities that will ensure we become the highest ranking officers of our army. The happy chosen few.

But what you stinking infidels fail to realise is that I come from an affluent, already powerful family. Because of this privilege I have been educated and am comfortable in elite social circles. Your leaders don't understand that my family always intended I join the military. That I was groomed from childhood to play an important role in the running of our country. We already have politicians and religious leaders in our extended family. But there was no one in the military. Until now.

I have learned my lessons well. I can be suave and sophisticated if needed, yet a ruthless leader of men when required. Bringing fear into their eyes, ensuring their utter devotion to me and our glorious cause.

The soldiers I lead are mostly from poor backgrounds. They have little or nothing of their own.

In many instances they are illiterate. They do not have electricity or running water in the hovels they live in. Therefore it falls to people like me, their leader, to shield them from the modernism of the western ways. To ensure they are immersed in the teachings of the Qur'an as well as in the ways of basic fighting. So when the time comes there will be fighting forces all over our country that will be ready, willing and able, to rise up against the infidel invaders. To claim back our country in the name of Allah and expel the evil force that is poisoning our land.

Therefore my task here is twofold. Firstly, to learn from your precious army. To learn all your ways, so that I may understand you better and therefore be able to outsmart you in battle. Secondly, to strike a blow against you unbelievers. Thirdly to do so without harming myself. For I am destined to be an important leader. A call I cannot ignore, nor would want to. For I am the chosen one. And as such am invincible.

Day 11

The crash from above had Crane racing up the stairs.

"Tina!" he called as he took the stairs two at a time, following the sound to the bathroom door. "Tina, are you alright?" he called again, pushing the door.

Nothing. No reply from Tina and no movement from the door. It remained solid in its rigid frame. An innate object, oblivious to Crane's concern for his wife.

"Tina, for God's sake!"

This time he heard a slight moan, muffled by the pine.

"What the hell did you lock the door for?"

He rattled the door knob, although he knew it was useless. The door was locked from the inside by a small bar, pushed across from the door to the lintel. He would have to break in.

Taking a few steps backwards, he hesitated. He daren't shoulder the door open, God knows what damage it would do to the weakened bone. Luckily the landing wasn't wide and so supporting his back and hands on the railing he gives a well placed flat footed kick to a point just above the door knob. The door gave way, causing some damage to his foot in reprisal.

Crane burst into the room finding his wife dazed and confused in the bath, entrenched in slimy water. Grabbing her arm, he tried to lift her out, only to find she was as slippery as a piece of cod from the fishmongers in the High Street. Her arm flopped out of his grasp and slithered back into the water.

"What the hell?"

Pulling the plug to let the water out of the bath, Crane reached up to the shelving above the toilet, grabbing the first large towel he could find. Wrapping this around Tina's back and under her arms, he managed to lift her to her feet holding her as she stepped out of the bath. Throwing the now sodden towel to one side, he watched as she wrapped herself in a towelling dressing gown and shuffled from the bathroom to the bedroom. Leaving her there to rest, he went downstairs to make a cup of tea and tried to calm down. Bloody stupid woman, what the hell did she think she was doing? It was probably some sort of home beauty treatment he thought, knowing Tina.

"My hero!" she grinned as he returned to the bedroom, two mugs of tea in his hand. His with three sugars in for the shock.

"What the hell was that all about?" Crane sat on the edge of the bed.

"Just fancied a bath," she smiled tentatively, her damp hair hanging round her face, sticking to her neck and shoulders. The precious bump barely contained by the bathrobe.

"What the hell did you put in the water? I still can't get the grease off my hands," Crane rubbed them together to prove his point. "And I'll have to change my shirt."

He looked down at his grease splattered white shirt

that more than likely needed throwing away.

"Baby oil," Tina answered. "I read somewhere that if you put it in your bath water, it helps to keep your skin supple so you don't get stretch marks."

"Jesus, had you put the whole bloody bottle in? Can you stick to showers in future, Tina? Please? If it means having you in one piece but with stretch marks, then so be it. And don't lock the door! Understood?" Crane's fear made him shout.

"Understood, Sergeant Major," Tina grinned. "Now shouldn't you be getting to work? Sorry I've made you late."

"It's okay," Crane replied, but glanced at his watch all the same. "Look, why don't we go out for dinner tomorrow night. I know I haven't been able to spend much time at home lately, but I'll make sure I can get away on time tomorrow. Deal?"

"Deal. Now bugger off," and she sank back on the pillows cradling her mug of tea.

Crane was, in fact, quite glad to bugger off, although he was accompanied by the guilty hot pin poking his brain as he drove to work. He felt guilty for not spending more time with Tina, who was alone during her maternity leave from her job at the bank, not only during the day but well into the evening on most nights. The scan had gone well and she'd begrudgingly shown him the photographs, carefully pasted into the 'Our First Baby Album'. He hadn't expected his businesslike independent wife to be so soppy, but it looked like becoming a mother was changing her.

He also felt guilty when he went off duty, worrying something would happen on the garrison whilst he was away. He'd be glad when the athletes went. Still, the thefts from Sergeant Major Dunn's stores had been sorted out. It turned out to be a couple of opportunists from the civilian staff, who were now spending their time going to the Jobcentre Plus instead of peeling potatoes. The thefts of jewellery still hadn't been solved, but the undercover WPC was in place and hopefully ingratiating her way into an unsuspecting, thieving group of cleaners.

Crane was fed up of feeling guilty. Was this a forerunner of things to come he wondered? Will he spend the rest of his army career feeling torn between his family and the army? Probably, he decided as he swung into the car park in front of his barracks.

Unfortunately his day didn't improve, as the first thing he saw when he entered the office, was the sallow face of the Intelligence Operative.

"Good morning, Sergeant Major," Lance Corporal Dudley-Jones called standing to attention. "I wonder if I might have a word."

"Very well, Lance Corporal, wait in my office and I'll be with you in a minute."

Crane took his time making his morning coffee. Then had a quick look through the memos and lists left by Billy and Kim from last night and checked if the forensic report had come in on Lance Corporal Simms. It had. So he read it. Only then did he go into his office, lean back in his seat and look at the Intelligence Operative.

"Right, what can I do for you?"

"Well, sir. There's been a fair amount of chatter on the airwaves over the past couple of days."

Crane closed his eyes, bloody hell this was all he needed.

"We have reason to believe the talk was about a plan to be implemented soon."

Crane opened his eyes and fixed them on the Intelligence Operative.

"What's the plan?"

"Um, at the moment that's a bit vague."

"I see. Who was this chatter between?" When he got no reply, Crane tried again, "Is it from any of the Afghan officers on the garrison?" Dudley-Jones was beginning to try his patience.

"Not exactly, sir."

"Not exactly?" By now Crane was very pissed off.

"No, sir, none of them were involved as far as we know."

Crane got up and walked into the main office with the Lance Corporal trotting behind him and stood by the large scale map of the garrison. Taking a deep breath he tried out his foundling diplomatic skills.

"So, as I understand it, Lance Corporal, you are warning me that there is increased activity on the airwaves, which may or may not indicate that there is a terrorist plan afoot." Crane's fists were clenched at his sides.

"Exactly right," the Lance Corporal beamed. But with his sallow skin it looked more like a Halloween leer.

"This may or may not involve one or more of the Afghan officers on our garrison."

"Indeed, sir." The leer was still in place.

"However, as I also understand it you have not one piece of physical evidence or any witnesses to support this." By now Crane's jaw was clenched as well as his fists.

The leer started to wobble. "Well..."

"Just as I thought. The thing is, Lance Corporal, I am just a simple detective working with dead bodies, victims, forensic tests and witnesses."

Crane put his hand out to stop the other man speaking.

"In other words, physical things. Things I can hold in my hand, evidence I can see and people I can talk to. These are the tools of my trade, if you like, just as intel is yours."

Crane stuffed his hands in his pockets and walked around Dudley-Jones.

"So, you are telling me that perhaps something may be happening, either shortly or in the distant future. Is that right?"

He stopped and stared at Dudley-Jones who nodded in agreement. At least Crane thought he did. It was difficult to tell as the young man had his head on his chest, staring at the floor. Crane picked up the file containing the forensic tests on Corporal Simms.

"The difference between us is that I can tell you that someone was definitely with Corporal Simms on the night he died. Simms had a jet black hair on his shoulder. Which is all very well, you might say. Until I also tell you that Simms was blond and none of the other soldiers who were on patrol with him that night had jet black hair."

The Lance Corporal didn't speak.

"So, as a number of the Afghan officers currently on the garrison have jet black hair, I wonder if it may be a better use of your time to get back undercover and see if you can hear any 'chatter' from them." Crane put quotation marks in the air around the word chatter. "And, don't forget to pick up any stray black hairs you may find. Dismissed." Crane emphasised the final word by shouting it.

Watching the Lance Corporal's back as he left the

office, Crane mulled over the conversation, feeling that his diplomatic skills still needed work, as they were more akin to sarcasm. He rubbed his beard, fingering the scar. Dear God, he thought, still twenty-nine days left.

Night 12

Crane's guilty hot pin had been working overtime, meaning the day had been full of additional tension, as he was determined to get away on time and not let Tina down. Eventually he rushed into the house, had a quick shower and changed into clean clothes, whilst Tina waited on the settee, pretending to be absorbed in the local news. She had on her best maternity dress and to Crane looks absolutely wonderful, her skin glowing and her hair a shiny, soft curtain falling down her back.

As Aldershot was not noted for its plethora of fine restaurants, Crane had opted for El Pic, the Spanish tapas restaurant near the Atrium, in Camberley. Thinking that something different would make it an extra special evening. As long as the food was good. And they could get a table. Maybe he should have booked? And so the worrying went on as he negotiated the back roads though Camberley's leafy suburbs that he knew Tina aspired to live in.

Crane's worries were unfounded. When they arrived at the restaurant, he felt they had stepped into another world. Crane saw Tina's eyes widen as she took in the ambience of the Spanish restaurant. Dark wooden bar, dark wooden round tables and chairs, authentic Spanish memorabilia on the walls and Spanish guitar music playing softly in the background. The only thing Crane wasn't sure about was the Spanish flag bunting strung around the bar, which to him struck a slightly garish note in the otherwise authentic atmosphere.

They had a drink at the bar whilst waiting for a table, which was accompanied by an appetizer of fresh tomato and garlic on toast. Crane and Tina studied the menu together.

"What do you think we should have, Tom?"

"Oh, well, it depends on what you fancy."

"So, in other words you don't have a clue either," she laughed.

Rubbing his beard, Crane had to agree that he hadn't a clue and called over a waiter to help them decipher the menu and advise them what to have. They decided to have a couple of tapas each, which would give them four dishes they could share. He knew Tina was finding it difficult to eat a lot of food, as the baby and her stomach were fighting for the limited space left in her belly. At the moment, the baby seemed to be winning.

After eating their tapas, which they both declared delicious, Crane kept glancing at the small garden at the rear of the restaurant.

"Tell you what," said Tina, "why don't we take our coffee outside?"

Crane collected the coffee cups and followed Tina into an oasis of green shimmering under soft lights, pulling out a packet of cigarettes as soon as he sat down.

"I've had a lovely evening, thanks, Tom," Tina leaned back in her chair.

"Well, I thought it might be the last chance we'll get

for a while." Seeing the alarm in Tina's eyes, he quickly added, "When the baby comes, I mean."

"Thank goodness for that. For a minute there I thought you'd brought me here to break the news of a posting."

"No love, nothing like that. This was just a nice treat."

"We'll have to do more things during the day when the baby comes, I suppose. Remember, 'have baby will travel'. I don't intend to be the sort of mum who won't go anywhere, who's afraid to leave the house and who's careful not to make any noise indoors in case the baby wakes up."

"Talking about travelling," Crane thought out loud. "How would you feel about uprooting when I do get another posting? You know, leaving your mum and all that and moving to the other end of the country, or even abroad?"

"I must admit I've not really wanted to think about it," Tina tucked her hair behind her ears. "I guess I'll just have to face it when it happens, unless..." her voice trailed away.

"Unless?"

"Well, unless you leave the army," Tina fiddled with her unused sachet of sugar.

"What's brought this on?" Crane struggled to keep his voice even.

"Oh, obviously having the baby. I've been thinking about the future, about stability for our family, about keeping you safe." Her eyes strayed to his scar.

"I didn't realise it was a decision we had to make," he replied.

"Well, you've nearly done your twelve years. So you can take a lump sum re-settlement grant and still get a pension when you're sixty-five."

"I know that," Crane lit another cigarette, "but the pension would be much bigger if I left after eighteen years or went all the way to twenty-two. Maybe even taking a commission and serving until I'm fifty-five. Even I appreciate I've have to retire then!" Crane tried to inject some humour into the conversation, but it fell flat. So he finished with, "That's got to be a big consideration, Tina."

"So has the family." She stirred her coffee.

"I'm sorry. I thought I was considering the family. The future of our family." Crane crushed his cigarette in the ashtray.

"What about your safety?"

"My safety?" Crane's voice rose.

"For God's sake keep your voice down, Tom, or do you want the whole garden joining in our discussion?" Tina hissed. "Your safety record hasn't been too brilliant lately, has it? What with a piece of shrapnel embedded in your face in Afghanistan and then being shot twice in a bloody church of all places!"

Tina struggled to move into a more comfortable position on her chair.

"Yes, well, what exactly do you think I would do if I wasn't in the Branch?" he asked, deliberately putting her on the spot. Pulling up short of poking a finger in her face as he asked his question.

"I don't know. Security or something?"

"Security? Tina are you out of your mind? I tell you, I would be if I had to take a job like that. I'm an investigator for God's sake, not a babysitter. That's what I've been moaning about for the last eleven days. And anyway, the army's not just a job, you know that. It's a way of life. It's a community, a family."

"I'm not sure I want to join that community."

"Sorry?"

Crane hadn't the first idea what she was talking about. As far as he was concerned Tina was already part of the army community by virtue of being his wife.

"I mean moving onto the garrison, Tom. You know I don't want to do that and join the community of wives."

"Not even if I get posted abroad and you can't come?"

"No. I'm not sure I could take the gossip and nosiness of the other wives. And the restrictions on whom you can fraternise with. It's the same for the women as well as the men, Tom. The rank system filters down to the wives. It drove me nuts."

Crane finished his coffee and pushed the cup and saucer to one side. Leaning across the table towards Tina he tried to explain.

"Then we have a problem, Tina. As far as I'm concerned the army made me what I am today. It became the family I never had and gave me a reason to get up every morning. A vehicle to channel my energies into. And I've experienced so many things I wouldn't have had a chance to do in civvy street. But now I'm to have another family. You and our baby son."

Crushing out his cigarette, he stood and took the car keys out of his pocket.

"Both are equally important. Don't make me choose between the army or you and the baby, Tina. That's not fair."

Day 13

Crane banged on Staff Sergeant Jones' window. As Jones raised his head, Crane jerked his, more of a demand that he meet him outside than an invitation. Crane paced up and down the car park as he waited, pulling deeply on a cigarette.

"Morning, Crane," Jones called as he ambled out of Provost Barracks into the sunshine, wearing his short sleeved summer uniform. "Much nicer place to have a meeting, out here in the fresh air."

Crane didn't hear the words, however, as a lorry rumbled by, belching diesel fumes into the air. And anyway he was too busy adding to the pollution with his cigarette.

Once the traffic cleared, Jones tried again.

"Morning, Crane. What's up? You've got a face like a summer storm."

"Indigestion and bloody Edwards!" Crane started to pace, treating Staff Sergeant Jones as the friend he was and not a subordinate.

"Ah."

"And the bloody Intelligence Corp!"

"Ah," Jones nodded his sympathies.

Crane stopped his pacing and whirled round to face Jones.

"Bloody pompous prigs! They've just spent the last half an hour going on about intelligence chatter and mobile phone calls. None of which I could make head or tail of. It's like chasing shadows, or the wind. None of it means anything in terms of physical evidence or real life sightings." Crane threw away the dead end of his cigarette which joined a pile of discarded butts and promptly lit another one.

"Could you just calm down a minute, Crane and tell me in English what the hell you're going on about." Jones leaned again the barracks wall his hands in his pockets.

Forcing himself to relax, Crane joined Jones leaning against the wall.

"It appears that the Intelligence Corps are getting jittery. They think there's something going on, but they have no idea who, what, when, where or why. Just monitored mobile phone calls talking about seeing old friends and making new ones. I tell you Jones it's all double-dutch to me. If there is a threat to the garrison, it should come from proper hard evidence. You know people in the wrong place at the wrong time, murders, thefts, that sort of thing."

Crane turned to look at Jones.

"You agree with me don't you?"

But Jones was pale and remained silent.

"Staff?"

"I think you better come inside," Jones croaked and hurried off.

Crane took a couple of minutes to finish his cigarette, before joining Jones in his office. As he arrived at the door, he watched the Staff Sergeant rummaging through the papers on his desk. Obviously not finding what he was looking for, Jones then began lifting up his computer keyboard, in tray, out tray and finally his telephone.

"Thank God for that," he breathed, holding a piece of paper in his hand.

"Thank God for what?"

"Oh, right, sit down, Crane."

As Crane complied Jones explained he received a telephone call from the Gurkha Welfare Office in Aldershot, reporting two sightings at night by an old Gurkha called Padam Gurung. He reported seeing a possible intruder, somewhere in the vicinity of the sports centre, late at night. Jones had to admit he'd forgotten all about it due to other pressures.

"What night?" Crane demanded.

Pulling a calendar towards him, Jones calculated. "The first one was thirteen nights ago."

"Bloody hell, Staff, that's about the same time Corporal Simms was murdered."

"Murdered? Jesus Christ! I thought it was an accidental death." Jones ran his hand over his head.

"I never did," Crane growled. "Especially when we found a jet black hair on his body. And now it looks like we've got a bloody witness who can say there was someone acting suspiciously around the sports centre that night." Crane stood and strode towards the door. "Get the bloody welfare office on the phone, find this Padam Gurung and bring him in." Crane slammed the door behind him as he left the office, then changing his mind, put his head back around the door shouting, "And don't forget an interpreter!"

As Crane climbed into his car, he winced as his indigestion worsened, forcing him to take two Rennies with his cigarette during the uncomfortable journey to Aldershot Police Station.

Luckily Derek Anderson was in his office when Crane arrived, enjoying his ubiquitous cup of tea and sugary cake.

"Want one?" he asked, pushing the plate towards Crane.

"No thanks, Derek, my stomach's bad enough as it is." Crane sat opposite Anderson and pushed the plate back towards his friend.

"Stress?" Derek asked with his mouth full.

"That and unfamiliar Spanish food. I took Tina out for a meal last night. The food seemed good at the time, but I'm not so sure this morning."

"And the cause of the stress?" Anderson tried to brush cake crumbs from his jacket, but merely succeeded in rubbing them in.

"Need you ask?" Crane smiled. "Anyway, I need to talk to you about the on-going investigation into the thefts from the Team GB living quarters in St Omar Barracks."

As Derek brought him up to date, Crane's concentration kept being broken by thoughts of an old Gurkha possibly being a key witness to the murder of Corporal Simms. Plus the failing of Staff Sergeant Jones to, firstly see the relevance in the message from the Gurkha Welfare Office and secondly, not acting on it.

"So, I think it will take a few more days."

As the silence stretched, Crane realised Anderson had finished his summing up of the operation.

"Oh, sorry, thanks, I'll pass that on," Crane rose to leave.

"Are you alright?"

"Yes, of course, Derek. Just things on my mind."

Crane scratched his scar. It had been itching a lot lately.

"Anything I can help with?"

Stopping at the door Crane replied, "Not at the moment, but I'm going to need your co-operation if I have to lock down the garrison."

"What the hell? Lock down the garrison. Crane come back!" Anderson's shouts followed Crane out into the corridor, but he ignored them.

Night 13

I am afraid of exposing myself too early. Sometimes I feel like I am being watched; at night when I am scouting out possible targets and during the day when we are undergoing training. But it's nothing I can't handle. During the day I am the model Afghan Army officer and during the night a Muslim playing my part in the Jihad.

The death of the soldier was a tricky one. I was unprepared - but the Prophet Mohammed kept me safe and I was able to engineer a suitable solution. The soldier fell quickly, his dead body unable to defy the force of gravity. Landing in a heap of bones and uniform, never to rise again. I was just about to scour through his belongings when I heard his colleagues call for him on his radio, so I had to leave immediately. Next time I will make sure I get what I need.

Today we were taken on a tour of some of the facilities on the garrison. On the way we passed the athletes practicing for the Olympic Games. They were parading around half naked, preening and grooming themselves in public, like peacocks. The males strutting around as though they were ready for rutting with the females who were similarly if not more skimpily attired.

We were shown a stadium where rugby football teams play each other. Apparently frequent matches are held between various factions of your Army, Navy and Air Force. Personally, I think a stadium where males worship their bodies rather than God should be turned into a meeting place for the people, where they can watch thieves and adulterers take their punishment. A public arena for stoning and whipping. To help the people understand what happens if you ignore the teachings of the Prophet Mohammed and the laws written in the Qur'an.

But I dared not give voice to my idea. The mask - remember? It is still in place. So as I am unable to persuade with rhetoric, I will had to find another way of teaching you infidels what the punishment is for attacking the one true religion. And believe me, I will.

Night 14

Crane put the pair of night vision goggles over his eyes and scanned the surrounding countryside. Taking care to stop and examine each clump of bushes and trees. He'd been with Sergeant Billy Williams for nearly two hours, positioned near the sports centre, searching in vain for any sign of either an intruder or an old Gurkha. His growing unease about the delay in locating and bringing Padam Gurung to the Royal Military Police Barracks had necessitated tonight's vigil. But he was also plagued with a growing unease about leaving Tina at night. What if something happened to her when he wasn't there? But conversely, what if he didn't find Gurung and something happened to the athletes? Either way, he'd have to learn to live with the guilt. Overlaying all of these fears was the growing need for a cigarette. He really had to stop smoking. Looking at the luminous dial of his watch he saw it was nearly 02:00 hours.

"Boss!" Billy's whisper interrupted his reverie. "Got something. Heat source at 11 o'clock."

Crane swung his head to the left, where he could see a dull orange patch, flickering like the flame of a

Bunsen burner through the swirling green mist of the background trees. They continued to watch it for a few minutes and as the heat source remained stationary Crane decided to move.

"Right, Billy, it seems it could be a man not an animal foraging. Let's go."

Billy led the way through the undergrowth, towards the dim heat source. It looked like Crane's decision to position themselves far behind the trees bordering the sports centre had been a good one. That way they could creep up behind anyone staking out the building without revealing themselves. Any potential intruder would be facing forwards, towards the target.

As they drew near, Billy halted and Crane pulled out his 9mm pistol. On Crane's signal Billy ran and jumped on the figure, with Crane close on his heels. Billy hauled the struggling figure to his feet, smoothly turning him to face Crane's outstretched hand.

Crane gazed at the wizened brown face inches from the end of his gun, whose eyes were so wide and wild they dominated his face. His bottom lip was trapped between clenched teeth. Slowly lowering his arm, Crane put his index finger to his lips, nodded at Billy and together they marched the old Gurkha through the grass towards the car and onwards to Provost Barracks.

Still not speaking, Crane and Billy entered an empty interview room and sat the person they presumed to be Padam Gurung at the only table, ignoring the pleading looks aimed at them. They left the room, locking the door behind them.

"Well done, Billy," Crane spoke for the first time in over ten minutes. "Rustle up the interpreter, oh and cups of tea and sandwiches if you can. I don't know about the old Gurkha, but I could do with a brew."

While Billy was carrying out his orders, Crane sloped off outside for a cigarette. He once again checked that his mobile phone was turned on and set it from vibrate back to ring and vibrate. The last thing he wanted to do was to miss a call from Tina. He really wanted to phone her, but knew that was pointless. Waking her up was not an option.

Fifteen minutes later they were ready. The interpreter, a serving Gurkha currently based at the garrison and Billy, who had poached refreshments from a nearby mess and arranged them on a large metal tray.

The interpreter went into the room first and once he had established the person they had detained was indeed Padam Gurung, Billy and Crane joined them and doled out tea and sandwiches. It was clear the kind gesture was appreciated, as Padam enthusiastically attacked the sandwiches. But for some reason Crane couldn't understand he kept smiling and nodding at them, repeating the word, "Tesco."

To Crane's amusement Billy replied, "Yes, we shop there too," grinning and nodding his head, before realising he wasn't being understood.

They then began the slow and painstaking process of interviewing Padam through the interpreter.

Padam's initial reaction was fear and confusion, but Crane explained that he wasn't in any trouble. He said they were glad Padam was watching the sports centre two weeks ago and were very interested to hear what happened. But Padam was insistent they hear about both occasions when he saw the smudge and proceeded to go through both events in detail.

Crane bit back his frustration and listened carefully while Billy took notes, but his interest wasn't piqued until, between bites of sandwich, Padam recalled the second time he saw the smudge. When it apparently disappeared and then magically reappeared. Deciding to come back to that point, Crane allowed the old man to describe what happened when the smudge ran towards him.

"I stayed as still as I could, hoping that whoever it was would mistake me for a rock or mound of earth under the trees. I held my breath so I wouldn't move and rustle the leaves or break a twig." Padam smiled with satisfaction and looked at Crane and Billy as if for confirmation he had done the right thing. "I remembered these things from when I was in the army," he finished proudly.

"Well done, Padam. You did very well, but what happened next?"

"This person, he or she, ran straight to me, suddenly swerving out of my way and disappearing behind me. I stayed still for a long time, to make sure I was out of danger before finally coming out from underneath my coat and leaves. So it seems I did look like a rock after all." Once again Padam beamed and nodded at the three men in the room in turn.

"Yes," Crane agreed. "You did look like a rock, but what did the shadowy figure look like?"

"Just that. A shadowy figure. Dressed from head to foot in black. I think the face was covered by something, as I could dimly see eyes and a mouth, but nothing else."

Unable to get any further information from Padam, who clearly had no idea of the height, weight or sex of the person, Crane suggested they go back outside so Padam could show them where the smudge had disappeared against the sports centre wall. Padam readily agreed, as long as he could take the uneaten sandwiches with him.

At the end of their recce, the interpreter drove the old man back to his flat in Aldershot. Crane and Billy stood outside the SIB office talking, before Billy continued his night shift and Crane went home for a few hours sleep, before returning to do the twelve hour day shift.

"So what do you think, boss?"

"I think I'm going to give Captain Edwards a headache tomorrow when I tell him I've got evidence that Corporal Simms was murdered and I'm locking down the garrison."

Day 15

It was only 09:00 hours and already Crane was fed up of people shouting at him. First of all Tina, when he told her what was about to happen and then Staff Sergeant Jones when he got to the office. Captain Edwards would be next to have a go, although he didn't know it yet, quickly followed, no doubt, by DI Anderson.

Crane stood outside the Captain's door, took a deep breath, knocked and entered.

Edwards was pouring over Dudley-Jones' Intel and raised his head as Crane walked in. "Morning, Crane, glad you could join us," looking at his watch as Crane sat down.

"Sorry, sir just had to go and see Staff Sergeant Jones."

"Really? Why was that more important than being on time for our morning briefing?"

"To give him the heads up that I'm going to have to shut down the garrison." Crane lobbed his grenade and waited for the explosion.

Captain Edwards was just taking a mouthful of coffee as Crane spoke and spluttered most of it out. "What did you just say? Shut down the garrison?"

Crane nodded.

"Are you mad? What the hell for?" Edwards managed to control himself this time and his voice returned to something like normal. Dudley-Jones, the Intelligence Operative, didn't say anything. Anyway he couldn't because he was of a lower rank. Who would think that those four simple words 'shut down the garrison' could cause such a furore! Crane thought they were emotive responses to his carefully considered and necessary action.

Edwards spoke again. "Come on, Crane, let's have it. And it better be bloody good."

"Well, let's look at the facts, sir. A soldier has been killed on the base." Crane continued despite Edwards trying to interrupt. "I have a witness who saw a black clad figure disappear through a back door of the sports centre and then reappear some thirty minutes later, at the very time Corporal Simms was killed. And there was a rogue black hair found on Corporal Simm's shoulder." Crane was stretching the truth somewhat as Padam wasn't on the base the night that Corporal Simms was killed, it was the night after. But that particular small detail didn't bother Crane.

"I'm not sure that I can totally agree with that assessment," Captain Edwards made to rise from his chair.

Unwilling to let Edwards try his usual superior ploy Crane said, "If I could carry on, please, sir?"

As Edwards slowly sat back down Crane continued, "And of course there's the intelligence angle."

Edward's face froze. "Intelligence angle?" he finally managed.

"Yes, sir. Unless I'm very much mistaken, you and Dudley-Jones here have been strongly advocating that I should take notice of all the intelligence chatter that's been going on. Seriously consider it as a threat. So you'll be pleased to hear I've also taken that into account. In fact the intel persuaded me that locking down the garrison was my only option. I'm sure the higher echelons of command will want us to be doing our best to protect not only our soldiers but Team GB as well." Crane finished speaking looking around in satisfaction.

In the end he agreed to increased security rather than a complete lock-down. That meant armed soldiers at every entrance to the garrison, with the right to stop and search each vehicle and person that entered. A right which Crane would make sure the lads fulfilled with enthusiasm.

After the negotiation was complete, Crane said, "Well, if there's nothing else, sir, I think I better visit St Omar Barracks. Speak to the Olympic representatives and then the local police. Unless, of course, you'd like to do that, sir?"

Receiving no reply Crane retreated from the office before anyone noticed the grin breaking out from behind his rigid mask of respect. The last thing Crane wanted was for Edwards to realise that increased security was his goal all along. He needed to save total lock down for another day. Keeping it as his ace up his sleeve.

After telephoning Jones and confirming the increased security, authorising barricades at every entrance, he then faced the Olympic representatives and athletes. He explained that due to a higher level intelligence threat, the army felt increased security was necessary. Nothing to alarm anyone. Just a precautionary measure. And, as the athletes didn't leave the garrison, it wouldn't affect them at all. In fact it could make things a lot quieter for them, he reasoned. There should be less gawkers, as local people probably wouldn't be bothered to wait in traffic jams and undergo a vehicle search just to come and watch the athletes train.

Driving to Aldershot Police Station, Crane was rather proud of his diplomatic skills, or was that manipulative skills? Crane didn't really care as long as it got him the desired result.

DI Anderson was just leaving the police station when Crane arrived, so he had to walk alongside him back to the car park, pleased to be out in the fresh air after the interminable morning meetings. On the way to Anderson's car, Crane outlined the reasons for the tighter security and vehicle searches at the garrison. Swearing Anderson to secrecy as to the real reason, of course.

"Alright, Crane," Anderson sighed as they reached his car and he fished his car keys out of his pocket. "I understand what you had to do, but I'm not happy about it. Purely because of the crap we'll get from angry residents. But my more immediate problem is these petty thefts from St Omar Barracks. The undercover WPC reported that a couple of the cleaners are acting suspiciously but she has no hard evidence. And on top of that the Witch of the North is ringing me daily for a report! I'd really like to get her off my back. Any suggestions?"

Crane leaned against Anderson's car. "Well, you never know, the increased security may throw something up. We'll just have to wait and see."

At that point Crane's mobile rang. Looking at the caller display he grinned at Anderson and said, "Speaking of the devil," before answering the phone call from Juliette Stone.

He immediately held the phone away from his ear as Juliette Stone launched into a very loud tirade of complaints. The volume was such that even Anderson winced before laughing and waiving to Crane as he drove away. This time Crane didn't bother with his diplomatic skills, not that they would have done any good, as he couldn't get a word in. The veritable Ms Stone didn't seem to pause for breath. At the end of the diatribe he was ordered to attend her office, in person, immediately and she then put the phone down. A bemused Crane simply added her to the list of people who had shouted at him that morning and made his way back to the garrison.

He didn't get very far.

The queue started just past Hospital Hill. With a smile playing across his lips Crane settled down to wait, deciding to take the opportunity to check in with Tina. By the time they had finished chatting he was near the front of the long line of vehicles waiting to drive through the garrison. Now he could see what had caused the inordinate wait.

After showing his ID to the armed soldiers on duty and driving through the barricade, he parked up and wandered back down to the cordon, with the air of a man out for a stroll in the warm sun. He watched a small knot of very angry people converging on the young soldiers, demanding to know what was going on. The placid yet determined air of the soldiers fuelled their anger rather than dissipating it. But they stoically continued to refuse to let any vehicle through without a thorough search. Any pedestrians and those on bicycles were subjected to a personal search.

Crane heard a strident voice ring out, "This is

absolutely ridiculous. You can rest assured I will be putting all this down in my article!"

The voice belonged to Diane Chambers, self appointed investigative reporter for the Aldershot Mail. Crane watched the young woman direct her photographer, encouraging him to snap the most inflammatory pictures he could, to go with what would probably be her equally inciting article. Unfortunately Diane Chambers caught sight of the smiling Crane.

"Ah, Sergeant Major Crane," she called, striding towards him in her uniform of jeans and tee-shirt, her short dark curly hair framing her young face. "I'm glad you find the anger of the Aldershot people so amusing. Perhaps you could let us in on the joke?"

Diane Chambers thrust a small recorder in his face.

"Good morning to you as well. I'm afraid my smile is nothing more sinister than enjoyment of this beautiful weather. Or doesn't the sun make you feel happy Diane?"

"Quite frankly, the weather is irrelevant to me. I'm working. And personally I find it difficult to smile when the decent hard working population of Aldershot are subject to bullying by the army."

"Bullying?" Crane looked around, his incredulity equally directed at both the bullying accusation and the claim that the population of Aldershot were decent and hardworking. "I don't see any incidents of bullying, Miss Chambers."

"What do you call this then?" Diane emphasised her point with a large sweep of her arm.

"Soldiers carrying out their job of protecting Team GB and the local community, with dignity. I don't see one soldier being rude or abusive to anyone. They are merely trying to do their job in what is clearly a very difficult situation. So, if you'll excuse me, I'd better go and give them a hand."

Crane walked away. He wanted to say much more, but knew he had to curb his tongue. The last thing he needed was to be misquoted by a zealous reporter. He was sure the article was going to be bad enough without him adding to the damage. And anyway, something had caught his eye.

The people going through the barrier into the garrison weren't the only ones being searched. Those leaving the garrison were also subjected to the same procedure. This applied equally to those merely travelling through the garrison as to those leaving after visiting or working there. Crane's eye had been caught by a group of people waiting to go through the barrier from the garrison side, towards Aldershot town centre. They were travelling in an Aspire Defence mini-bus and had been obliged to leave the vehicle and wait in turn to be searched.

What Crane had seen was the young WPC from Aldershot Police Station, currently working undercover in St Omar Barracks. She looked at Crane and very slightly inclined her gaze towards two women standing to one side of the group from the minibus. The two women were agitated, eyes averted from the soldiers, their arms crossed as though hugging themselves to keep warm.

Crane casually approached the soldiers and stood next to them whispering instructions. As the queue shuffled forward, Crane saw the WPC join the two women, attempting to distract them and thus separate them further from their Aspire Defence colleagues. So the three women were the last of the group to approach the barrier where they were confronted by two armed soldiers and shepherded to one side of the road.

Speaking over their protests Crane explained that the soldiers needed to search the carrier bags they were holding.

"Bloody army!" shouted one, "who the hell do you think you are?" Her garishly painted mouth twisted into a snarl and she pushed back hair as yellow and brittle as the drought stricken grass she was standing on. Her Aspire Defence bib, worn over a tired once white shirt, was blotched and stained.

"Why can't you leave decent people alone and concentrate on catching bloody terrorists?" her companion spat, her words slurred by the tongue and mouth piercings she sported. She tried to pull her tattooed arm out of the grasp of soldier.

"Ladies, please." Crane used the description sarcastically but doubted it would register with either woman. "We simply want to check your bags."

"Not fucking likely!" Straw hair swung her bag into the face of an unprepared soldier, twisting out of his grasp and turned to run back towards the garrison. But she only made it as far as the WPC's foot. As she sprawled on the floor, displaying her laddered tights and red underwear, the two soldiers quickly pounced, taking a woman each and handcuffing them, ignoring the foul words spewing from two equally unattractive mouths.

Night 16

Crane replaced the telephone and slumped back in his office chair before stretching out the stiffness in his limbs. A large yawn reminded him how tired he was and how much he was looking forward to going home to Tina. As the time for the birth of their son drew nearer, he was finding it more and more difficult to detach himself from his personal life whilst at work. He often found his hand caressing the mobile phone in his pocket, in fear of missing the vital call. The one calling him to her side at the hospital as labour had started. No more had been said about him leaving the army since their visit to the restaurant. As though by tacit agreement, neither had raised the subject again. But he was well aware that didn't mean it would go away. His musings were interrupted by a knock on his door.

"Boss?"

"Yes, Billy what is it?"

"DI Anderson would like a word."

"Okay, put him through." Crane nodded towards the telephone.

"No, he's here in the office."

"Oh! Fair enough, rustle up coffee would you?"

Crane stood up and tried to smarten his appearance, although as he tucked in his white shirt and did up his tie, he realised there was not much he could do to improve it. His shirt looked like it had been put in the tumble dryer for too long with the resulting creases fused into the material by the heat. No amount of smoothing down made a difference. Glancing at the glass panels in his office wall, he saw his face reflected back at him, showing the strain of the past few days. New lines were appearing around his eyes and his beard was beginning to look straggly instead of short and smart.

The man who walked into his office looked no better. Anderson clearly didn't do warm weather. His shirt was damp, his tie long since discarded and his trousers had the appearance of clothing purchased from a pile of screwed up garments in a charity shop sale bin.

"Jesus, it's hot," Anderson exclaimed sitting in the chair opposite Crane. "I thought it would get cooler at night."

"Coffee, sir?" Billy had followed the DI into the office and placed a mug in front of Anderson and then Crane.

"Rather have a cold pint of larger," Anderson grumbled, but grabbed the mug anyway.

"How's things?"

"That's why I came. Thought I'd bring you up to date on my way home."

"About the thefts?"

"Mmm," Anderson slurped his coffee. "Got those two women banged up for theft. Well done on that one, Crane."

"Thanks, but it was more a case of being in the right place at the right time than any detective work. If you remember, yesterday the Witch of the North had just ripped my head off over the phone, as more items had been stolen. She was annoyed to say the least that we hadn't got the people who took the first ring and watch and more jewellery going missing added insult to injury."

"The WPC was closing in on them, though. She'd already identified them as being the most likely suspects."

"Yes, but she had no proof until they were stopped at the barrier. Then by running, they gave us the excuse we needed to apprehend them. A shifty couple of women they were too. It didn't take much to figure out that they were probably holding the stolen items."

"Yeah, well, thanks anyway." Anderson saluted Crane with his mug.

"Derek, it was just a good example of co-operation between the army and the local police. And anyway you got the arrest. I don't need to worry about targets like you do."

"Don't get me started on targets." Anderson finished his coffee, placing the empty mug on Crane's desk. "Well, I'm off home. What about you?"

Crane rose and walked with Anderson out of the office. "I'll be off soon," he said, once more fingering the phone in his pocket.

"Good. Try not to leave Tina on her own too much."

As the two men walked out of the building into the balmy dusk, Crane ignored the lovely view of the playing fields stretching out before him towards Farnborough and turned to Anderson.

"How do you manage to juggle work and home life?" asked Crane.

"I don't," was the blunt reply as Anderson patted his pockets looking for his car keys.

"But you're married. Sorry, I don't understand." Crane fished in his pocket for his cigarettes and lighter.

"I don't worry about it. My wife copes with it, not me."

"Come again?"

Anderson climbed into his car and spoke to Crane through the open window. "When we got married, I was already a policeman. Jean and I had a long talk and I explained that she wasn't going to have a normal life being married to a copper and an ambitious one at that. I wasn't being selfish. She just had to understand what she was getting into. Long hours, disrupted nights, broken promises, missed holidays, birthdays and anniversaries. It's hard, but that's the way it is."

"Doesn't she ever complain?"

"Oh yes, she often grumbles about being more like a single parent than a married woman, but I know it's nothing serious. Just her letting off a bit of steam. Understandable really."

"Did you ever think of getting out of the force?"

"Yes, but I couldn't see the point really. I'm a copper through and through. It's who I am. I could never really do anything else."

Anderson started the engine and drove away, leaving Crane smoking his cigarette and thinking.

By the time he'd finished it Crane had made a decision. About work though, not his turbulent domestic arrangements. Returning to his office, he called an impromptu meeting with Billy, Kim and Staff Sergeant Jones, who Kim managed to catch before he left the barracks.

"Right," Crane began after everyone was seated in

the open plan office in front of the board detailing the murder of Corporal Simms. Covered with pictures of the soldier, both dead and alive. "I just wanted a quick word about the Afghan officers we have on the garrison."

Jones groaned, "For God's sake, Crane, not again. Is this what you called me in for? Jesus, man, I want to go home."

"Hear me out, would you." Crane paced in front of them. "I just think that with the increased security level on the garrison it gives us an ideal opportunity to keep a closer eye on them."

"In what way, sir?" Kim perched on the edge of a desk, as cool as ever, despite the humidity.

"Well, as there are so many Royal Military Police around at the moment, I think we could place a few more eyes and ears around them without arousing suspicion."

"But what about the Intelligence Operative, sir?" Billy asked between gulps from a can of cold drink. "Isn't he supposed to be under cover with them?"

"Supposed is the word, Billy. Have we had any useful reports from Lance Corporal Dudley-Jones?"

"Well, now that you mention it, boss, no."

"Exactly. But go through them again tonight anyway and double check," Crane ordered. "So what do you think, Staff?" Crane turned his attention back to Jones.

"How am I supposed to achieve this, Crane?" Jones sighed and rubbed his bald head.

"Just alter the rosters a bit. You've got extra men already because of Team GB and even more now because of the increased security level. So all you have to do is to introduce New Mons Barracks into your patrols. Keep switching the men, so the Afghans don't get suspicious by seeing the same faces. Kim can work out the details for you tonight if you like. Can't you, Kim?"

"Of course, sir, glad to help." Kim was already jotting down notes.

"There you go then," Crane grinned.

"So what did the Captain think of your new plan?" Jones asked a smile playing on his lips.

"Let's just say that on a need to know basis, I don't think he needs to know about this. Do you?"

Day 17

UNDER SEIGE
by Diane Chambers

Aldershot is living under siege conditions after the recent tightening of security at the garrison.

According to a military spokesman, the measure was necessary because of an increased security threat and the obvious need to protect Team GB. But this is causing real problems for many local residents. Armed soldiers at check points with stop and search authority are producing long traffic delays and giving people a feeling of being intimidated.

"It's horrible," one local commented. "Gun toting soldiers insisting on stopping and searching every vehicle. Raking through our personal possessions. It made me feel like a criminal." Others who need to use the garrison as a cut through to North Camp are finding the long delays badly affecting them. One driver commented, "Yesterday it took me nearly an hour to get through the garrison. I had to ring my employer to tell him I was going to be late for work. It's totally unacceptable."

Delivery companies are also having problems, unable to meet the tight time schedules imposed by their companies as they are forced to either wait in long queues or drive miles out of their way.

Yet the military were unrepentant. When asked what he felt about the situation, Sergeant Major Tom Crane merely commented, "The soldiers are just doing their job." Well, a job it may be. But innocent residents should not be the ones to pay the price.

Diane Chambers welcomes any comments from local residents. She can be contacted by email on: chambers@aldershotmail.com

Captain Edwards threw the paper at Crane. "See what you've done now? The whole of Aldershot is furious because you decided to up the security level at the garrison borders."

"With respect, sir," Crane countered.

"Respect! That's something you seem to be lacking in at the moment, Crane. I quote," the Captain peered at the paper. "'The soldiers were just doing their job.' Unquote. Couldn't you come up with something a bit more conciliatory?" Edwards threw the newspaper down as though it was on fire and about to burn his fingers.

"That's what I'm trying to tell you, sir. Diane Chambers used my words out of context. I said more than that, but she's chosen not to print all of it."

The row was taking place in Crane's office for a change. He was glad that Billy and Kim were on nights and not there to witness it. But he guessed word would soon get round from other members of the SIB who he could see listening intently, whilst trying to look busy.

"Well that's nothing new is it? You've had run-ins with her before, so you should know what to expect by now." Captain Edwards paced around Crane's small office, like a caged lion. First one way and then the other. Over and over again. Crane's next words made him stop.

"I got the petty thieves through the stop and search procedures, sir, surely that counts for something."

"Of course it does, Crane, but no one knows about it, do they? All they know is that the army are making their lives difficult and Diane Chambers intends to fuel the fire as much as she can."

Crane was still standing behind his desk. He had risen from his chair when the Captain entered his office and had not been given permission to sit down.

"May I remind you, sir, that you authorised the stop and search, as did the brass upstairs."

"No you may not!" Edwards shouted pointing a finger at Crane. "Don't try and turn this back on me."

"Sorry, sir. Shall I just cancel the whole thing then? And bugger the consequences?"

"Consequences?"

"Yes, sir. Terrorists trying to smuggle bombs or bomb making equipment into the garrison, hidden in vehicles. Or had you forgotten the increase in the threat level recommended by Intelligence?"

"No, Crane, I hadn't forgotten. Look, just try and handle it a bit better. Perhaps you should call Diane Chambers." Edwards rubbed his long aquiline nose. "No. On second thoughts, stay well clear of her and any other reporter that may want a comment. Speak to DI Anderson instead and see if he can do anything to defuse the press. Dismissed."

When Crane didn't move, Edwards looked around the room as if only just realising he was in Crane's office and not the other way around. Two spots of colour appeared on his cheeks and he rushed out of the door without even collecting the offending newspaper.

Smiling, Crane sat down and pulled the newspaper towards him re-reading the article. He then turned over the page where an interesting headline caught his eye.

HOMELESS GURKHAS A DISGRACE

Once more written by Diane Chambers, the article was an inflammatory diatribe against the elderly Gurkhas who had flooded into Aldershot and Farnborough with no money, no jobs and nowhere to live. They were being blamed for all sorts of things: for looking untidy; hanging around street corners, which some residents found threatening; begging; muggings and break-ins. Local charities were quoted as 'doing their best' but that was clearly not enough as far as the paper was concerned. The main thrust of the article was that the streets needed to be cleansed of this menace. Diane Chambers, as usual, taking an inflammatory point of view without offering any balanced argument.

Crane thought back to his conversation with Padam and knew the reality was very different. Many of the old Gurkhas were destitute, arriving in England with scant possessions and no money. He had read previous articles in the national press which said that Gurkhas who arrived in England needed about £2,000 each to pay for accommodation and basic furniture - about the equivalent of three year's pension for the old men. A sum of money totally beyond their means as they had already sold their farms and land in Nepal to pay for their visas and flights, or taken out huge loans which they would never be able to repay. A sad ending for soldiers who had a long history with the British Army. Being interested in military history, Crane knew that in World War II over 250,000 soldiers from the Nepalese hills served Britain in her hour of need. Ten Victoria Crosses were awarded to them, as befitting a fighting race, whose motto, to this day, was 'Better to die than be a coward'. Crane thought he should mention this article to Anderson as well.

When his mobile rang, he was still thinking about the Gurkhas.

"Tom? Tom can you hear me?" the panicky voice of Tina's mother sounded tinny in his ear.

"Yes, Brenda, what's the matter? Is it Tina?" Crane stood up and walked towards the door.

"Yes. We were having coffee in town and she went all dizzy and pale and then broke out into a sweat. She said she had a bad headache and just felt unwell. I called an ambulance and she's on her way to Frimley Park Hospital."

"Is she having contractions?" Crane was walking through the main office.

"No, they think it's her blood pressure. I'm on my way to the hospital now in my car."

"Right. I'll get back to you." Crane snapped shut the phone and ran up the stairs to Captain Edward's office. He knocked on the open door and put his head through the gap.

"Sorry, sir. But Tina's just been rushed to Frimley Park Hospital." Crane stayed where he was, half in and half out of the office.

"Oh it's you, Crane. Come in."

Crane hesitated in the doorway. "I was just letting you know I was leaving, sir."

"Leaving? Is the baby coming?"

"No, sir, they think it's her blood pressure apparently."

"Have you talked to DI Anderson yet?"

"Well I was just about to but then..." Crane's voice tailed off and he looked at his mobile phone which was still in his hand.

"Then request denied. You were making a request weren't you, Sergeant Major?"

Crane moved further into the office and stood to attention. "Yes, sir, I was making a request." He drew out every word.

"That's what I thought." Edwards tilted his head so his nose was in the air. "Request denied. Carry on, Sergeant Major."

"But, sir, Tina?"

"Crane, you said yourself the baby isn't on the way. And as you keep reminding me we have an emergency situation on the garrison, so I'm afraid I can't spare you."

"For f….." Crane didn't finish the word as Edward's disdainful stare cut off the expletive.

"Sir." Crane mumbled and left the office, clenching his jaw to stop him saying something he would regret for the rest of his army career. But in his mind he was calling his Officer Commanding every foul word he knew. He wanted to grasp Edward's neck and squeeze hard, wiping the sneering expression off the Captain's face for good.

Once back in his office he grabbed his cigarettes and headed for the car park. He wasn't going anywhere. He just needed the nicotine crutch whilst he called Brenda.

After making the call he closed the phone and then his eyes, wondering how the hell he was supposed to survive the next twenty-four days with his sanity intact.

Night 17

My brothers, have I told you about the lessons I learned at school? Islamic lessons, of course, in an Islamic School. One of the big lessons I learned there was that looking like a non-Muslim is forbidden. Those who do not look like Muslims are disbelievers or infidels. I was taught not to be fashionable in society. By that I mean wearing Western style clothing. I tell you, it is true that adopting western dress is a way of enslaving Muslims. The first step by the West in their programme of mind control.

Yes, mind control. We Muslims must fight it with every part of our being. These Western governments will enslave us, controlling Muslim minds, making us do what they want us to do. Brain washing Muslims into adopting Western customs and attitudes.

So now I ask you, my Muslim brothers here with me in England, are you part of those who prefer that way of life over the way of the Prophet? You should hate the sinful nature of non-Muslim society. Be aware of all the evil on the streets. Evil that can come from Westerners and Muslims alike. Beware of those Muslims who do not wear the Hejaz properly. Beware of those Muslims who smoke.

I tell you, you should hate walking down the streets of Aldershot. As you do, you should be mindful of the words of the great Prophet Mohammed who showed us how to live our lives for the glory of Allah.

We must be vigilant and condemn the ways of non-Muslims. Do not emulate those from any other religions; be they Jews, Christians or Atheists. Do not copy anything! Remember who heaven has been prepared for – us Muslims. So I urge you to forget any friends from outside Muslim society and think only of your religion.

Remember that Allah has described the disbelievers as the worst of all people. Do you still want to follow them, their ways and their practices? You must not. It is not the right thing to do.

I denounce the concept of integrating into British society or any Western society that wants to impose its ways on our glorious country. This is NOT the right thing to do. Even as bad as some Muslims have become, being brain washed into living a Westernised way of life - even they are not as bad as infidels or kaffir. For never will a kaffir enter heaven, until a camel can enter the eye of a needle.

Day 18

Nearly twenty hours after her admittance to hospital, Tina was responding well to treatment. So great was Crane's relief, tears blurred his vision and threaten to leak out of the corners of his eyes, but he gulped them back. When he turned to Tina he saw that she hadn't suppressed her emotions and tears were spilling down her cheeks.

"Do you understand?" said Tina

"Understand what?"

"What the doctor was saying about pre-eclampsia."

"Not really," Crane had to admit, letting go of Tina's hand and falling into the chair by her bed. He'd had very little sleep. Rushing to the hospital after work and refusing to leave. He knew he'd have to get back to the garrison soon, but decided against risking a peek at his watch.

"Well, it seems that my blood pressure was too high and apparently I've got protein in my wee. But they are giving me Magnesium…" she paused, searching for the right word and failing, "something or other, which is helping my blood pressure come down. So it seems I won't develop full blown eclampsia after all."

"As long as you follow orders."

"Exactly, Sergeant Major," Tina laughed. "As long as I follow orders and stay here in hospital, in bed and rest for a couple of days. Speaking of orders," her expression turned serious, "shouldn't you be getting back to the garrison?"

Crane looked at his watch, as Tina had brought up the subject, not him. It was perilously close to 07:00 hours.

"I'm afraid so, love. Are you sure you'll be alright?"

"Of course, Tom. I'm in hospital aren't I? And anyway Mum's coming in later today during visiting hours."

"Look, about yesterday…" he began, but as usual couldn't seem to finish the sentence.

"Tell you what," Tina said, "why don't you see if you can make me a cup of tea before you go?"

Crane left Tina's bedside and enquired about tea at the nurse's desk. They pointed the way to the kitchen and told him to help himself. As he was waiting for the kettle to boil and hunting for clean cups, he wondered why he found some conversations with Tina so difficult. He knew he either refused to talk about whatever subject she'd brought up, or turned all defensive, deliberately making an argument out of a discussion. He was sure she wanted to talk to him again about leaving the army, but he just couldn't face that particular discussion at the moment.

He realised he couldn't let her down too many times before it caused a rift between them. Did she know how guilty he felt? Probably. Then again, possibly not. He had never told her about the hot pin of guilt that poked his brain. The one he tried to ignore as much as possible.

By now he was back with Tina offering her the cup of tea.

"I know you want me to leave the army," he blurted. The blunt words not coming out as he intended, as usual. Thoughts spilling out of his mouth before he'd engaged his brain.

"What? Where the hell had that come from? Did I miss the beginning of a conversation you've just had with yourself?"

"Probably," Crane admitted. "I was just thinking in the kitchen." He looked at his wife, lying in the bed. Her long dark hair tied back, emphasising her pale face.

"I appreciate you realise it's something we need to talk about," she said. "But not yet and certainly not now. Remember, no pressure, no excitement and definitely no stress."

"Is that me or you?"

Crane reached for his jacket, ducking out of the way as Tina took a swipe at him, then bent down and kissed her cheek.

"I'll see you tonight after work. Unless something happens to you or the baby. You will get them to phone me at once won't you?"

"Of course, Tom, now bugger off to work."

"Yes Ma'am," he saluted. Turning away he tried not to run out of the ward. He had a clean shirt at work and a washing kit, so he shouldn't look too bad. Perhaps if he sat down most of the day, no one would notice his creased trousers. Lost in his thoughts, he didn't see Tina wave goodbye.

Nor did he seem to be aware of the traffic on his way to work, until he arrived at the queue of cars waiting to enter the garrison. He'd been thinking about his conversation with Derek Anderson yesterday when he went to the station, as the Captain had insisted. Together they'd agreed the wording for an explanatory press release, about the increased security requirements, which they hoped would be included in next week's edition of the Aldershot Mail. But personally Crane wasn't holding his breath. He didn't trust Diane Chambers as far as he could throw her.

Last year he had pushed her a bit too far. Offering access to him in future investigations and an exclusive interview, after the successful capture of a megalomaniac, intent on persuading fathers to kill their sons and to then commit suicide. But Crane hadn't kept his side of the bargain. Not that he'd had any intention of keeping it in the first place. So now Diane was determined to portray the army in general, and Crane in particular, in the worst possible light. Anderson had promised to have a word with her. Maybe the threat of limited access to the police would do the trick.

Leaning out of his side window, Crane saw there were only three cars before him waiting to go through the barrier. As he watched the soldiers interviewing a driver, prowling around the vehicle, putting mirrors on long poles underneath it and walking sniffer dogs around the bodywork, he caught a glimpse of a slim young woman with short brown curly hair wearing a checked shirt. Mindful of Captain Edward's words, he turned the car around, causing even more traffic chaos, on his way to finding another route into the garrison. Avoiding Diane Chambers was preferable even to being late. He could always say that he had been monitoring the stop and search procedures should anyone ask.

Day 19

The steps outside the Princess Theatre and the adjoining gardens in Aldershot, had long been used for civic parades and receptions, and today was no different. The fitful sun flitted from behind the clouds every now and then only to run away, as though playing its own version of hide and seek. The crowd were following its game, pulling off cardigans and coats when it shone brightly, only to don them again when it hid behind a cloud. The large banner displayed across the front of the Theatre read 'Aldershot Welcomes Team GB'. An odd banner to use, as this was a farewell ceremony, Crane thought. But then he'd never really understood the workings of Mayor Braithwaite's brain.

Crane was mingling with the crowd, standing out like a sore thumb, dressed completely different to the majority, with his short sleeved white shirt and tie worn under a dark suit. Everyone else was in casual summer clothes. Crane may as well have been in full military uniform, he looked that incongruous.

Someone had obviously been handing out Union Jack flags, as Crane saw several children waiving them in a burst of national pride. As he watched more closely he saw they were also being used as effective weapons, to hit other children over the head with, poke up bottoms and in one instance into an unsuspecting eye. The affected child started to wail. The mother, more intent on drinking her can of larger than looking after her child, simply looked down at the bawling girl, told her to 'fucking shut up' and added a slap to make her point. Crane turned away, sickened.

The sound of microphones being checked brought his attention back to the large steps in front of him. "Testing one two three," rolled around the gardens from strategically placed loudspeakers and was met with jeers from the crowd.

"Get on with it then, mate!" someone bawled in Crane's ear. "We ain't got all day you know – the pubs open soon!" The jester glowed with pride at the raucous laughter that followed his comments. God help us if this is Aldershot's finest, Crane thought.

A commotion on the steps heralded the arrival of Mayor Braithwaite, complete with robes and gold chain. The sun also decided to make an appearance, obviously not wanting to be left out of the proceedings, resulting in large drops of sweat rolling off the Mayor's pockmarked face onto his robes within minutes. Quickly grabbing a proffered handkerchief from his wife's hand, he dabbed his face and began to speak.

"Citizens of Aldershot, thank you for turning out in your hundreds to wave Team GB goodbye and wish them good luck in the forthcoming Olympic Games!" Whilst the Mayor raised his own Union Jack flag and waved it in the air, Crane looked at the fifty or so people gathered around him and suppressed a smile at the Mayor's powers of estimation.

"The team will be passing by shortly. In the

meantime please show your appreciation for the Aldershot Town Band."

Desultory clapping was soon drowned out by the sound of brass instruments played inexpertly, yet more or less in time. A discordant sound that most people ignored, merely raising their voices to carry on their conversations over the music. Crane slipped under the police cordon and showed his ID to the nearest constable before crossing the road to the steps of the theatre. Angling sideways as he climbed, he headed for DI Anderson who was standing on the edge of the steps.

"Doesn't this make you proud to be British?" asked Anderson by way of greeting.

Guessing it was an ironical statement, Crane merely nudged Anderson's arm and nodded his head towards the Mayor and the figure standing beside him. Diane Chambers, clearly revelling in her role as reporter for the Aldershot Mail, was interviewing the Mayor, thrusting a small recorder under his nose.

"This should be fun, Derek," Crane said, listening in on the interview.

"This is a proud moment for Aldershot," the Mayor was saying.

"But do you think the price the good people of Aldershot had to pay was worth it?"

The Mayor looked perplexed and muttered, "What price?"

"The disruption. Increased security at the garrison. Harassment by the army. Long traffic jams. Need I go on?"

"Surely, a small price to help the pride of our nation on their way to victory, Diane." The Mayor had a nervous smile playing on his lips, clearly not sure why the interview was taking such a bad turn.

"So you condone the actions of the army and the police?"

"Condone?"

Crane laughed out loud as the Mayor, frantically looked around for someone to get him out of the situation, but no one was taking any notice of him.

"Yes, Mayor Braithwaite. Condone. Or if you prefer, excuse or pardon the heavy handed actions of the army."

"I'm… I'm sure they only did what they thought necessary..." Mayor Braithwaite was now craning his neck and spying the coaches containing the athletes he said, "I'm sorry, Diane, you'll had to excuse me. Team GB are on their way."

As the Mayor rushed to his wife's side, Diane Chambers looked around for another victim. Crane turned his back to her before she could spot him.

"Coward," laughed Anderson.

"Too right," agreed Crane, remaining where he was, only turning around when Anderson assured him the coast was clear.

The first bus pulled up and some passengers disembarked. Representatives from Team GB, the IOC and BOA climbed the steps, where they were greeted by the Mayor. They shook hands with assorted local dignitaries, waved to the crowd and got back into the bus. To the sound of the brass band, the buses filed past the waiting crowd, athletes waiving from the windows. As the last bus left, the sun got bored and disappeared, leaving the straggling crowd shivering as they dispersed.

"Thank God that's over," said Crane, lighting a cigarette.

"Aren't you going to give those up?"

"I'm supposed to when the baby comes."

"Good luck with that then."

"Which, the baby or giving up smoking?" Crane flicked ash onto the road.

"Both I reckon. Still at least this is finished," Anderson indicated the Team GB banner. "You must be relieved."

"Yes. Now just twenty-one days left." Crane ground the stub of his cigarette under his foot.

"Twenty-one days?"

So Crane explained his theory that he'd been pushed into the wilderness for forty days and forty nights, looking after the Olympians and Paralympians and co-ordinating their security.

"So now I've got the Paralympians arriving tomorrow." Crane finished. "I tell you, Derek, both teams had better win lots of bloody medals after all this!"

"You'll be prouder than anyone when they do, Crane. It will all have been worthwhile."

"I guess so."

Crane stared across the steps towards Aldershot Garrison which could be seen in the distance, on the other side of the dual carriageway. The wind was starting to get up and Crane's tie fluttered in the breeze, causing him to do up his jacket to keep it in place.

"But in the meantime, I've got a dead soldier, no leads and a load of Afghan officers on the garrison. And on top of that there's still the job of co-ordinating security, as well as looking after the Paralympians."

"No problem for a man like you," Anderson smiled, his grey wispy hair blowing in the now cold wind.

"I'm not so sure anymore, Derek."

Crane looked at the ground and studied his shoes, shivering slightly as the wind cut through his lightweight suit.

Night 19

At last I have been given my chance – nothing can stop me now. I can sense everyone thinks the threat is over. People seem more relaxed on the garrison, laughing and joking and drinking alcohol. The security level should be downgraded soon and I will then be free to roam around, putting the finishing touches to my master plan.

Talking of roaming around the garrison, do you know what I saw today? People lying prone on the grass. Nothing wrong with that you might think? But what about when some of them were scantily clad couples practically fornicating? Practicing in public what should only be done by a married man and woman in the privacy of their own home.

One of the young women I remember in particular. She was with a group of men, boys really. I watched as she lay down on the grass, then got up again and teasingly removed her outer clothing, revealing milk white skin, her upper body covered by a scanty piece of silk. I could see the boys ogling the shape of her breasts and the sliver of skin revealed between her top and her skirt as she stretched out. I watched as she languidly hitched up her skirt revealing bare thighs and lay back once again with her arms stretched above her head. Her uncovered head. Her soft brown hair framing her face, some of it tumbling down her chest, like fingers stretching and craning towards the mound of her breasts.

Suddenly I remembered where I was and had to quickly gather my thoughts, replace my slipped mask and turn my face towards the army officer giving us instruction. But all the time, in the back of my mind, was the image of the young woman I had seen. Poisoning my thoughts and my body. A body that was threatening to expose my basest instinct. This, my friend, is why Muslim women and indeed all women should be covered in public. So they can't taint the thoughts of good true Muslim men. See how that image threatens to divert my thoughts from the one true path? But I am strong, both mentally and physically. I will resist the temptations of your Western ways.

And so, back to my plan. Things are falling into place. I have chosen a location and now have made a mental list of things I need. Not a written list. I have been instructing my Muslim brothers in the ways of the Qur'an and now it is nearly time to reveal to them what we have to do to glorify the name of Allah.

Nearly, but not quite.

Day 20

Crane was in the meeting being held in the open plan office of Provost Barracks. It was a mixture of de-briefing and forward planning. De-briefing on the security for the Olympians and a briefing about the arrangements for the Paralympians, due to arrive that afternoon. Crane looked around and saw all the usual suspects. Captain Edwards in command, if not control. Staff Sergeant Jones resigned to twenty one more days of rosters, plotting the movement of his own and drafted in Royal Military Police. Sergeant Billy Williams, his youthful zeal undaunted by 20 straight 12 hour shifts of night duty. Sergeant Kim Weston, as usual surrounded by files, notebook in hand, the epitome of efficiency. Lance Corporal Dudley-Jones, trying to look competent and knowledgeable by burying his head in computer print outs, and failing. They had just finished the de-briefing of the past nineteen days.

"So, any problems?"

Crane looked around the table and when no one else responded to Captain Edward's question, he said, "Well, sir, I consider the unresolved murder of Corporal Simms as a problem."

"In what way?" Edwards steepled his hands and pressed his finger tips together.

"Well, because it's unresolved, sir."

Closing his eyes, Captain Edwards said, "I know that, Crane. Can you be more specific?"

"I feel this matter should be factored into our security arrangements for the coming days." Noticing Captain Edward's hard stare, he slowly added, "With your permission, sir."

Predictably Edwards rose and began pacing up and down the side of the rectangular table. Stopping in front of Crane he asked, "How?"

"By keeping the increased security level."

There was a spluttering sound from Staff Sergeant Jones at the other end of the table. Ignoring it Edwards called, "Dudley-Jones!" The young man began to rise from his seat, before realising there was no need. He sank back down and replied, "Yes, Captain?"

"Would you inform Sergeant Major Crane here, of the recommendations from the Intelligence Corps?"

"Very well, sir." Grabbing one of his computer print outs, Dudley-Jones cleared his throat and began. "The Intelligence Corps have reviewed all recent Intelligence and as a result recommend that the security threat level be reduced."

"On what basis?" Crane wanted to know.

"Oh, um," Dudley-Jones ruffled pages and read, "on the basis that the previous high levels of 'chatter' have dwindled. They believe that if there was a threat to Team GB, it may well have moved on with them to the Olympic Stadium." Dudley-Jones sat back.

"May well have?"

"Um, let me see…..," more ruffling, "the exact wording is 'it is highly likely that any threat would have moved on with them'."

"Thank you, Dudley-Jones," the Captain said. "So, Crane, as I always thought, the murder of Lance Corporal Simms, if that's what was, appears to have nothing to do with any Olympic athletes. And even if it had, it has moved on with them. Request denied. Now, after that unnecessary delay, let's get on with the arrangements for the Paralympians."

There were to be no civic receptions, no welcoming committee. The whole operation far more low key than for the able bodied athletes. In some ways Crane felt it was a shame for the Paralympians not to have their efforts equally recognised, but on the other hand it was understandable. The Olympic Games were starting in less than a week and the whole entourage following Team GB had moved on to the Olympic Park. It also meant that the Paralympians could train with a greater degree of privacy than that afforded to their able bodied counterparts. Something at least to be grateful for. Crane felt there was enough pressure on everyone as it was both the athletes and the army. Most probably the situation would change and they would start to come under intense media pressure as the starting date of Paralympics drew nearer. Crane was just glad they'd have gone from the garrison by then, to other training camps.

By the end of the meeting, it was decided Billy and Kim would continue on nights and Staff Sergeant Jones would continue to co-ordinate with Crane. Crane would in turn co-ordinate with the BOA, Juliette Stone and Uncle Tom Cobbley and all, including Dudley-Jones. Crane couldn't fathom out what Captain Edwards was doing. So he gave up trying to.

"Excellent," Edwards concluded. "Thank you all,

meeting closed. Dismissed."

Everyone got up, stretched and collected paperwork before drifting away. Crane and Jones headed outside by mutual, unspoken consent.

"Jesus Christ," Crane lit his cigarette the way a dying man would suck in oxygen.

"You alright, Crane?" Jones lit up himself, but without such intensity.

Crane exhaled loudly before speaking. "Yes, fine, just fed up with all this bloody stuff. Meetings, co-ordination, liaison. If I'd have wanted all this shit I'd had gone into Administration or Logistics, not the Special Investigations Branch."

"Fair comment, but it's a good learning curve you know. Different skills can come to the fore when you're placed in stressful situations."

"Stop spouting that official line bollocks, Jones." Crane snapped.

"Well stop bloody whingeing then," Jones shouted.

The silence between them became a roar in Crane's ears as he stared at Jones, every muscle in his body taut. Incensed that a man of inferior rank, albeit a friend, would talk to him like that.

But Jones wouldn't back down and held the stare. Eventually breaking the silence by asking, "How's Tina?"

The simple question diffused Crane's anger, turning it into hot tears only held back by sheer willpower. He realised this was what his anger was all about. Not just the job, but also the uncertainty over Tina and the baby. Averting his gaze he said, "Still in hospital."

"But doing well?"

"Yes thanks." Crane coughed the emotion from his voice. "Should be home today or tomorrow."

"Look, Crane, it's not for much longer. Twenty days. Just under three weeks."

"If that's the case then," Crane said after a moment, turning to smile at Jones, "could we still keep the Afghan officers under close observation?"

"Fucking hell! Oh all right then. But it's not produced anything so far."

"Maybe not, but it just might. You never know. Anyway," Crane threw away his cigarette and pulled his car keys from his pocket, "I'm off. A meeting with the Wicked Witch of the North."

"Who in hell's name is that? No, let me guess, Ms Juliette Stone." Jones emphasised the Ms.

"The very one. See you later."

During the short drive to St Omar Barracks, Crane was delayed by a cavalcade of motorised armoured vehicles. Whilst waiting for them to turn right into Clayton Barracks, Crane used the hands free set on his mobile phone to call the hospital, where he was once again re-assured that Tina was fine. Her vital signs were good and she was resting. He urged the nurse to tell Tina he rang, before ending the call.

During the conversation, his eyes were drawn to the soldiers and machinery passing in front of him. The men standing proudly in the turrets, at one with their vehicles; dressed in muted colours to match the body work, with the same camouflage nets on their helmets as those draped over their transport. Crane knew that clearly defined roles were the mainstay of the British Army. Everyone had a job to do. They knew exactly what it was and what was expected of them. He didn't have that certainty. Not in his professional life, where he felt like a leopard stuck in a cage of tigers, nor his personal life, where he seemed to be separated from

Tina and the baby by a pane of glass. He felt helpless. He could see them, but was unable to reach them. The last of the vehicles moved away, allowing the traffic to flow again along Queens Avenue. As Crane drove to his destination, he wondered if a leopard could change his spots.

For once Juliette Stone was not prowling the corridors and rooms of St Omar Barracks, but sat in her office.

"Come in," she called, "Coffee?"

"No thanks, this is just a quick visit to make sure everything's alright."

"All in order, Sergeant Major." The abrupt reply tempered by a smile in her eyes, if not in her lips. "By the way, thanks for your help in catching the thieves."

"All in a day's work, Ms Stone."

"Maybe so, but it's still appreciated." Now the smile reached her lips and she lifted her cup of coffee, looking at Crane over the rim.

Oh my God. Is she flirting with me? Crane's stomach tensed at the thought and he was part flattered, part terrified.

The telephone interrupted their exchange much to Crane's relief and he got up as Juliette answered the phone. But she reached out to him and motioned he should stay where he was with a flap of her hand. Pulling a clean piece of paper towards her, she started scribbling. After asking the caller for a written report as soon as possible, she replaced the receiver and handed the paper to Crane, accompanied by a flick of her ponytail and a question.

"Are you going back to your barracks, Sergeant Major?"

"Yes, why?" Crane glanced at the scribbled message.

"Could you pass this onto Staff Sergeant Jones for me? It appears we've had a break in at the stores. They're doing a full inventory at the moment and will let me know in writing what's missing as soon as they can."

"Any initial ideas?"

"It seems to be cleaning materials. But the landscape contractors were storing stuff there too, so I guess we'll have to check with them. Tell the Staff Sergeant I'll let him know as soon as we know."

"So in the meantime I'm to act as messenger boy?"

After running her index finger along her bottom lip she asked him, "Why? Do you have a problem with that?"

Night 20

The absence of barriers with armed soldiers was good news. It meant he could enter the garrison at night again. Not that there weren't any armed soldiers around, of course. There were still lots of Royal Military Police on patrol. Driving around the garrison in jeeps, or walking around with dogs. But it was easy for someone with military training, such as himself, to keep out of sight, in the shadows.

Padam was not going to the sports centre tonight. He saw the athletes in their buses a couple of days ago, so he knew they weren't on the garrison anymore.

As he ambled along, he found himself in an area of the garrison he had not explored before, beyond the Military Cemetery. Walking up the steep hill, on his right hand side he saw a long, squat building, with an outside area sporting benches. Thinking it may be a mess, he walked past without much interest, deciding to cut across the field behind the building, hoping it would bring him back into the main body of the garrison. It was a dark night, with clouds obscuring the moon, making it difficult to see. He walked over extremely hard grass. It scrunched under his feet, as though all the life had been sucked out of it. A legacy of the fine weather perhaps? It made walking quite difficult and Padam stumbled. Suddenly the grass under his feet on his left hand side was gone and he tumbled sideways, sliding down a large incline. The hard, prickly surface scratched his hands and face. He was glad he had trousers on and a pair of shoes he found discarded in a bin, as protection for his legs and feet. It was several moments before he reached the bottom and stopped sliding.

Taking a few moments to recover, he rolled over onto his back, slowly wiggling his fingers. They all worked, so there was nothing broken. He touched his face, wincing at the pain, his fingers sliding over some of the cuts, which must be bleeding. He struggled to his feet, hampered by the pain in his hands, his old knees joining in the protest. As soon as he stood, his legs felt cold from a slight breeze. Examining the only pair of trousers he owned, he found they were torn.

He limped along the bottom of the hill, reluctant to try and climb back up the incline. As he walked he felt a change underfoot. Here the grass was soft and springy. Intrigued, Padam squatted down to feel the two different surfaces. How could the grass be so dry on one side, as hard and unyielding as a stiff brush, yet green and soft on the other? As he looked around, the moon peeped out from behind a cloud, the cold white light glinting off poles in front of him, reaching skyward, back up the hill. One behind the other, as if on parade. Grabbing the first pole by the T bar at the bottom, he made his way carefully upwards. The poles were not fixed and swung backwards and forward making them difficult to use. Still they were better than nothing and he needed assistance to climb back up the hill. He couldn't imagine what they were for, or why they were there. Once at the top, he decided to return the way he had come, down the road, having had enough adventures for one night. As he walked he passed a large sign with 'Alpine Snowsports Centre', written on it, which he didn't understand.

As Padam walked down the road the quiet of the night was disturbed by the chugging of a diesel engine. Ducking down behind a low hedge, he watched through the foliage as three soldiers drove by in a military vehicle. Just before a curve in the road, they stopped. Two of them got out, with the third one staying behind the wheel and driving away. The two on foot then split up, one running off in the direction of nearby houses and the other staying where he was. After a few moments, the remaining soldier inclined his head as though listening to something. Padam remained motionless. The soldier walked towards the entrance of the Military Cemetery, on the opposite side of the road from Padam, and disappeared inside. As he couldn't be sure how long the soldier would be, Padam sat down, made himself comfortable and settled down to wait.

After a while Padam saw a soldier emerge from the entrance. A different soldier. Dressed in an entirely different uniform. A short dark moustache on his face. Not the soldier who had run towards the houses earlier, nor the man who had gone into the cemetery. Moustache man made his way down the road. Padam decided to wait some more. After Padam estimated he'd waited an hour and as no one emerged from either the houses or the cemetery, he made his way to the end of the road, deciding to return to his flat. He had no idea what was happening, but perhaps the Royal Military Policemen he met several days before would be interested. He would go and see them in the morning. In the meantime, he had the feeling it would be safer to leave the garrison to the soldiers.

Day 21

Crane's mobile rang just before 07:00 hours, as he was driving into work. Punching the button on his hands free set he said, "Tina?"

"Sorry, boss, it's me."

"Oh, morning, Billy, what's the matter?"

"Missing soldier, sir. Last seen on Gallwey Road, opposite the Military Cemetery."

"Are you up there?" Crane negotiated a sharp right hand bend.

"Yes, boss, with Kim and Staff Sergeant Jones."

"Okay, I'm just entering the garrison; I'll meet you in a couple of minutes."

Crane clicked off the phone and muttered, "Oh shit." A missing soldier. And if that wasn't enough he had to pick Tina up from the hospital later that morning. "Shit!" Crane accelerated past St Omar Barracks, ignoring the speed limit, pulling up behind Billy's car a few minutes later.

He was greeted by Jones who succinctly explained the situation. "Good morning, sir. One of my guards is missing. Corporal John McInnes. He wasn't in place, here outside the cemetery, when the duty driver arrived to pick him and his partner Private Stuart Cable up at about 05:00 hours."

"Was Private Cable there?"

"Yes. The duty driver brought him straight back to barracks and reported to the Guard Commander. Apparently McInnes and Cable decided to split up for a bit." Jones emphasises the 'apparently'.

"That isn't normal procedure is it? To split up and patrol alone?

"Strictly speaking, no. Looks like the silly sods were pulling a flanker and it's backfired on them. Cable is in the Guard Room now, trying to explain himself. Although the word amongst the lads is that his baby is ill and he was worried about it. So," Jones paused, "I think it could be that McInnes thought he would help out by letting Cable pop off home and check everything was alright, as he only lives a few hundred yards away. If that's the case, it's the end of Cable's army career."

Crane closed his eyes and breathed deeply as he listened to the story, wondering at the stupidity of the Corporal, whilst understanding how torn the man must feel. There but for the grace of God and all that. "You've started a search of the cemetery?" he asked.

"Yes, sir, some of the Royal Military Police are in there together with search teams from A Company. But it's a large area to cover, over 15 acres. Some of it heavily wooded. And the whole bloody lot is enclosed by large holly hedging. If something's happened to McInnes in there, it could take us some time to find him. If anyone sees anything the first signal is a whistle."

"Alright, thanks, Jones." Crane turned away and called, "Billy? With me."

"Okay, boss," Billy bounded over like an excited

puppy, forcing a smile from Crane. How could someone who's just finished a twelve hour shift be so bloody energetic?

Crane crossed the road and paused at the entrance. He couldn't help but be intimidated by the cemetery. Even after all these years. When he was younger, much younger, he had pulled a night guard duty that included patrolling the cemetery. He was with a black lad called Cobb. When you worked at night with Cobb, all you could see were the whites of his eyes and teeth and the red of his lips and tongue. He was reminiscent of a voodoo doctor when the idiot insisted on prancing around. As he was doing that night. Giving Crane the creeps.

They were on patrol checking along the perimeter of the cemetery. It was slowly beginning to get light, with a mist floating just above the ground, as though the clouds had fallen from the sky to coat the earth. As they went through a particularly dense patch of mist, Crane saw something hanging from a tree. As the mist swirled around it, he glimpsed what he thought was a broken branch, hanging lifeless from the tree, held on by a thread. But it turned out to be a broken man. Swinging from the end of a rope. As the man's face came into view, covered with vaporous tendrils of mist, Crane had to stifle a scream. But Cobb seemed less affected. Commenting that maybe the soldier had decided to commit suicide in the cemetery, so he'd have company when he passed over to the other side.

Taking deep breath and pushing the image away, Crane pulled on his coat for protection against the early morning chill.

"Pretty old this place isn't it, boss?" Billy kept pace with Crane as they ventured down one of the many tarmac paths that criss-cross the area.

"Mmm, it was established soon after the army first set up camp here in Aldershot in the 1850's."

"It's well looked after."

Looking at the undulating landscape, Crane could see what Billy meant. Neat crisp rows of white headstones, set amongst close cut turf. For Crane the atmosphere in here was different from that of other military cemeteries. Not just because of his earlier experience, but because of the landscape. Numerous trees had been allowed to grow; breaking up what would otherwise be a stark scene. The harsh lines were softened by Oak, Pines, Firs and Chestnut trees and yet in other, older parts, the cemetery had intentionally been allowed to return to the natural heath land it once was.

So in one section you could clearly see the difference between the recent white headstones and the older, grey ones alongside them. Crane found these areas particularly poignant. The old stones looked like they were slipping and sliding down the hill, canting at odd angles and for him were visual illustrations of the passage of time. He wondered if he himself would be buried here and if in a hundred years anyone would know, or care, where his plot was. Shivering, Crane wrapped his open coat around him.

The shrill call of a whistle made Crane jump out of his reverie and he and Billy set off at a run towards a remote part of the cemetery. They stopped at the outskirts of a dense group of bushes, where a Royal Military Policeman was waiting.

"Corporal McInnes?" Crane nodded into the undergrowth.

"Think so, sir. He's jammed in behind the pillbox.

136

All I could see was a pair of boots, so I immediately retreated and whistled."

"No sign of life?"

"None, sir. There were drag marks in the leaves and earth, but I couldn't see any footmarks. The ground's too hard."

"Good work, lad." Crane reached for his phone.

Jones answered, breathless, as though he too was running towards the sound of the whistle.

"Looks like we've found him, Jones. Bring the tape and we'll seal off the area. Doesn't look like the scene's been contaminated. I'll call Major Martin and Billy can do forensics."

After that there was nothing else to do but wait. Crane sent Billy off in search of coffee and his forensic kit and Kim back to the office to prepare the paperwork, including pulling Corporal McInnes' Military Record. He also puts in a courtesy call to Captain Edwards, who was still at home enjoying his breakfast and seemed fully intent on staying there. "No need for me to attend, Crane," he said. "This one's down to you."

Luckily the Captain then terminated the call, obviating the need for Crane to confirm the order with a 'sir', which he hadn't felt like doing.

At 09:00 hours he called Tina's mother. The silence that followed his request saying more than any insult she could have thrown at him. He then called the hospital, asking them to pass a message onto Tina, that due to an 'incident' at work, he wouldn't be able to go to the hospital and take her home but had arranged for her mother to be there. He was diverted from the stab of guilt from his hot pin by Major Martin emerging from the bushes.

"Right, Crane, you can go in now. The body was jammed behind the pillbox with just the boots visible. I've had to move him for ease of examination, but don't worry, Billy's taken lots of photos. The whole area is surrounded by Holly bush and overhanging trees, so we've found pieces of cloth attached to some of them, along with a couple of blood stains. Not sure yet who's blood it is obviously. Could be from scratches on McInnes as he was dragged in, or from the perpetrator."

"Time of death, sir?"

"Difficult to say straight off as you very well know. I need to take into account the ambient temperature overnight and this morning and do some calculations, but I'd say maybe between 04:00 and 06:00 hours. Give or take. Once you've had a look I'll have him moved."

"Cause of death, sir?"

"Looks like a broken neck."

Crane and Billy looked at each other. Words were not necessary. But Crane uttered one anyway, "Shit."

Night 21

The post mortem of Corporal McInnes took place later that day. Crane, for once, decided not to attend and sent Billy in his place. Billy returned to the barracks as happy as if he had just had afternoon tea with Major Martin, not watched him cut up a dead body. The results were as they suspected. Death by a broken neck, this time with bruising from the perpetrator's hands clearly visible. Lividity, pooling of the blood in the body, suggested McInnes had been dragged behind the pillbox and left there for a couple of hours, with time of death confirmed between 04:00 hours and 06:00 hours.

Two things concerned Crane now. Firstly, the murder of a second soldier on the garrison (although Captain Edwards still maintained the first one was an accident) and secondly, a lost weapon. The gun McInnes was carrying couldn't be found. It contained live ammunition and an extra magazine was also missing. Jones had kept his lads and A Company searching in the cemetery but now at 18:00 hours there was still no sign of either. They had beaten and battered every bit of undergrowth they could and found nothing. A lost gun. Live ammunition missing. An ongoing threat. As per the chain of Command Edwards had bawled out Crane over the missing weapon, Crane had bawled out Jones and Jones had bawled out the Platoon Commanders. It hasn't achieved anything, but had made them all feel better. Apart from the poor sods at the bottom of the pecking order, that was.

What would really make Crane feel better, he decided, was going home to Tina. Which he couldn't do for another hour, so he went out to the car park for a cigarette and called her on his mobile, for about the fifth time that day.

"Hey," he said as she answered, "Are you alright?"

"Tom," she laughed, "Yes I'm fine, just as I was an hour ago."

"Sorry."

"What for?"

"For everything really. For not being there to bring you home from hospital. For not being there now….." he tailed off, not sure what else to say, apart from sorry.

"Tom, stop it. I know you have a job to do and what job is more important than finding the killer of a soldier?"

"Thanks love, but…."

"But what?"

"Oh, I don't know. Lots of things." Crane leaned against a wall and paused to smoke his cigarette. "Anyway, I thought I'd bring home a take away for dinner. What do you fancy?"

"Chinese," Tina replied without hesitation. "Then I can just pick if I get too full. Anyway I'm busy doing the food shopping on-line. Did you know there was nothing in the cupboards and just a load of stuff gone off in the fridge?"

"No, sorry, love. I haven't bothered with shopping

for food whilst you've been in hospital. I've eaten in the mess."

"Well, never mind. I'm home now, so I can order it tonight and get it all delivered tomorrow."

"Okay, see you between 7.30 and 8. Love you."

"Love you too, Tom, now get back to work."

Crane closed the phone and went back inside. Kim had come on duty early and was working on the incident board. "Any forensics in yet?"

"No, sir, not until tomorrow and that's at the earliest."

"What are they checking?"

"Blood collected from the scene, pieces of cloth from the bushes, scrapings from under Corporal McInnes fingernails."

"Boss?" Billy called from the other side of the office. As Crane turned Billy said, "Staff Sergeant Jones wants you to go over and see him."

"Now?" Crane glanced at his watch.

"Yes, sir. Can I tell him you're on your way?"

"Yes, Billy, but it better be bloody important."

Crane repeated that sentiment to Jones when he got to his office.

"It is, Crane. Very. Your favourite neighbourhood Gurkha was here. Clearly trying to tell us something about last night. This was the best I could do without an interpreter." Jones handed Crane a crude drawing.

Crane sat in the visitor's chair. It creaked and groaned under his weight as he wriggled to get comfortable.

"For God's sake, Jones, can't you change this bloody chair?" Looking at Jones, Crane saw the suppressed grin. "No, I suppose not."

Crane looked at the drawing in his hand and stopped

moaning. It depicted a vehicle, parked by the cemetery, with one soldier walking towards the graveyard and the other running across the fields. "Padam was there."

"So it would seem. Take a look at the second one." Jones handed Crane another piece of paper.

"Bloody hell," was all Crane could manage as he stared at the second drawing. This showed a third soldier leaving the cemetery. "Have you managed to get an interpreter?" he demanded.

"I can't get anyone here until tomorrow morning."

"Well we can't work with Padam without one. If he really did see the killer and can identify him, we need a proper interview that will stand up in court. So we'll have to be careful." Crane struggled out of the chair and headed for the door. "Set it up for as early in the morning as you can, Jones. Keep Padam here overnight, so we don't lose him. Give him a hot meal and comfortable bed, he'll be happy enough."

Jones nodded his agreement. "This is bad, Crane. Two soldiers dead. It's getting personal now."

"Getting personal?" Jones' words stopped Crane in the doorway. "With me it always was personal, Staff, from the first one."

"But why were they killed? What's been achieved by their deaths?"

"At the moment I've no idea," Crane had to admit.

"Where are you off to now?"

"Home. Via the Chinese take away."

Day 22

The Chinese take away from last night was giving Crane indigestion. He'd been in the barracks for hours, interviewing Padam with an interpreter. At the moment Padam was with an artist trying to come up with a composite picture of the soldier seen leaving the cemetery. Crane took a copy of his signed statement off the desk in front of him and decided to have a walk around the car park.

The movement seemed to ease his stomach problems and the fresh air cleared his head, as he studied the statement again. McInnes must have heard something, a disturbance in the cemetery perhaps and went to investigate. Once inside McInnes must have encountered the murderer, who broke his neck and pulled him behind the pillbox. The pillbox was in a remote part of the cemetery, so maybe McInnes tracked the suspect for some distance. Or had he been lured there? That was more likely, but if so it indicated that the perpetrator had some training, military or otherwise and a degree of cunning.

What was the reason for the death? The act of killing itself, he wondered? Counting Lance Corporal Simms, there were two murders. Perilously close to becoming a series of killings. Which meant there could be more to come. But what motive would someone have for picking off soldiers and with such precision?

As Crane walked he tried to look at the puzzle from another angle, lighting a cigarette to aid his thinking. The missing weapon could be the key. Perhaps that's what the suspect was after. But if that's the case, what was he after the first time? Nothing was taken from the first soldier. So if nothing was taken, maybe it was to stop him either seeing something or reporting something. But Crane had no bloody idea what could be under the swimming pool that they shouldn't see. They had searched it again since the death of Corporal Simms. But they'd better search it one more time. Exhaling the smoke from the last drag of his cigarette, he marched back into the barracks.

Crane managed to catch his Officer Commanding in his office, but unfortunately Captain Edwards didn't share his views. As usual.

"How can you be sure this old Gurkha is telling the truth?" he demanded.

"I beg your pardon, sir?" Crane couldn't keep the incredulity out of his voice.

"This old man had been lurking around on the garrison in the middle of the night," Edwards warmed to his theme. "What was he doing?"

"Well, just keeping an eye out I guess." As he spoke Crane realised how lame that sounded.

"Keeping an eye out! For God's sake, Crane. You should be treating him as a suspect, not a witness. He could be making the whole thing up. A cover story for killing a soldier who found him trying to break in somewhere or steal something."

"Break in? Steal something? In a cemetery?"

"I understand these Gurkhas are very poor. Living on the breadline."

"Yes sir, it's an appalling state of affairs," Crane agreed.

"That's as may be, but that sort of vagrant tends to turn to stealing to survive."

Crane began to realise Edwards didn't have much sympathy for the plight of the old Gurkhas.

"I see there were items stolen from the Aspire Defence stores," Edwards looked down at the files on his desk, indicating one at the top of the pile.

"Yes, sir." Crane wondered where this was going.

"Any progress with that?"

"Um, not as yet, sir and we're still awaiting a full list of the items missing from Ms Stone."

"Well, chase it up, Crane. And search the old Gurkhas' flats or wherever it is they live."

"Search them? Why, sir?"

"Because they could be our culprits. The ones who have been stealing from the stores."

"But we've no reason to suspect that, or any jurisdiction in Aldershot and Farnborough, nor any authority to do it, sir."

"Well then, see DI Anderson and get some authority. Dismissed."

Crane tried to speak again but the Captain kept his head resolutely down, studying the files on his desk.

Crane covered the couple of miles between the garrison and Aldershot Police Station in record time. Anger drove the car, crashed the gears and gunned the engine in hopeless retaliation. By the time Crane arrived, he was shaking from the adrenalin rush and sweating profusely. Grabbing a bottle of water from the glove box he stayed slumped in the car seat with the door wide open. The water tasted metallic on his tongue and failed to wash out the bad taste in his mouth from his conversation with Edwards. Screwing the cap back on the bottle, he threw it into the glove box, slammed the lid closed and got out of the car. The door suffered the same fate as the glove box and Crane only stopped himself from kicking the car bodywork by reaching for his cigarettes and lighter.

He was marginally calmer when he arrived at Anderson's office. The usual clutter needed moving before he could sit down and he then brought Anderson up to date with events.

"So, another dead soldier," Derek commented when Crane had finished.

"'Afraid so. But this time we have a witness. We have confirmation from the post mortem as to cause of death, a broken neck with bruising from unknown assailant's hands. So, taking all that into account, coupled with the position of the body, which was dragged behind a pillbox, I can safely call it murder." Crane ran his hand through his hair and then over his beard.

"But?"

"But what?"

"Come on, Crane, your body language is giving you away. Look at you, slumped in your chair, fiddling with your hair and beard. You're obviously pissed off. So, there's a 'but' in there."

"It's the witness," Crane sighed.

"What about him? Don't you think he's reliable?"

"Oh I do," Crane threw his file onto Anderson's desk.

"So who doesn't? Edwards?"

"Exactly. He's ordered me to treat him as a suspect."

"A suspect? A 60 odd year old man? Thinner than a twig and shorter than you and me and just about everyone else I know?"

"Yes. I guess Captain Edwards thinks that if you turn it around the other way and look at him as a suspect, Padam killed McInnes because he caught him in the act of stealing something or at least trying to break into somewhere."

"What could he be stealing in a cemetery for God's sake?"

"Buggered if I know." Crane scratched his scar. "But Edward's theory is that there could have been more than one of them at the scene. You know they hang around together, are rarely seen alone and then there's their situation to consider."

"Situation? What does that mean?" By now Anderson was scratching his head.

"The fact that they have no money, no jobs and no support from the state. Being broke and hungry can change even the strongest man."

"So, Edwards thinks they're stealing to support themselves, out of desperation."

"Well, I get the impression he's not much concerned about their desperation, just their vagrancy." Crane shook his head, disgusted by the attitude of his Officer Commanding.

"Are there any reports of more thefts on the garrison?"

Crane grabbed the file back off the desk and opened it. "Unfortunately, yes. Various items were stolen from Aspire Defence stores. Here's the report." He handed over the flimsy bit of paper. "I still haven't got a full list of what's missing from the Witch of the North."

Crane's description of Juliette Stone caused Anderson to smile for the first time during their conversation. "And Edwards thinks the Gurkhas may be responsible?"

"Looks that way. So…" Crane let the word hang between them. Anderson merely lifted his eyebrows, waiting for Crane to continue. "So," Crane started again, "Edwards wants their homes searched."

"And where do they live?" Anderson's eyebrows reached even further towards his hairline.

"You know bloody well where. In Aldershot and Farnborough mostly."

"But not on the garrison."

"No, Anderson, not on the garrison."

"For fuck's sake, Crane. I know we work closely together and all that, but this is a bit thin."

"How about if I pad it out for you a bit. Provide a full detailed report for you to use to get a search warrant."

"It better be good." Anderson leaned back in his chair.

"Don't worry, it will be - I've got my orders."

Day 23

"Boss?"

Yes, Billy, what is it?" Crane wasn't happy at the interruption.

"Sorry to bother you, sir, but Lance Corporal Dudley-Jones would like a word."

Crane lifted his head to look through his office window. Dudley-Jones was pacing up and down, a buff file in one hand and a slim black net book in the other.

"Oh, very well." Crane saved and closed the file on his computer, secretly glad to get away from the report he was finishing off for Anderson, requesting a search warrant of the Gurkhas' homes. "Why are you still here?" he asked Billy looking at his watch.

"Just off now, sir. Had a couple of things to finish off for Sergeant Jones."

"Okay, see you tomorrow morning. Send in Dudley-Jones on your way out."

Dudley-Jones quick-marched into Crane's office and stood in front of the desk.

"You'll never guess what's happened, sir," he exclaimed as Crane indicated he should sit down.

"Lance Corporal, I don't engage in guessing games.

If you've got something to tell me, get on with it. Otherwise get out of my office."

"Oh, yes, sir, sorry, sir." The Lance Corporal's sallow complexion suffused with colour. "We've had an Intel report in overnight, sir," he continued, jiggling about on his seat like a seven year old at school desperate to tell the teacher the answer to his question.

Crane's response was to close his eyes. "And?" he asked, slowly opening them again.

"And there's definitely something going on."

"Dudley-Jones, that's what you said last time and nothing has happened."

"But this time it's more concrete. Can I, sir?" The Lance Corporal indicated his net book. Taking it to mean that he had something to share, Crane nodded reluctantly.

The Lance Corporal lifted the lid and hit the power button with a flourish. "This is a recording of a conversation monitored last night."

Dudley-Jones opened a file. The sound of hissing filtered from the tinny speakers on the net book, followed by a conversation between two men. The voices kept fading in and out and Crane strained to hear some of the words.

At the end of the recording Crane said, "I take it you have a transcript."

"Of course, sir," and Dudley-Jones fished out a piece of paper from the file he was balancing on his knee.

INTELLIGENCE REPORT
DATE: 24.7.2012
TIME: 03:00 hours
PREPARED BY: Sgt P Smith

Below is a transcript of a mobile telephone conversation recorded at 01:00 hours on the 24ᵗʰ July.

PERSON 1: How is our friend?

PERSON 2: Getting better, thank you.

PERSON 1: Good. Did you manage to get everything he needs?

PERSON 2: Yes.

PERSON 1: Excellent, I'm sure it means a great deal to him. When will he be completely recovered?

PERSON 2: In a day or two.

PERSON 1: You can't be more specific?

PERSON 2: Not at this stage.

PERSON 1: Very well, keep me informed.

The connection was then broken. The call lasted 60 seconds and originated from a mobile phone in Helmand Province, Afghanistan. The receiving mobile phone was in the Aldershot/Farnborough area. At this stage no information is available on either mobile phone number, with regards to the registered user or network provider, although enquiries are ongoing.

Crane read through the transcript and then asked Dudley-Jones to play the recording again, so Crane could compare the two. This helped clarify the words, but not the meaning.

"What do you think, sir?" Dudley-Jones' eager expression once more reminding Crane of a school boy.

"I think I need a coffee. White, two sugars." As Dudley-Jones scampered across the office for the coffee, Crane read through the brief transcript a third time.

"So why is this seemingly innocuous telephone call significant?" Crane waved the paper in Dudley-Jones' face before taking the proffered mug and leaning back in his chair.

"Well, sir, for several reasons. One – the call was made from Afghanistan to the Aldershot area. Two – neither man said the other's name, or the name of the third person they referred to. Three – it is proving difficult to trace the owners of the mobile numbers. And, of course, four – the content of the conversation."

"Seems innocent enough to me," Crane said, placing his coffee mug on his desk. "Just someone enquiring about a friend who is ill."

"On the surface, yes, sir. But we need to read between the lines."

"Alright, read between the lines for me then, Lance Corporal."

"Well, sir," Dudley-Jones stood and moved behind Crane's desk to stand next to him. Leaning forward he said, "The line *'is our friend better'*, for that read *'is our friend ready'*." He put his finger under the line to emphasise it. "Then," he continued, "See the words *'did you manage to get everything he needed?'* That isn't necessarily medicines, but equipment."

"Okay," conceded Crane. "Anything else?"

"Oh yes, sir. This line. *'I'm sure it means a great deal to him. When will he be recovered?'* So the equipment is obviously very important and the caller then wants to know specifically when everything will be in place. They then decide in a day or two." Dudley-Jones straightens up. "We'll obviously be monitoring the airwaves closely for the follow up call."

Crane motioned the Lance Corporal to move back to his seat while he thought for a moment. Personally he considered it to be load of bollocks. But on the other hand…

"Good work, Lance Corporal." Crane beamed at the young man in front of him. "I think we should take this to Captain Edwards immediately. Don't you agree?"

Once they gained access to Captain Edwards, Dudley-Jones did his party trick once again, whipping out his net book and regaling the Captain with his Intel.

"Well," Edwards leaned back in his chair. "I think we should take this very seriously, don't you, Sergeant Major?"

For once Crane was happy to agree with his boss. "Indeed, sir. Seems pretty significant to me. Added to that two mur…err….dead soldiers," Crane quickly changed the word in response to Edwards's raised eyebrows. "Not forgetting the thefts from the stores."

Edwards eventually spoke into the silence. "At the moment I don't see that the thefts are relevant to this intel." Frost coated Edwards's words. "I've already told you how to deal with those, Crane. I take it you have followed my orders?" The blue eyes above the long nose peered at Crane.

"Of course, sir. It's all in hand." Crane said holding the Captain's stare.

"Be more specific please, Crane."

"I've already had a meeting with DI Anderson about obtaining a search warrant for the Gurkhas' accommodation. In fact I was just finishing a full and detailed report for him to use with his request for the warrant when Dudley-Jones here came to see me."

"Um, sir," Dudley-Jones interrupted at the sound of his name and looking at Edwards said, "What shall we do about security on the garrison?"

Captain Edwards rose from his chair and paced the office. When he spoke he forced the two men to swivel around to look at him, at his position by the office door.

"Increase security on the garrison. Same procedures as last week."

"You feel that's necessary, sir?" Crane asked innocently.

"You know it bloody well is, Sergeant Major. The brass will have my guts for garters if we don't react to this intelligence. So, as you've got a lot to do now, Crane, you'd better get on with it. Dismissed. Both of you."

As the two men clattered down the stairs after leaving Captain Edwards, Crane hissed, "Perhaps, Lance Corporal, now you'll stick like glue to the Afghan officers, as I requested."

Night 23

Rumours abound. They think I can't understand their whispered conversations in the Officers' Mess, but of course I can. Two soldiers are dead. Why? What's happening? Who's behind it? It makes me laugh to myself, as I alone know what's going on. It is interesting to see how animated conversations stop as soon as I approach. The outsider. On the surface treated with respect. But underneath, treated with suspicion. They cannot hide their true feelings, no matter how they try.

I have now formulated the how, what and where of my little plan and obtained the materials I need. So the next part of my mission is to earn the respect of my fellow British officers. Lull them into a false sense of security. Show I can be trusted. That I am a true friend of the British Army.

It is also time to tell the others of my plans. Plans that will throw your security services into disarray. So they don't know what's going on, or which way to look, nor have any suspects. I shall enjoy watching that. Knowing that I am in control. Knowing that they are reduced to reacting to my disruptions.

I have had the go ahead from home; they will be

watching and waiting for news of my success. In essence, I have to succeed. I will succeed - for I know with every fibre of my being that Allah will reward my faith, and not the faith of you infidels! For Allah is good! Allah is great! Allah is the way to eternal salvation!

But I also understand that to achieve eternal salvation requires more than a Muslim just leading a good and humane life. It requires - no demands - certain achievements in one's life. Those achievements could be conquering land, converting non-believers or destroying infidels - all in the name of Allah.

Here in your country I know I cannot conquer land, nor convert non-believers. So I must destroy you infidels. As many as I can. And I will.

Day 24

Crane entered Aldershot Police Station and waved his security identification at the desk sergeant. As he walked through the large open plan office towards the CID area, Crane was puzzled. There were lots of staff in the office and they were all on the phone. Fragments of conversations drifted towards him, then swirled away to become lost in the general melee.

"We can only apologise…."

"Tightened security was necessary I'm afraid…"

"A series of thefts….."

"I understand you are being inconvenienced but….."

Crane stopped at the door of Anderson's office, looking in with some trepidation. When he saw Anderson was also on the phone he knew he was in trouble.

Replacing the receiver with a bang, Anderson paused for a moment before picking it up again and dialling a number. Preferring to leave un-noticed, Crane nevertheless knocked on the door to gain Anderson's attention.

Jerking his head up at the interruption, Anderson

stared at Crane.

"Morning," Crane called from the door. Receiving no reply Crane's eyes swept the office and his smile became more of a grimace. Still Anderson didn't speak.

"Are you alright?" Crane hovered at the door, uncertain whether to enter.

Eventually Anderson spoke. "No I'm bloody not."

Crane noticed the elongated words and stiffness in his friend's body. "Ah…not a good time to call then."

"Not at all, Crane." Anderson seemed to force himself to relax, leaning back against his chair. But his crossed arms remained a barrier between the two men. "I was just going to call you, ask you to come over, so you could see the fruits of your labour." Anderson indicated the crowded space outside of his office.

"Ah…" was all Crane could manage.

"I know you had to increase the security at the garrison again, but Jesus Christ, Crane, we've never had so many phone calls!" Anderson rubbed his head, adding to the general disarray of his grey wispy hair. "Everyone from civilian support staff, to constables and all the way up the ranks to me, are apologising to the local population."

"Sorry," Crane replied, "but you know it makes sense," and he was unable to suppress the grin which spread across his face crinkling his eyes.

This seemed to diffuse the situation, as Anderson smiled a wry smile in return and shook his head. "I actually think the excuse is making things worse," Anderson said.

"Why?"

"It sounds so feeble, reports of thefts from the garrison."

"Surely it's better than telling the truth? That we

think there are terrorists getting ready for an attack somewhere in the vicinity."

"I suppose so," but Anderson didn't sound convinced.

"Believe you me, a load of pissed off residents is a whole lot better than terrified people, afraid to leave their homes in case the local Tesco is bombed."

"All right," Anderson sighed. "But you're going to have to deal with the local press. This was your call and you're going to have to take some flack."

"Be glad to, Derek." Crane glanced at his watch. "But I must go, duty calls. Have to inspect the front line. Back up the lads at the barriers."

Once outside, before crossing the car park, Crane paused between a couple of police cars parked nose into the building, to light a cigarette. He ducked his head inside the flap of his jacket to keep the flame out of the blustery wind. As he raised his head a familiar but definitely unwelcome figure was standing directly in front of him, blocking his way.

"Sergeant Major Crane," Diane Chambers said, "just the person I wanted to see."

After taking a moment to drag on his cigarette, Crane exhaled. "Sorry, Ms Chambers. No comment at this time. Please direct all enquiries to the press office."

"Oh, Sergeant Major," Diane purred. "This isn't an official request for a comment. More of a, how can I put it, off the record chat."

"Sorry, I don't do off the record chats. Now if you'll excuse me?" Crane made to step forward, but was stopped by Diane turning sideways and leaning backwards onto one police car, with her legs stretched out and feet nearly touching the wheel of the one next to it. Her legs were clad in their usual denim, but today her feet sported sandals. Seemingly her only concession to the July heat, as she was also wearing a white tee shirt under a partially open checked shirt.

"In that case, I'll chat and you listen."

Realising he was defeated for the moment, Crane continued to smoke his cigarette.

"You see," she said, "I was sitting at my desk this morning thinking about the increased security at the garrison and that got me wondering about the Afghan officers who are currently in New Mons Barracks." She paused for dramatic effect, staring straight at him.

Crane struggled to keep his face blank.

"It seems more logical, don't you think, Sergeant Major, that there could be a link between them and this lock down. Personally, I think all this talk about thefts from the stores is just a smoke screen. As ineffectual as the smoke from your cigarette."

Crane looked at the butt in his hand and quickly threw it on the ground.

"Any comment now, Sergeant Major?" Diane smiled, obviously very pleased with herself.

"None whatsoever. I'm afraid I don't know what you're talking about."

"Oh but I think you do." Diane straightened up and turned to face Crane. "You're in charge of security on the garrison at the moment aren't you?"

Crane didn't answer the rhetorical question.

"So therefore you know the location and movement of everyone on the garrison. Surely, it can't have escaped your notice that there are a handful of, shall we say, unusual visitors?"

Forcing himself to relax Crane smiled. "Sorry, Diane, I don't know what you're talking about. Security has been increased on the garrison due to a number of thefts. I'm afraid that, as usual, you've heard some incorrect rumours and put two and two together to make five."

"Not this time, Crane. I have my sources on the garrison and I've heard this piece of information more than once," she gestured to the ever present recorder in her hand. "So, I can confidently do a piece on possible terrorists in our midst."

Crane realised his fists were clenched at his side, just as Anderson's had been a few minutes earlier. Forcing himself to uncurl them, he crossed his arms and asked, "Do you think that's wise?"

"Why wouldn't it be? The people of Aldershot have a right to know what's going on. That they could be in terrible danger."

Crane could see the screaming headlines and rhetoric that would drip off Diane Chamber's poisonous pen. But the question was - how to deal with her?

"What do you want, Diane?" he sighed.

"An in-depth interview with you, about how the garrison dealt with having Team GB and then the Paralympians on site. That way I get a double page spread. The one I should have got last year, only you reneged on the deal."

"I was ill in hospital, as you very well know."

"That's as may be. But this gives you a chance to make up for it."

"And you'll wait until the Paralympians had gone?"

"Of course, Sergeant Major," triumph gleamed in her eyes. "See you in a couple of weeks then," she called as she wove her way through the car park and disappeared inside her battered VW Beetle.

Crane made a mental note to have Captain Edwards call the editor of the Aldershot Mail, just in case Diane Chambers decided to go back on their apparent deal. If she did write such a piece, the Captain would ensure the editor pulled it, in the interests of national security, never mind Aldershot security. Edwards would also make sure the editor rejected any idea she may have of writing a piece on security arrangements for the Olympians. After all, no one was allowed access to that kind of information, particularly not the press. Her editor would understand the need to keep such things under wraps, even if his naive young reporter didn't. He hoped. As Crane went to his car, he checked the time on his wristwatch, noticing the date. Doing a quick calculation, he found he still had seventeen days to go. Seventeen more days of chaos.

Night 24

Padam could sense the tension in the air on the garrison. It was a palpable thing. He could feel it on his skin and taste it in his mouth. Could see the strain on the soldier's faces as they held their weapons just a little too tightly, the whites of their knuckles clearly visible. Saw the way they rolled their necks to release pent up anxiety. Apprehension in their eyes as they waited for the next person to come up to the barrier, requesting either access or exit from the garrison.

Padam strolled up to a barrier, to see what would happen if he attempted to walk through, instead of infiltrating the garrison through little known gaps in the security. He was instantly dismissed as a threat. In fact, instantly dismissed full stop. No one even wanted to look in his Tesco carrier bag. The soldiers waved him through, as though trying to be rid of him as quickly as possible. Other people waiting in the queue looked through him as if he was invisible. But he was used to that. It was clear the residents of Aldershot don't quite know what to make of Padam and his friends. They couldn't communicate with them, as they didn't understand them and vice versa. But it seemed to be more than a language barrier. It was more that they didn't seem to understand why they were in their midst at all. So they did what most people do to those they don't understand. Ignore them. Pretend they're not there.

Once inside, Padam was still ignored. The focus seemed to be on the barriers, the normal ways in and out. It was as though everyone was looking outward and not thinking about who was actually around and why. So Padam was able to stroll along Queens Avenue, up towards the sports centre. But, as he came to the road that led to the centre itself, he found armed guards at the barrier. So he doubled back and entered the grounds from a more oblique angle. After all he had no legitimate reason for going to the sports centre and the only people being allowed through were the athletes and vital members of their entourage.

Settling down in his favourite clump of trees, Padam opened his carrier bag and enjoyed a small picnic of fresh fruit that a market trader had casually thrown to him earlier in the day. As he looked more closely at the apple and banana, he saw they were badly bruised. But it was of no matter. Fruit was fruit whichever way you looked at it. He also had a small bottle of water. An old bottle he'd filled from the tap in the flat. It tasted stale and a bit metallic, but he soon got used to it.

As night fell, he became more conscious of his vulnerability and lay down on the ground after making a bed of leaves. He pulled the army greatcoat over himself, making sure he tucked his carrier bag under the coat by his leg. Suitably disguised he settled down to wait.

He thought he was asleep and dreaming when he saw his son, walking, no running, crouched over with a bundle of wood clasped in his arms. Knowing it couldn't possibly be his son, he shook his head, blinked his eyes and then pinched his arm for good measure. But the figure was still there, steadily gaining ground on the sports centre. As he focused, Padam saw it was the smudge. And it wasn't carrying wood, but long bundles that resembled sticks. It was also carrying something else, a tin or bucket, dangling by the handle from one of its hands.

As Padam expected, the smudge stopped half way down the side of the sports centre wall. It paused for a moment probably making sure it was alone and unobserved, Padam surmised, before disappearing as before. Morphing into the wall.

It was nearly dawn by the time the smudge reappeared. Padam, bored and stiff nearly missed the fleeting figure as it raced towards the safety of a clump of bushes. Without its bundle of sticks.

Day 25

It was the smell that hit Crane first. Then the heat. Then the noise. There were over fifty elderly Gurkhas in the open plan office space in Aldershot Police Station, along with police officers, Royal Military Police and interpreters. Interviews were being conducted at four tables with long lines of Gurkhas waiting for their turn. Military and civilian police were going along each line taking names and inspecting documents.

Crane watched the moving piles of old clothes. It seemed that some of the elderly men were wearing every stitch of clothing they owned, despite the oppressive heat in the room from the sheer number of bodies. Others wore little, their shirts and trousers hanging off their emaciated limbs, old sandals covering bare feet. It looks like a scene from Belsen.

Threading through the crowd Crane escaped into Anderson's office.

"Happy now?" Anderson asked as Crane walked through the door.

"Jesus Christ, Derek…I've never seen anything like it." Crane sat and put his elbows on his knees but the images had followed him into the office.

166

"Well, so much for Captain Edward's theory. This lot couldn't steal a box of tissues and carry them home, never mind sacks and boxes from the Aspire Defence stores."

"It makes me want to take pictures of ...that…that… debacle out there and then throw them in Edward's face."

"Apart from the fact that you'd lose your job."

"I suppose so," Crane managed a grin. Straightening up he said, "I've got to ask the question. Anything of use so far?"

"Not a dickey bird. Nothing suspicious at any of the squalid boxes unscrupulous landlords call flats. And not one of the Gurkhas has seen or heard anything about thefts, or been offered that type of stolen goods. Not that they could afford to buy them even if they were." Derek threw a selection of reports at Crane.

"What are they saying then? They must be saying something, there's a lot of noise in there."

"Let me see. What about, 'how can I get a job?' 'How can I get any money off the welfare state?' 'What do these documents mean?' 'Can you translate these papers for me?' 'Where do I go to get my rent paid?' Do you need me to go on, Crane?"

"No." Crane stood.

"What are you going to do now? Aren't you going to help with this lot?"

"Sorry, Derek got an urgent appointment with Captain Edwards, although he doesn't know it yet."

"Be careful, Crane," Anderson warned.

During the drive back to the barracks, Crane fumed whilst on the phone to Tina. He damned Edwards to hell and back for wasting his time, the resources of the

Aldershot Police and the Royal Military Police. Then he went on to damn his Officer Commanding for giving him the job of babysitting. Overseeing perfectly good Royal Military Police staff sergeants who had their own chain of command. But most of all, for hindering his investigation of two murders. Well, one possible and one definite as Tina pointed out. Crane also told Tina that Edwards had vetoed the general circulation of the artist's impression of the foreign looking soldier seen leaving the cemetery. Restricting it to Royal Military Police circulation only. Even the lads on the barrier had no idea Crane was looking for a mystery soldier, nor what he looked like. How the hell was he supposed to do his job properly with that idiot in charge he wanted to know?

By the time Crane arrived back at the barracks he had cooled down and decided to heed both Anderson's and Tina's warnings to be careful. Standing to attention he made his report in a purely professional and unemotional way. He finished with, "Unfortunately, sir your excellent idea of actively investigating all the Gurkhas in the immediate vicinity has regrettably come to naught." Zero, zilch, nil he added in his head.

"Very well, Crane," Edwards reached for a document on his desk. "In that case, let me know how you intend to proceed with the investigation into both the untimely deaths and the thefts. By tomorrow morning. Dismissed."

Crane just about managed to hiss, "Sir," before fleeing the building for a cigarette.

Once in the car park, Crane decided to go for a walk around the open playing fields to clear his head. As he walked he tries to clear his mind of all the negative feelings and thoughts about the current investigations in general and his Officer Commanding in particular. Lifting his eyes from the ground, he watched the disabled athletes train.

In previous weeks the ground was littered with discarded clothing from the able bodied Olympic athletes. Track suits, shoes and shirts. This time Crane saw discarded wheelchairs, prosthetic legs and running blades. A sight that was at once both heartbreaking and inspiring.

He watched the Paralympians for a while as they trained. Their determination clear from their decisive movements. He watched efforts made with a smile, despite the pain written on their faces and sweat running down their bodies. The entire endeavour topped with euphoria when a movement or race went well. Quite a number of the athletes were ex-forces personnel who had been injured in Iraq and Afghanistan and were forging new lives from the wreck of their old one, as disabled athletes. Crane felt humbled in their presence. And a bit of a twit, if he was honest. Here was a field full of people triumphing over adversity and all he could do was whinge.

After another circuit of the field, he strode back into the barracks to make a couple of phone calls.

Day 26

Crane saw Lance Corporal Dudley-Jones hesitate at the door so called, "Come in, Lance Corporal, we won't bite!" The 'we' being Crane, Billy and Kim. The gangly young man made his way to the conference table, placing his files on the Afghan officers on it, then perching on the edge of a chair.

"Right," Crane said. "I've called this meeting because it's about time we got a handle on the Afghan officers on the base. Thanks for bringing your files, Dudley-Jones."

"Haven't you been reading my reports, sir? The information I have on the officers was all in there."

"Really? Then in that case I must have missed something. What do you think, Kim? You're the office manager. You've read all the reports and background information on the officers as well. Have I missed something?"

Kim merely smiled at the question. Or rather, just turned up the corners of her mouth. The smile didn't reach her eyes. Her pristine uniform as usual accentuating the coolness of her demeanour.

"That's what I thought. So," Crane turned back to

Dudley-Jones, "as I see it there are several questions to be answered."

"Are there, sir?" Dudley-Jones had turned that peculiar puce colour again.

"Yes, son and you are just the person to answer them for me, or get the answers I need. Kim, would you put the questions up on the board as we go?"

Crane nodded at Billy.

"Right, sir," Billy said. "Firstly I think we need to know who is in overall charge of the group."

"Good place to start. What do you think, Lance-Corporal?" As the Lance-Corporal stayed silent, Crane prodded. "Come on, Dudley-Jones, please join in. This is a group brainstorm, not a witch hunt."

With some gentle and not so gentle persuasion, Crane's list was made. He wanted answers to information such as: who was in charge; who had the officers been meeting with; were any splinter groups forming; anyone seeing each other covertly; anyone acting suspiciously; anyone not where they should be sometimes. Unfortunately there were very few answers to the questions.

"Right then, so, what's the best way of getting the rest of the answers?" He asked all of them, but it was Dudley-Jones who answered, "Um, me, sir?"

"Excellent, Lance Corporal. Glad you're volunteering. I know you've been around the Afghan officers before, but this time I want you to focus your energies. Look at the demographics of the group. Just because one man is the senior officer, doesn't mean he's the one these people look to for support. A bit like in the British Army where the men look to an experienced Sergeant Major over an inexperienced officer, don't you think?"

Dudley-Jones looked stricken, as though just realising his mistake of possibly over estimating Captain Edwards and most certainly under estimating Crane. Kim merely turned up the corners of her mouth again and Billy went to get more coffee. "Kim," Crane continued, "I want you to get itineraries for the group as a whole together with any differences for individuals. Since they arrived on the barracks, mind. Back dated information is as good as forward planning. Go over them tonight and leave a report for me to look at in the morning. Billy?"

"Boss?"

"When you've finished your coffee, pop over to the Sergeants' Mess. See if you can hook up with anyone who has had even the slightest dealings with any of the Afghans." As Billy beamed, Crane added, "Don't forget you're on duty, coke only please."

"And you, sir?" asked Dudley-Jones.

"And me what?"

"What are you going to do?"

"Walk you outside, so I can have a cigarette."

The puce colour on Dudley-Jones face, brought on by his latest gaff, had faded somewhat by the time the two men were outside.

"I, um, that was, sir….." Dudley-Jones mumbled. Deciding for once to keep quiet, Crane waited for the young man to speak again. "It's just that you seem rather good at this."

"Why thank you, Lance Corporal." Crane took a drag of his cigarette to mask his smile.

"I thought you hadn't understood this intelligence stuff, but you do don't you?" As Crane nodded, Dudley-Jones warmed to his theory. "All those questions that need to be answered about the Afghan

Officer's movements - that's the sort of thing they do on the ground in Afghanistan." Again Crane just nodded. The young man rushed on. "So I was just wondering, sir, why you're not in the Intelligence Corp?"

"Because, Lance Corporal, here in the Special Investigations Branch, we are hands on. We *do*. We don't report stuff so others can do things. We actively investigate, not just watch over things. How can I explain? It's a bit like that old adage, 'those that can do – those that can't teach'."

Crane ground his cigarette out under his foot and made for the door. Then he stopped and turned back to Dudley-Jones. "And rest assured, Lance Corporal. I have every intention of 'doing'."

Crane's idea of 'doing' involved knowing exactly where the Afghan officers were at the moment. Kim quickly looked up the information.

"They're in the Officers' Mess, sir. Gathering for a formal dinner in their honour."

Crane made his way to the mess. The hum of chatter and clatter of knives and forks reached Crane as he entered the mess, by the back door into the kitchen. A Sergeant Major can't enter the Officers' Mess, unless by invitation. Each rank has their own mess as no soldier could be seen fraternising with someone of a higher or lower rank. Yet another clear example of the army's rank structure. Crane stood at the swing doors from the kitchen into the dining room. None of the staff paid him any heed, his dark suit and ID around his neck signalling him out as SIB and no one was brave enough or reckless enough to draw attention to themselves. The head chef clocked him of course, but merely nodded.

As the guests were all enjoying what appeared to be their main course, there was a lull in the comings and goings of the waiting staff through the swing doors. So Crane was able to stand there for some time, looking though the round glass covered holes cut into the top of the doors. The Afghan officers were easily identifiable just by their looks, let alone their different uniforms. Crane was searching for someone who fitted Padam's description of dark skin, dark moustache and dark hair. To his dismay he found at least six of the twelve looked like that. The rest were either clean shaven or had full beards. From his vantage point he was unable to see if the clean shaven ones showed signs of paler spots on their faces, where a moustache or beard had been removed. All the officers seemed relaxed and able to understand a modicum of English, being engaged in conversation with their fellow diners. Even though he was officially off duty, Crane decided to sit outside in his car for a while, to observe the Afghans as they left the mess.

Unfortunately a Ford Focus wasn't the most comfortable car to sit in for prolonged surveillance and after a while Crane became restless and uncomfortable, deciding to conceal himself outside. As he hid in the shadows of some trees, he saw a group of four Afghan officers emerge from the mess. They seemed to be deep in conversation. Crane watched as the group whispered to each other. They then each hugged one man in turn, before he peeled away in the direction of the sports centre. Just as Crane made the decision to follow the lone officer, his mobile phone vibrated in his pocket. Looking at the caller ID he saw the call was from Tina.

"Tina?" he hissed. "Are you okay?" He knew something must be wrong. They'd already agreed she would only phone tonight in an emergency.

At first all he heard was panting, then, "Tom?" gasped Tina. "I think the baby's coming!"

Shit, Crane thought, but said, "Are you having contractions?"

"No, I always bloody sound like this!"

"Alright, Tina, calm down. I'm on my way. Have you called the hospital?"

More panting. Then, "Yes. For God's sake, Tom hurry up!"

Day 27

Crane arrived home, waking up most of the street with his screeching tyres as he pulled up in front of the house. He sprinted indoors, leaving the car engine running. He wanted to make sure he was ready to get away as quickly as possible, so the baby wasn't born in the house or, dear God, on the back seat of his car. As he burst into the sitting room, tie askew and shirt tails hanging out, he found her relaxing on the settee, seemingly having recovered both her composure and control over her body. Her hair was still damp around her face from sweat, and as he folded her into his arms as best he could around her large bump, her breath against his neck was still fast and ragged.

"Sorry, Tom," she whispered into his shirt collar. "False alarm. A combination of Braxton Hick's contractions and panic."

After Crane had made a cup of sweet tea and found a blanket to cover her with, she explained to him all about Braxton Hicks contractions. Not that she'd remembered about them in her panic. It was the maternity ward at the hospital that made the diagnosis. As Tina calmed down under the soothing voice of the midwife on the other end of the phone, she found that, as predicted, the contractions became less strong and less frequent. After sipping most of the tea she seemed to suddenly remember what she had interrupted.

"Oh my God, the Afghans! What happened?"

"Nothing much, I kept watch for a while, but didn't see anything suspicious. So it looks like we both had false alarms tonight," Crane had laughed.

But he didn't feel very jovial the next morning. His head a tangle of thoughts, as he tried to figure out what the lone Afghan officer could have been up to. Feeling claustrophobic in the office, he gave up trying to read Kim's report and decided to go to the sports centre. The large grey building was in stark contrast to the older mellow red brick of Provost Barracks and the nearby New Mons and Clayton Barracks. Crane first took a turn around the outside of the building, missing the company and sharp eyes of Billy. He stopped at the grey metal door the mystery smudge disappeared into and out of. He closely examined every inch of the door, but couldn't see signs of anyone trying to force the lock. Unless, of course, it had been picked. And as it was a door for maintenance personnel, it was rarely used.

Deciding to take another look at the spot where Corporal Simms was found dead, Crane went back to the front of the building making his way through the busy complex, showing his pass several times along the way. He collected a maintenance man to unlock the doors, so he could explore underneath the swimming pool. It wasn't possible for the two men to have much of a conversation, as the noise from the pumps, pipes, water, and muted shouts and screams from the athletes above their heads in training sessions, drowned out their voices. Try as he might, Crane learned nothing new from his walk around the cavernous space and reluctantly made his way back to the office, where he wanted to look up the details of the men on guard duty at the complex that night. At the very least he needed to check their reports and get one of the team to talk to them again to see if they had seen anyone or anything incongruous during their time on duty at the sports centre, not just around the time they lost Corporal Simms.

He was also wondering where Padam Gurung was. No one had seen anything of him since the rounding up of the Gurkhas at Aldershot Police Station. Crane thought that after a grilling from the Royal Military Police and then the Aldershot Police, it was no wonder the man was lying low.

Another layer of worry to add to the clutter of his thoughts was Tina. There was no way he wouldn't have gone home last night he reassured himself. And he had been free to leave the garrison as he wasn't on duty. But as it turned out to be a false alarm, he now wished he could have stayed and watched the Afghan Officer. But that made him feel guilty all over again. Would he really put the job before Tina? Crane hoped not. But there was always that niggling doubt. He guessed, of course, that's what Tina realised. That one day Crane would have to choose between the army and his family. If that time came, which way would the sword fall? Either option was fraught with problems. Jump one way and he could lose his job and the other way possibly his family. By the time he arrived back at the Royal Military Police Barracks, Crane's head was spinning.

Night 27

I am beyond rage. Every fibre of my being is on fire with hatred for the infidels. The kaffir. Do you know what they wanted my Muslim brothers and I to do? To attend a church service! Can you believe it? The impudence. The effrontery. The audacity of these people. They said it would foster love, tolerance, integration and understanding of other religions. I have no need for any of that.

The Prophet decreed that you must show no sign of love or affection in your heart for a kaffir. That love, fornication and freedom are not allowed for Muslims. The only guidance I need is the Holy Qur'an. The word of God which is written to guide mankind forever. The Holy Prophet Muhammad is the perfect model of Islamic teachings, whose example shall be forever binding on every Muslim to follow.

We believe that, as the principles and teachings of religion reach perfection and completion in the Holy Qur'an and the example displayed by the Holy Prophet, it follows that the Qur'an is the final Book of God and that Muhammad (may peace and the blessings of Allah be upon him) is His Last Prophet, after whom no other

Prophet can appear. The Qur'an requires Muslims to follow in these footsteps. To develop the highest personal attributes and moral virtues and display these qualities, even at the cost of their own individual or even national, interest.

So I say again, there is no God but Allah, and Muhammad is the Messenger of Allah.

Therefore, I and my Muslim brothers will not go into any other church apart from a Mosque. For all other churches are the meeting places of devils. And the angel of death will come and rip out their souls.

Day 28

Crane was returning to the garrison for a team meeting, one he hoped to get to on time, as at the moment he was stuck in the queue of cars at a barrier. The temperature was still high despite it being nearly 17:00 hours, so all the drivers had their windows open, encouraging people to lean out of their vehicles and chat. This in turn bread moans and groans at the absurdity of the situation, along the lines of those Crane heard at the police station. Horns beeped, arms waved and invectives flew from frustrated drivers either trying to get home, back to the office, or complete a delivery. One pedestrian noticed Crane's identification badge around his neck and proceeded to lean into his car through the open window to berate him.

Once the cars inched their way to the front of the queue, the soldiers become sitting targets. Insult after moan peppered them and Crane was impressed with the stoicism of the lads, their faces remaining impassive, refusing to rise to the bait.

Because of the hold up, Crane entered the office at a run. He was greeted by Billy, holding out a cold bottle of water for him, while the remainder of the team settled down around the conference table. Crane stayed standing at the incident boards that he'd been working on. He had moved the four free standing white boards and put them together in a row. The first detailed the investigation into the death of Corporal Simms. The second covered the work done on the death of Corporal McInnes. The third was the thefts from the Aspire Defence stores and finally the fourth covered the information they had gathered on the Afghan officers. Dudley-Jones had already briefed Crane on the Afghans. It seemed the Lance Corporal was making some progress with his observations of the dynamics of the group and had realised a faction of four tended to stay together, centred around an officer called Captain Fahran Popal. Crane had put the four names on the board and asked Dudley-Jones to keep a closer eye on them.

"Right. What I want to do," Crane said, "is for us all to go through the information we have on each of these separate incidents, so we can update each other and make sure all salient points and connections are on the board. So let's look at the Simms case. Kim, has anything else come in from forensics or statements that we should be aware of?"

"Um, sir," Dudley-Jones interrupted. "I thought the death of Corporal Simms had been deemed an accidental death."

"Maybe, maybe not, Dudley-Jones. For now, I want to keep it on a board. Kim, anything?"

"No, sir, nothing. The statements taken from the lads in his battalion show Simms was well liked and a very enthusiastic soldier. It just looks like he was in the wrong place at the wrong time. No new forensics, only that one black hair."

"I went over the statements from those on guard duty with him that night," Crane said "but didn't see anything of interest. Billy, did you re-interview them?"

"Yes, boss. Not one of them noticed anything untoward during any of the times they were on duty at the sports centre."

"Oh well, worth a try. Anyone else have anything to add? Right then let's move on."

After going through each whiteboard, Crane said, "Now let's do it again, but this time looking for links." Crane ignored the groans. "Come on you lot, any sort of link will do. Billy, you first."

"Right, boss. How about Padam Gurung? He has links with both deaths. Seeing someone or something, first around the sports centre and then in the vicinity of the cemetery."

"Good," said Crane, writing the name with a linking arrow to both boards. "Anyone else?"

"Black hair on both bodies," called Kim, "which links the deaths to each other."

"Um, how about a possible Afghan soldier seen in the vicinity of the cemetery?" Dudley-Jones called, his puce coloured face showing he was anxious, but Crane was pleased he was plucking up the courage to join in.

"Thanks, Dudley-Jones," Crane said putting a linking arrow between the Afghan board and the McInnes board.

"How about linking the Afghan officers with both deaths, because of the black hair?" Sergeant Jones asked.

"Why not?" Crane agreed, drawing yet another linking line. "By the way, Kim, any further forensic analysis on the hairs?"

"Sorry, sir, still awaiting DNA and also ethnicity."

"Let me know as soon as those come through." Crane turned back to his boards.

"No links with the missing stores, boss." Billy observed.

Crane thought about that, rubbing his scar and scratching at his beard. "What stuff is actually missing, Kim? Have you got the updated list from Ms Stone yet?"

"Yes, sir, it came in this morning. I've not had time to look at it as I've just come on duty. Here it is."

Crane took the proffered piece of paper and wrote on the board: bleach, various cleaning materials, a mop and bucket, broom, large rolls of paper and some paint brushes.

"Sorry, boss, but I still can't make a connection with these thefts and the other boards," Billy shook his head in frustration.

"There must be a connection," Crane mused, "I just can't see it at the moment."

A ringing telephone interrupted him, followed by a second and then a third. As Kim and Billy rushed to grab the ones on their desks, Crane answered the main office line.

"Crane."

"Ah, Crane, glad it's you," said Captain Edwards. "Bit of a problem at New Mons Barracks. Go over and sort it out will you?"

"What sort of problem, sir?"

"Missing person."

"In that case I'll just send Sergeant Jones and the Royal Military Police to start with, sir."

"Not this time, Crane. I need you to go personally. With your team if possible."

"Very well, but may I ask why, sir?" For God's sake

184

give me a bloody clue, Crane thought. It was like pulling teeth.

After a pause Edwards answered, "Because the missing person is one of the visiting Afghan officers."

Night 28

The missing man was Captain Azar Niaz. So Crane and Billy were in New Mons Barracks finding out what they could about the last known movements of Niaz. They needed to interview Second Lieutenant Collins, the officer responsible for the exercise on nearby Ash Ranges, which was the last time Niaz was seen. Crane found Collins's office, knocked and walked in.

"Sorry to disturb you, sir, Sergeant Major Crane, SIB. I need to talk to you about Azar Niaz."

The Second Lieutenant, open mouthed and probably about to bawl Crane out for the interruption, closed his mouth and invited Crane and Billy to sit down. Crane silently thanked those who drew up the Army Regulations, giving SIB carte blanche to talk to anyone they needed to, without having to adhere to the rigid army structure of command.

"What can you tell us about the exercise today please, sir," Crane said as Billy took out his notebook.

"Well, Sergeant Major, the group of twelve Afghan officers were split into three groups of four, with their objective being to find and infiltrate an enemy position, without detection. This exercise will then be expanded in several days time, with each Afghan officer being expected to lead a team of British soldiers with a similar objective. They were doing really rather well at it..."

"It's of no interest to me, sir, how good they were at being officers," Crane cut in. "Can we please focus on Azar Niaz. Who was he training with?"

"Um, let me see," Collins fiddled with his paperwork. "I need to look it up. Perhaps you should be talking to my Sergeant, Sergeant Tomkins. He would know straight away."

"That won't be necessary, sir, if you could just find the information please?"

"Ah, here it is. The group of four men training together were Fahran Popal, Dehqan Khan, Behnam Freed and Azar Niaz. Is that what you wanted to know?" Collins removed his glasses and looked at Crane.

"Yes, sir, thank you for your time." With a nod at Billy, they left the office. As they got to the door Crane turned and said, "Did you notice anything unusual about any of the Afghan officers, or about these four in particular, sir?"

"Good gracious, no, Sergeant Major. Whatever are you suggesting? They are exemplary officers, making the Coldstream Guards extremely proud of them, not to mention their own Afghan Army. I hope you're not casting doubts about their credentials and reputation?"

"Of course not, sir, heaven forbid I should criticise an officer," Crane said as he left, sure that Collins wouldn't have recognised the sarcasm. Junior officers rarely did. Billy and Crane left the office to find Staff Sergeant Jones, who was conducting a search of Ash Ranges with his Royal Military Police and soldiers from the Coldstream Guards. The least the Guards could do, after losing one of their important visitors, was to help with the search.

"What do you reckon, boss? Do you think he's just lost?" Billy asked as they drove from New Mons Barracks, towards Ash Ranges.

"Well, Billy, as I see it we have to try and determine whether Niaz is simply lost, or has disappeared on purposes. If the latter is the case, he constitutes a threat."

"A threat, sir?"

"Oh for God's sake, Billy, wake up man. With two dead soldiers already, it isn't difficult to leap to the conclusion that Niaz could pose a terrorist threat. Why else would the bloody man go missing? Is he the person who killed them? What the hell is he plotting? What surprise does he have up his sleeve for us?" Crane punched the steering wheel. "So many fucking questions and absolutely no bloody answers."

Billy was quiet for the rest of the journey, no doubt smarting, but Crane didn't much care.

Kim was already hard at work when Crane arrived back at the barracks after dropping Billy at Ash Ranges, striding in and issuing orders as he took off his suit jacket.

"Right, Kim, make arrangements for Niaz's picture to be given to the soldiers at each of the barriers in and out of the garrison. Oh and include that artist's impression - the one of a suspect drawn from the information provided by Padam Gurung."

As he finished speaking Kim began obeying the orders, but he was very much afraid it was a case of bolting the stable door. Crane went into his office to answer his ringing phone.

"Ah good evening, Crane, Major Brownlow here,

Coldstream Guards."

"Yes, sir, how can I help you?" Crane began to loosen his tie with one hand, the other clutching the phone.

"It's more a case of how I can help you, Sergeant Major. Just wanted to let you know we've had an informal chat with the remaining three Afghan officers."

"Really, sir?"

"Yes, Crane, thought it might be better coming from us, rather than you lot in SIB."

"Really, sir?"

"Don't be difficult, Sergeant Major. Anyway, it seems they have no knowledge or understanding of where or when they saw their colleague last. So there's no need for you to interview them. Anyway it's a bit difficult with the language barrier you know."

"No I don't actually. I distinctly remember seeing all four Afghan officers conversing with their English colleagues at the Officers' Mess. So I'm somewhat surprised that they now seem to have lost both their memory and their ability to speak English."

"Crane," Major Brownlow rumbled a warning.

"Also, sir," Crane emphasised the 'sir', "I have other information that you are unaware of. I have been closely monitoring the activities of this particular group as they have been seen behaving suspiciously. So thank you for your input, sir, but I will be interviewing them tomorrow, with an interpreter present, of course."

Crane replaced the receiver with exaggerated care, cutting off the Major in mid sentence.

Day 29

Before Crane began interviewing the Afghan officers with Dudley-Jones, Crane read through the background information the Intelligence Corp had on them. All four came from the same region in Afghanistan and joined the army in their mid 20's. There was precious little information on their activities before joining up.

"There's not much to go on in here," Crane said to Dudley-Jones, throwing down the file in his hand and reaching for the photograph of Azar Niaz. "He looks uncannily like the description that Padam Gurung gave us." He passed the photo to Dudley-Jones.

"Yes, I see what you mean, sir, but then, so do the rest of the four." Dudley-Jones spread out all four photographs for Crane to compare.

"You're right. They all have olive skin, swept back dark hair and a moustache. Shit. Is the interpreter here?"

"Yes, sir, waiting outside."

"Okay, but remember, don't let on you understand any Pashtu. I want to see if you can catch anything they say that perhaps the interpreter misses or misinterprets."

"Don't you trust him?" Dudley-Jones asked in surprise.

"I don't trust anyone, Lance Corporal. I've always found that to be the best policy."

"Oh, right, sir. Are we interviewing Fahran Popal first?"

"No, if he really is in charge of this little cell, he'll be the hardest to get information from. So I want to start with the other two."

The 'other two' gave Crane nothing. They sat sweating in the stark interview room that was hotter than the 80 degree heat outside and insisted they knew nothing. Had seen nothing and had no idea where Niaz might be, or what he might be doing. Both men had shifting eyes, that didn't keep still. Neither really looked at Crane, but mostly at the interpreter, whom they fixated on, as though they were adrift at sea, in danger of drowning and he was a life saving plank of wood.

But Captain Fahran Popal was different. Crane could feel it as he entered the room. Popal had an arrogant way with him and Crane watched him relaxing in the chair, with a slightly quizzical expression on his face, making Crane feel Popal was laughing at them. But his manner was polite, if not deferential.

"Do you have any idea why Niaz would disappear?" Crane demanded.

The interpreter offered a negative reply.

"When did you last see him?"

The interpreter said Captain Popal couldn't remember in the confusion of the exercise.

"I find that rather strange," Crane said. "In the British Army it is vital that we work together as a team. Each team member must be aware of where the others are at all times and trust they are watching your back."

The interpreter indicated that Popal didn't understand the term 'watching your back'.

Stifling a sarcastic comment, something along the lines of in that case the Coldstream Guards weren't doing a very good job, he instead said, "being there to support you".

The interpreter said that Captain Popal and his fellow countrymen found the exercise very confusing which was probably why they failed to notice Niaz wasn't there.

"What do you think has happened to Niaz?"

Popal simply shrugged his shoulders and continued to stare at Crane.

"Does he know anyone else in this country?"

Again the shrug.

"Captain Popal, any information you can give us about Niaz and his background may help us find him. Are you sure there is nothing you can tell us?"

The interpreter relayed Popal's apologies and his sorrow that he couldn't help, not having known Niaz before coming to Aldershot. But Crane noted the slight smile playing around Popal's mouth. His eyes held none of the sorrow he was professing to feel and instead of his gaze sliding away in shame, he continued to hold Crane's stare. Feeling he'd get nothing more from the man, Crane ended the interview.

Leaving the boiling hot room, Crane pulled Dudley-Jones into his office and closed the door. He'd rather have gone outside for a chat and a cigarette, but needed privacy for their conversation.

"Well?" he demanded of the Lance Corporal.

"Arrogant bastard."

The reply took Crane by surprise.

"That's a bit strong for you, Dudley-Jones."

192

"Well, sir, I don't much like being called scum, even by a superior officer." Crane watched Dudley-Jones throw his files and notes on the desk.

Crane laughed, "Well he's not exactly a superior officer, but I know what you mean. Scum, eh? Interesting. The interpreter never mentioned that bit."

"No, sir. It was when he was introduced to us. Popal asked why an officer was being interviewed by lower rank scum and it was explained to him that you were in the Special Investigations Branch and I was in the Intelligence Corp and that we had the authority to interview any rank, even those above us. What a creep!" Dudley-Jones sat in the chair by Crane's desk.

Crane walked around the office to his own chair. "Yes, he was arrogant and a bit smarmy with it and I'm not just talking about the amount of oil in his hair. You'd think he'd be more concerned about his fellow officer wouldn't you?"

"Any normal person would, but I don't think he's normal."

"No, Dudley-Jones, neither do I. Get Intelligence to dig up as much background information on those four as they can. Surely someone on the ground in Afghanistan can fill us in. We need to know what they did before they joined up and also need to know if there's any evidence they knew each other before coming to Aldershot."

"Yes, sir, but it may take a few days."

"I realise that, which was why you need to get onto it right away. Oh and I also want a voice analysis done against Captain Popal's interview today and that tape your boys made of the mobile phone conversation. See if it's the same voice."

"But Popal hardly spoke, sir."

"Yes, Dudley-Jones I did notice. I wonder why that was?"

Day 30

Padam packed the precious letter away in his plastic carrier bag. It had arrived that morning and he wanted to open it when he was alone. He was planning to try to see his friends in the Royal Military Police as he should tell them about the bundle the smudge was carrying. But that was before the letter arrived. So Padam decided he would firstly go and read his letter and then see the Royal Military Police later.

Peering out of the window he saw the good weather was holding, but he decided to take his army greatcoat with him anyway. For one he was old and felt the cold and for two believed his fellow Gurkhas could not be trusted. Someone could be tempted to take it for himself. He knew it was something of a prize amongst his peers who coveted it in readiness for the winter months ahead.

He had heard talk that the army practiced on a piece of land called Ash Ranges and he thought that today was a good day to go there. And anyway a nice bit of woodland would make a change from the mean streets of Aldershot or the sentries on the garrison. A friend had shown him the direction to take out of Aldershot and written Ash on a piece of paper, so he could follow the signs.

As Padam wandered along the road out of Aldershot he came to a large roundabout over a huge road choked with traffic. He saw the sign for Ash as he approached and surmised he had to cross the large circular roundabout. Unfortunately this meant trying to avoid the fast moving cars every time he had to cross a tributary road, making Padam think of several instances when he had been a serving soldier, where he'd had to run whilst dodging bullets. These smaller roads either fed traffic down to the huge thoroughfare where they were swallowed up once they arrived, or spewed the cars out that wanted to leave. It was as though the road itself was a huge breathing monster expanding and contracting with the flow of traffic.

By the time Padam was safely across he was covered in sweat and shaking. After a few hundred yards he sat by the side of the road, which already felt like a quiet backwater, shrugging off his coat and taking several gulps from his water bottle. Looking around he realised the huge road he had crossed marked a divide from Aldershot to Ash in more ways than one. On the Aldershot side were industrial units, a plethora of drab Victorian terraces and dilapidated blocks of flats. Yet here on the Ash side there was space, greenery, larger houses and no rubbish. Padam felt the pressure of his life in Aldershot lifting from him and he imagined all his worries were caught in a metaphorical balloon, which he let go of and watched float off into the sky. Until it was a tiny speck in the distance. Refreshed Padam struck out for the Ranges.

He found an entrance to the woodland a few hundred yards from a clutch of shops in what he imagined to be the centre of the village of Ash. All the shop units were taken, there were no boarded up premises here. He walked off the road onto a track, through wooden posts and was immediately engulfed by trees. He decided he would enjoy the scenery later, for now he just wanted a quiet spot to read his letter.

Padam eventually settled on a shaded knoll some way into the Ranges. He squatted down and pulled the envelope from his bag. Opening the letter with trembling hands, he settled down to read.

Dearest Padam

I have the most exciting news. People arrived in our village a few days ago. People from England. They said they were here to help the families of old soldiers who had once served with the British Army. Not to help them get to England, but to assist those who had already travelled there to come back to Nepal if they wanted to. They would be willing to pay for your flight back! Can you imagine? We could all be together again. I know we have nothing left anymore, no farm, no money, no job, but surely it is better to be poor together, than to be destitute so far apart. I told them where you lived and they promised to write to you in Aldershot through a place called the Gurkha Welfare Society.

Please come home my husband, we miss you so much.

Padam had to stop reading as he couldn't see the words any more, his vision blurred by tears. They were pouring down his cheeks, wetting the collar of his shirt. But he didn't bother to wipe them away. All he could think of was home. He couldn't believe it. He could go home. Home to his wife, son and daughter. Get away from the misery, poverty and drudgery that made up his life now. Back to everything familiar to him, a world away from this alien country called England. It seems his wife had forgiven him for selling their small farm and taking out such a huge loan in the hope of a better life in England, which had turned out to be a fallacy. All they both wanted now was to be together in their old age.

Padam was so caught up with emotion, that he didn't hear the faint rustling behind him. Didn't feel the man's breath on his neck. But he did feel the strong hands encircle it and felt the crack as his head was whipped to one side. He did feel his body go numb and saw the precious letter fall out of his now useless fingers and fly away on the breeze. His last thought was 'home' before he too floated up into the blue sky, just like his balloon full of worries.

Night 30

"To lose one soldier, Crane, may be regarded as a misfortune; to lose two looks like carelessness; but to lose three?" Major Martin couldn't keep the mirth out of his voice.

"Thank you, Lady Bracknell," Crane made a mock bow, acknowledging the misquotation from The Importance of Being Ernest. But their mirth was extinguished as they gazed on the body of the dead man from a respectful distance.

Crane had been briefed by Staff Sergeant Jones. Originally the RMP who had stumbled across it on Ash Ranges, had thought it was a bundle of old clothes left behind, or deliberately dumped. After all he was searching for an Afghan officer, not piles of discarded clothes. As the young soldier poked the rags with a stick he was using to examine the undergrowth, he realised there was more substance to the abandoned wool and cotton than he'd first thought. He immediately stepped back and called for Staff Sergeant Jones. As darkness fell, Jones called the Adjutant, set up a perimeter around the scene and had lights and a generator brought in. Crane arrived just after the pathologist, the retired Major Martin.

"Why do you think it's a third soldier?" Crane asked. Major Martin handed him a document Crane had seen before. A Lal Kitab.

"Jones found this a few yards from the body. In a Tesco plastic carrier bag."

For a moment Crane couldn't speak as he stared at the red booklet in his hand. Clearing his throat he said, "You're right, Major. He was a soldier, albeit many years ago. Padam Gurung served the British Army well in his youth and tried to carry on serving it in his old age. I'll, um, just go and see Jones."

Walking away, Crane took a few moments on his own, before approaching the Staff Sergeant. Upset that not only had an innocent old man been killed, but also his only witness.

"Sorry, Crane," was the first thing Jones said. "I was dropped on when I found the documents. I'm still waiting for Major Martin to confirm identity, of course, as we can't see much of the body at the moment. But judging by the size and the clothes, there's probably not much doubt."

"No, probably not," Crane said. He then noticed Billy clambering through the undergrowth.

As he reached Crane, Billy said, "Just heard, boss. Bloody shame. But why him?" he asked indicating the crime scene with his head.

"He was probably in the wrong place at the wrong time, Billy. I'd say Padam saw something he shouldn't have and got killed so he couldn't pass on the information to anyone."

"Seen, sir? Seen what?"

"My best guess is an Afghan officer, hiding out in here somewhere."

Crane's eyes swept the blackness of the rest of the ranges. The area was easily closed to the public by flying the red danger flags. Local residents were well used to military exercises in this area, which closed down the public footpaths and access to the heath land. A number of signs peppered the area explaining the red flag system and warning the public about picking up military debris, which may explode. The ranges themselves were part of a vast area of mainly Ash woodland and undulating heath land, which the army had purchased back in the 1920's for soldiers from the nearby Aldershot Garrison to use for exercises. At the moment Crane and the rest of the team were in an area of low shrub land, just off one of the tarmac roads that ran through the area. He looked into the nearby woodland, the bare trunks of the ash trees illuminated by a full moon hanging low in the sky. What secret was hidden within that army of tall black skeletal sentries?

Major Martin interrupted Crane's examination of the woods.

"Crane," he called. "Definitely Padam Gurung I'm afraid. Matches his photo identification."

"Cause of death? Let me guess. Broken neck?

"Looks that way, Crane."

"Any idea on time of death?"

"Bit early to say, but approximately eight to twelve hours ago."

"Thank you, sir," said Crane, stuffing his hands in his coat pocket and returning to Billy, with his head down, deep in thought.

"Why was Padam here, boss?"

"That's what I want you to find out," Crane said, lifting his head. "After you've finished collecting forensic evidence, rustle up an interpreter, then go and collect DI Anderson. I want the fellow Gurkhas he shared a flat with interviewed. Maybe one of them knows what Padam was up to."

When Billy left Crane went to find Staff Sergeant Jones, to explain what he wanted. Jones, Crane and a couple of men then set out across the ranges.

The tarmac roadway soon gave way to track. Neither of which were conducive to silent progress. On the tarmac the men's army boots thudded like a drum beaten with a cloth covered stick and on the track, the dry twigs, leaves and bracken underfoot became firecrackers on Chinese New Year. Moving as stealthily as they could, Jones navigated their way using only the light of the moon. Gradually the sound of the generator running the lights dimmed to a mosquito hum as they traversed deeper into the Ranges. Startled night animals become their only companions.

Crane was sweating and regretting keeping on the light coat he had on because of the chill of the night. His shoulder was starting to ache deep in the muscle stretched over the bone and during a short halt whilst Jones got his bearings, Crane tried to manipulate it as best he could. He was just wondering how much further they had to go, when the faint shadows in front of them became looming concrete structures. They had arrived at the flag butts, or buttresses, stretched across a section of the ranges, from where the red flags were raised to warn non-army personnel that the ranges were out of bounds due to army exercises. Jones had brought them to the front and side of the structures, so they could approach unobserved. The four men then circled round to search each structure in turn.

It was at the third butt that they struck lucky. Crane and Jones hung back as the two Royal Military

Policemen inched forwards to the edge of the buttresses before flinging themselves around the sides and flashing their torches into the interior. There they found Captain Niaz, huddled in the small space, curled into a foetal position, as though trying to hide within the safety of a womb. He was cocooned in a blanket and surrounded by debris that included an empty water bottle and food wrappers. As Jones and Crane approached they look down on the man pinned in the powerful torch beams like a hare in headlights. Too stunned to resist, Niaz allowed himself to be prised from the small area where the red flag raising and lowering mechanism was housed.

Leaving Niaz flanked by the two Royal Military Policemen, Jones and Crane moved to one side. Jones radioed for a vehicle to take them back to Crane's car and then onward to Aldershot where Niaz could recover at the Royal Military Police Barracks. In custody, of course.

"Good thinking, Crane, the flag butts," Jones said. "Do you think he killed Padam?"

"Probably, but we'll have to be careful, strictly following procedure in our efforts to prove it. There's going to be outrage from the other Afghan officers at Niaz's arrest, as well as from the Coldstream Guards. No doubt Captain Edwards will join in the general debate as well. Make sure Major Martin sends Niaz's clothes for forensic processing. Maybe there was some transfer from Padam to him, or indeed the other way round. Whatever, we'll have to be careful and play it by the book. He may be a suspect but it's still too early to have any evidence."

"And Captain Edwards?"

"I'll ring him as soon as I get back home. I've been

on duty for over eighteen hours now and I'm due back again at 07:00 hours, so I need a few hours sleep before starting any interviews. In the meantime can you arrange for the interpreter to be there at say 09:00 hours tomorrow morning? Oh and Dudley-Jones too, of course. Better not leave him out of this one."

Day 31

TERRORISTS IN OUR MIDST?

By Diane Chambers

Residents of Aldershot are in uproar for the second time in a month, at the draconian way the army have used their stop and search powers on innocent residents as they pass in and out of Aldershot Garrison. Long delays are once again the order of the day as people try to go about their normal daily business.

An army spokesman explained, "There have been a number of thefts from locations around the garrison and it is particularly important, therefore, to monitor traffic in and out. We must put a stop to this ongoing theft problem and I'm sure the residents of Aldershot will accommodate the extra security that is deemed necessary at the moment."

But this reporter has discovered this may not be the real reason for the increased security at Aldershot Garrison. It has come to light that there are a number of Afghan Army officers staying there at the invitation of the Coldstream Guards.

In these troubling times local residents are worried about the possibility of terrorists in our midst. One local resident said, "It's absolutely appalling that the army could take such a risk and let Afghanis onto the garrison. Everyone knows the problems our lads are having over in Afghanistan at the moment, so why increase the risk to the soldiers serving on the garrison, never mind the local people?" Another resident Jean Cooper said, "I tell you it makes me afraid to go out! Who knows where they will attack and when?"

The army press office refused to give an interview, or even publish a statement when approached by this newspaper with the concerns of the local population. Is this a case of on a 'need to know' basis, the wider area outside the garrison don't need to know? Until we get an official explanation, the residents of Aldershot can only wait and wonder what might happen.

Anderson threw the newspaper at Crane across the desk. "Any comment, Sergeant Major?"

"Come on, Derek, you know we couldn't explain the real reason behind the increased security at the garrison."

"I know, but now it's been leaked what the hell am I supposed to do?" Anderson ran his fingers through his unruly hair. "We've had local residents on the telephone wanting to know if we're going to put armed police patrols on the street to protect them!"

"That bloody Diane Chambers."

"Wait a minute, did you know about this, Crane?" Anderson leaned over his desk.

"Let's just say she threatened me with it. Unless I gave her an exclusive interview on how the army coped with the Team GB athletes on the garrison, after they'd gone of course. So I had to agree with her request, or should I say demand."

"And she reneged on the deal?"

"Looks like it, and before I could give the heads up to Edwards," Crane scratched his scar.

To his surprise Anderson laughed. "Well, she got her own back after all. I'd say this was payback for not giving her an interview about the investigation last year. Wouldn't you?" Anderson was still chuckling.

"Alright, Derek, don't rub it in. Anyway, for now the army are going to release a statement. Captain Edwards is working on that at the moment. It's going to be something along the lines that our Afghani visitors are all upstanding army officers and there's no question that they could be a terrorist threat."

"But is that true?" Anderson shrugs his shoulders, becoming serious again. "What about finding Padam Gurung's body last night and the lost Afghan soldier? How does all that fit together?"

"To be honest, Derek, I don't know what the hell's going on." Crane shook his head. "Dudley-Jones and I interviewed Niaz this morning, but got nothing out of him. It was a complete waste of time. The whole thing is bloody chaos. I've got another dead body, an Afghan officer who refuses to speak at all, a reporter acting like she trying for a Pulitzer Prize and an Officer Commanding who's wobbling like a jelly."

"Are there any connections between the three deaths?"

"Lots of connections between lots of events, but nothing that adds up to anything. I can't even come up with a motive." Crane smoothed down his tie and then not knowing what to do with his hands as he couldn't smoke in the office, started to play with his scar again.

"There's got to be something, Crane," Anderson examined his own tie, which sported an abstract pattern of food stains, so he dropped it with apparent disgust.

"I know, but whatever it is I can't see it at the moment. And being without Billy and Kim during the day makes me feel like I'm working with one hand tied behind my back somehow."

"Are they doing alright on their own at night?"

"Oh they're fine. Working well together." After a pause Crane added, "I rather think it's me that's not functioning properly."

As a grin started to break across his face, Crane stood so fast he knocked over his chair. "That's it, Derek! You're brilliant. Thanks a lot," and rushed out of the office.

Crane hadn't had time to implement his plan when Juliette Stone turned up at the barracks, looking for him. As a result, he was less than pleased to see her and more interested in seeing Captain Edwards and making a couple of phone calls.

Before she could open her mouth he put up his hands and said, "I know, Ms Stone. I can only apologise but I assure you there is no threat to any of your staff or to the athletes in St Omar Barracks."

"Sorry, Sergeant Major?"

"The piece in the Aldershot Mail," Crane indicated the folded newspaper on his desk. To his surprise Juliette Stone laughed.

"Oh that bit of rubbish," she said. "The stupid girl actually came to me for a comment and I sent her away with nothing more than a dose of reality." Ms Stone's jacket crackled like a piece of breaking ice as she perched on the corner of Crane's desk. "I'm actually here to give you the full report on what's missing from the stores."

Crane took the proffered piece of paper, but didn't read it. "Thank you, but you could have sent someone over with it."

"Sometimes it does us all good to get a way for a while, wouldn't you agree, Crane?" A smile played across her lips as she slowly crossed her legs. The light in her eyes reminding Crane of the way Tina used to look at him, before the demands of the baby on her body became paramount.

"Of course, but we also need to pick our moments, wouldn't *you* agree?" Crane held Juliette Stone's gaze.

"Ah, and this is not a good moment for you?"

"Definitely not, I'm afraid," Crane tried injecting a sense of regret into his voice, but wasn't sure he managed it.

"Some other time perhaps," she replied standing, but not leaving.

"Perhaps," Crane mumbled, picking up and looking at the piece of paper she'd given him, without seeing any of the words written on it. A pose he held until he once more heard the crackle of ice as she left his office. As he breathed in deeply, he smelled her alluring perfume and once again saw the teasing in her eyes. Feeling guilty for finding another woman attractive, he pushed the thought away, together with her piece of paper and got on with his work.

Crane eventually got his meeting with Captain Edwards. This time he didn't need to emphasis the seriousness of the situation. That was something Edwards started on as soon as Crane entered his office.

Leaving Crane standing to attention in front of his desk Edwards summed up the awfulness of their present predicament in every last gory detail, from the original death of Corporal Simms to the current position of having an Afghan officer in custody and an old Gurkha dead, with all the twists and turns in-between. He finally barked, "So what are you going to do about it, Crane?"

Edwards allowed Crane to sit once he realised there was a possible solution and listened like a prison inmate eagerly learning of plans to escape.

Night 31

Allah is Good! Allah is Great! Allah be Praised! Things are going better than I dared hope. As a result of my carefully laid plans, I have the security services on the garrison running around in circles, how do you say, ah yes, chasing phantoms in the wind, grasping at thin air.

I had the supposed privilege of meeting your chief investigator the other day. Crane is it? Or some such name anyway. It is of no matter. He struts around like a cock with his faithful chickens running around him, scratching for any bits of praise he may throw down at them. Pathetic. I spit on him, the infidel. He thinks he is so good, so clever, but I had him rattled.

For let me remind you, that I, with the power of Allah behind me, am more than a match for this evil one. He has no idea that the confusion is being orchestrated by me. Nor has he any concept of the chaos that I am about to rain on his head. No inkling that this torture is not going to end anytime soon.

He thinks it will, of course. He will think it's all over and that he's triumphed over what he perceives as the evil invading his garrison. But that will just be me lulling him into a false sense of security. For he can never win.

Never beat the truth that is the one true religion.

I will grind him down until he turns into nothing but a speck of dust under my boot. Just you wait and see.

Day 32

Crane alternated between pacing the corridor and sitting by Tina's bed. He was woken around 05:00 hours with Tina feeling light headed and breathless with swollen ankles. So he wasted no time in getting her into the car and over to Frimley Park Hospital. At the moment she was surrounded by a doctor and couple of nurses, leaving Crane to kick his heels in the corridor.

"Mr Crane?" It took a minute for Crane to react to the use of the term Mr. Normally he was addressed as Sergeant Major, or just Crane. Looking up he saw a doctor walking towards him. "Well, emergency over for now, I think."

"What's the matter with her, doctor?" Crane tried not to snap, but worry was making his voice harsher than normal.

"Flare up of the old pre-eclampsia again, I'm afraid. But we've been monitoring the baby's heartbeat and it's a strong as ever. So for now I want to leave things be."

"Oh good, so she can go home now?" Crane bent to collect his coat from a nearby plastic chair.

"Most certainly not. Mrs Crane must stay in hospital until the baby's born."

Straightening up and leaving his coat where it was, Crane asked, "When will that be?"

"One never really knew with babies I'm afraid, Mr Crane." The doctor consulted his notes. "But we won't leave her too long before inducing. Still, a few days yet, I should think." With that then he turned on his heel and walked away, then he turned back calling, "Oh, your wife is sleeping now, Mr Crane, so best leave her until visiting time don't you think?"

Looking at his watch Crane realised it was time to go to work anyway, so with one last look at Tina's sleeping form squeezed into a bed on the Maternity Ward, he sloped off. As he passed the cafeteria near the front doors, it was just opening, announced by the enticing aroma of freshly brewed coffee. Deciding to get a cup to take away and enjoy with his cigarette outside, Crane made his way to the deserted counter. As he was waiting for an assistant to emerge from the kitchen, he was joined by someone else, who began tapping his foot and looking at his watch. "For God's sake," the man mumbled.

"Desperate for coffee?" Crane said glancing at the person who had joined him.

As the man meet Crane's eyes he exclaimed, "Bloody hell, Crane! How are you?"

"Benson! Fine thanks and you?"

As the two men greeted each other like long lost brothers, an assistant finally came to take their orders. Benson decided to get a take away coffee as well and joined Crane outside.

The two men strolled down to the car park catching up with each other's lives. Benson was posted to Colchester a few years ago, at the same time as Crane and the two men worked well together and enjoyed each other's company.

"I didn't know you were posted back at Aldershot," Crane said when they were far enough away from the hospital buildings to light up. "When did that happen?"

"I'm not," Benson said looking out over the vast expanse of empty car park that would soon fill up as patients began arriving for appointments.

"Don't tell me you're out?" Crane was astounded. Benson was one of the most committed soldier's he'd met. A great outdoors man, he would volunteer for every course going and loved nothing more than to face new challenges and learn new skills. But looking more closely Crane saw slackness around Benson's face and a thickening stomach almost as big as the man's barrel chest.

"Yeah, couple of years ago now."

Benson began a close inspection of the ground by his feet. His hair, longer than Crane remembered flopping over his shirt collar, the dark brown now flecked with grey.

"Why? What went wrong? Weren't you enjoying army life anymore?"

"Nothing went wrong, Crane, and yes I was still enjoying army life, but the wife wasn't."

"The wife – Carol?"

"Yes, after we had our first kid, she changed somehow. Maybe it was being more tied to the house, oh I don't know." Benson started playing around with gravel under his foot. Rolling the small stones backwards and forwards. "She talked me into leaving. Told me it would be best for the family."

"And was it?" Crane looked at Benson keenly.

"Oh yes. For them, definitely." Benson finally looked at Crane. His face was smiling but his eyes were not. "It's been great seeing the kids grow up, you know, look here's a picture," and he fumbled in his wallet before passing over a small family portrait, well worn at the corners.

"Lovely," Crane tried to sound enthusiastic. "So what are you doing now?"

"Security." Benson avoided Crane's gaze by putting the photograph back.

"What, private stuff, body guard, that sort of thing."

"No," Benson laughed, the tinge of bitterness clear, "buildings. Anyway, best get back. If I'm not careful Carol will have had the baby without me and then I'll really be in trouble." With a wave of his hand, Benson walked off back towards the hospital.

Crane watched his retreating back and realised they hadn't made plans to meet up again. He raised his arm and went to call out, but seeing the stoop of Benson's shoulders and the hesitancy in his stride, Crane's mouth remained closed and his arm dropped back down. Probably not such a good idea. Best to leave things alone. What would they have in common now anyway, apart from joint memories?

Crane hurried to his car, glancing at his watch and hoping Billy and Kim would still be at the barracks when he arrived. As he drove away his mind kept going back to Benson's hunched figure as he walked away, a far cry from the proud, upright man he had known in the army.

Night 33

Crane endured Billy's grumblings. He knew he'd stop soon and anyway to a certain extent he had to agree with him. Being dragged out to the sports centre in the evening, after just switching to days, was not what Billy considered a good idea. But Crane knew that having the team back together on days was one of his better schemes and as Edwards was desperate for results, he'd agreed.

"What are we looking for boss?" Billy asked as they climbed out of Crane's car.

"Anything, nothing, oh I don't know. It's just that something's off kilter and I want to find out what. So keep alert," the tone of Crane's voice indicating the final statement was an order.

"Okay, boss."

Crane and Billy stood by the car which was parked in the sports centre car park and looked around. At 23:00 hours the Paralympians and their helpers were all back at St Omar Barracks, the sports centre was closed and armed Royal Military Police and soldiers on guard duty had the building on their patrol lists. Flood lights illuminate the car park and front of the building,

217

bathing Crane and Billy in harsh white sodium light.

"Are we going inside, sir?" Billy indicated the building with his head.

"Yes, but not through the front doors. Where are the Afghan officers tonight, Billy?"

"In New Mons Barracks, boss. It's a normal off duty evening for them, no formal dinner or anything like that."

"Right, in that case they're close and free to roam around. Come on."

Crane moved away from the car park towards a clump of trees about 100 yards away. By the time they arrived, their eyes had adjusted to the night and Crane paused.

"This is the spot where Padam saw the smudge gaining access to the sports centre through the side door there. Can you see it, Billy?"

"Vaguely, sir." Billy's face screwed up with the effort of focusing his eyes on the dark side of the sports centre.

"Well that's the way we're going in tonight. Come on."

Crane began to pick his way carefully out of the thicket and headed towards the building. On their arrival Crane produced a key, which he gently inserted into the lock. The night was so quiet they could hear the tumbling of the teeth as the key turned. Crane waited a few moments before cautiously opening the door, in case someone was waiting on the other side. He and Billy slipped in and Crane locked the door behind them.

The air was thick and heavy, smelling of dust and chlorine. As Crane and Billy switched on their torches, dust motes swirled, trapped in the twin beams of light.

Without speaking, Crane indicated Billy should go right and he would go left, sweeping around the space and meeting again in the middle on the other side.

Crane felt the tingle of unease playing over the back of his neck, his senses alert to any disturbance in the air. Playing his torch beam around the space in front of him he then looked up and carefully examined under and around the pipe work above his head. A spaghetti junction of plastic. Pipes ran adjacent to each other, under or above each other and canted off at angles. He knew that some were inlet pipes and some outlet pipes. Others allowed for the flow of water to be re-circulated through the filters and pumped back into the pool. Any one of them an ideal place to place a bomb. But on his half circuit of the space Crane found nothing. No smudges on pipes that shouldn't have been there. No tell tale tape holding explosives in place. No ticking of clocks. The other thing Crane didn't find on his arrival at the meeting point was Billy.

Standing with his back to the wall, Crane played his beam around and above the yawning space in front of him. Nothing. So he continued on his way, hoping to find Billy delayed by a piece of evidence. When Crane found him he realised Billy had indeed been delayed. Not by something, but by somebody and left lying prone on the floor, his torch several feet from his body, illuminating the back wall.

Crane's first reaction was to rush to Billy's aid, but his training stopped him and he stood still. Ears straining, eyes searching, his light insufficient to reach further than a few feet in front of him. Once he was satisfied there was no threat, Crane took the few steps that brought him to his sergeant. Still he didn't speak, putting his fingers to Billy's neck where he should feel a pulse. He closed his eyes in relief as he felt a strong, regular blip under his fingertip.

At Crane's touch Billy groaned, moving his head and then trying to get to his feet. Crane held him down, giving his young sergeant a few moments to come to, before attempting to stand. He then made sure Billy got upright in stages before supporting him on their slow journey back to the door.

Propping Billy against the wall, Crane took the door key from his pocket and turned it in the lock. Pressing down on the handle he pulled the door towards him. It refused to open. He tugged the metal door, but there was still no movement. It took Crane a few moments to realise he had just locked the door. Someone else had unlocked it and in his panic forgotten to secure it again.

The fresh air outside seemed to revive Billy and by the time they reached Crane's car, he said he was feeling better.

"Apart from a headache, boss" he said.

"What the hell happened?"

"No idea, boss. Never heard or saw a thing. Just bang and the lights went out!" Billy looked down at his dark clothing and tried ineffectually to brush the dust off.

"Any recollections at all? Here, sit in the car. Try and remember exactly what happened."

Crane got into the driver's seat and turned to face Billy. The colour was returning to his face and his pupils were becoming smaller, albeit slowly, a reaction to the overhead light in the car. Crane knew he should have Billy's head injury checked out, but needed to hear what happened first.

"I was walking along the side of the wall, looking above me at the pipes. I didn't see anything suspicious, so decided to sweep my light in front of me. I took a few paces away from the wall and the next thing I knew something must have hit the back of my head. I didn't see anyone, or hear anyone, sorry, boss." Billy turned to Crane.

"It's alright. Just take a few more minutes." Crane got a packet of cigarettes out of his pocket and went to light one.

"Oh boss, not one of those smelly things…Jesus Christ that's it! The smell, boss. There was a funny smell in the air."

"Well done, son," Crane said. "What was it?"

"That's the thing, boss. I've no idea. But I'll know it if I smell it again."

Day 34

Crane was pleased to see Billy at work the next morning, after being given the all clear at the hospital the previous night. Gratefully taking the steaming mug of coffee proffered by Kim, Crane sat in the open plan office looking at his white boards. There were now six. The first two were the investigation into the deaths of Corporal Simms and Corporal McInnes. The third one, the thefts from the Aspire Defence stores. The fourth covered the investigation into the four suspicious Afghan officers, with the fifth and sixth covering the disappearance and subsequent finding of Azar Niaz and the death of Padam Gurung. Billy and Kim joined him, drinks in hand.

"Right," Crane said. "I think it's about time we had another team briefing. Kim, call in Staff Sergeant Jones and Lance Corporal Dudley-Jones, so we can update the boards and see where we were."

"Nowhere, boss, if you ask me."

"Well I'm not, Billy," Crane said. "Stop being so bloody defeatist. I know you must have a headache, but still."

"Sorry, boss," Billy mumbled, rubbing the back of

his head. Crane had to smile at the pathetic attempt to try and elicit sympathy. Calling to Kim to let him know what time the others would be there, Crane went towards his office to call the hospital and find out how Tina was this morning. He stopped at the shrill ring from Kim's phone on her desk, looking at her questioningly as she answered it, just in case it was the hospital wanting him.

It was someone wanting him, but not the hospital. As Kim replaced the receiver, he saw her eyes were wide and heard the panic in her voice as she said, "Sir that was a call from the sports centre. They think they've got a suicide bomber."

Crane took a couple of seconds to assimilate the information. Although he had half expected something like this, the news threw him for a moment.

"Right, Kim, as the call came in direct, phone the following people." He saw her quickly reach for her ever present note pad. "Firstly the Adjutant, then Captain Edwards and finally Staff Sergeant Jones. Tell them all, but particularly Jones, that we need to lock down the garrison. Now. Oh and don't forget Dudley-Jones, I want him over at the sports centre in case we need an interpreter."

"An interpreter, sir?"

"Yes, the odds are it's one of the Afghan officers. Call the Coldstream Guards and find out where they all are, particularly Popal Faran, Dehqan Kahn and Behnam Freed. Come on, Billy." Crane ran for the door, where he stopped and called back to Kim. "Don't forget the boards, make a new one for this incident and if you get time update the others."

"Sir," Kim said in a steady voice, her earlier fear seemingly soothed by the orders.

Crane and Billy raced across the car park. At his car, Crane threw Billy the keys, so he could have a cigarette on the short journey to the sports centre. He always seemed to think better with a cigarette on the go. Barriers were already up when they arrived and they had to show their identification to gain access. As they parked, Crane climbed out of the car and threw away his cigarette butt.

Crane and Billy approached the front of the sports centre. Stopping at the bottom of the steps, they gazed through the large glass doors. Standing alone in the reception area was one of the Afghan officers. Crane thought it was Behnam Freed, but wasn't sure as the group of four officers they had been monitoring all looked the same to him, each having swept back black hair and a moustache. An abandoned coat, a plastic carrier bag, a couple of clip boards and some loose papers surrounded the man on the floor. His arms were held wide with damp stains spreading from his armpits, turning his light brown shirt a muddy colour. What at first appeared to be a bullet proof vest covered his chest. But on closer inspection, Crane could see it had been modified with pockets all around it. Each pocket held a small tube with wires coming from the top of each cylinder, which were interlinked. In Freed's left hand was a small rectangular box, the top of which was covered with his thumb and from the bottom ran a wire which disappeared around his back. There didn't appear to be any sports centre staff in there with him, unless they were hiding behind the reception desk itself. The only item on the counter was an abandoned telephone.

Crane turned his attention back to the car park, walking away from the front of the building. Members of the sports centre staff were huddled in one corner of the car park. In another, disabled athletes were being helped into wheelchairs and those who could walk unaided were being unceremoniously loaded into mini-vans.

As Staff Sergeant Jones ran up to them, breathing deeply, Crane ignored him, turning to Billy first. "Go and interview the staff, find out what happened and get the number for that telephone on the reception desk. Also check that all members of staff currently working here are accounted for. They had emergency evacuation procedures, so the marshals should have a list of staff with them."

As Billy rushed away, Crane said to Jones, "Go and speak to the disabled athletes, make sure your lads get their names and then release them back to St Omar Barracks. But I want them to stay there until you can interview them. All of them. Also find out if any of them are still in the sports centre. By the way, has the garrison been locked down?"

"Yes, sir, as soon as I got the call from Kim I contacted each entrance. No one can come in, or for that matter get out, at the moment."

"Good, now where is Dudley-Jones?" Jones shrugged his shoulders and moved off. Crane was pulling out his mobile, when he saw the young Lance Corporal jogging up the road towards the sports centre. By the time Dudley-Jones reached Crane, Billy had returned from speaking to the staff.

"Right, boss, here's the telephone number for the phone in reception." Billy handed Crane a piece of paper. "They think there are three members of staff missing. But they're not sure if they are still in the building, or had snuck outside for a quick break. All three of them were either between classes, or waiting for an activity to finish so they could set up another one. It seems the incident occurred at a quiet time this morning with not many athletes and staff on site."

"Good, go back and see if anyone has mobile phone numbers for the three unaccounted for. If so, ring their phones and find out where they are."

"Yes, boss," Billy acknowledged his orders and moved off again.

"Ah, Dudley-Jones," Crane turned to the Intelligence Operative. "Glad you could join us."

"Yes, sir, sorry, sir, got here as quickly as I could." Dudley-Jones panted out his reply.

"Right, well, I've got the telephone number for reception. So you and I are going to walk slowly and carefully back to the glass doors. I think it's Freed in there with a suicide vest on. We're going to call the number of the phone on reception and hope he answers it. If he won't speak English I'm going to need you to talk to him."

"Me?" Dudley-Jones' eyes widened in fright. "A, ah, are you s, s, sure, sir?"

"Positive. Come on, lad," and Crane walked away, leaving Dudley-Jones to scamper in his wake. Once they were in position, Crane and Dudley-Jones both lifted their arms to show Freed they were unarmed. Crane then held aloft his mobile phone and pointed to the telephone resting on top of the reception desk. Freed nodded in response and moved towards it, with his arms still wide, as though afraid to drop them and dislodge any of the wires or explosives around his chest. Crane dropped his eyes for a moment to his mobile as he dialled the number. As the phone inside began to ring, Crane lifted his eyes and he and Freed stared at each other through the glass.

Night 34

Crane was wired on caffeine, adrenaline and nicotine. He wanted nothing more than to go home, have a shower and change his clothes, before relaxing and pouring himself a very large drink. But he couldn't as he had to go to the hospital to see Tina. And he couldn't do that either, as Freed was still standing in the reception of the sports centre, with his bloody suicide bomb vest wrapped around him.

It turned out there were some Paralympians stuck in the sports centre after all, along with the three missing staff members. It had taken hours of careful negotiation between Crane and Freed, using Captain Popal as an Interpreter/go-between, for them to be released. A few at a time. Still not fully trusting either Afghan, Crane kept Dudley-Jones close by to whisper in Crane's ear if he felt there was a discrepancy in the translations. The young man had stopped being a cube of jelly and found some backbone. Crane thought the trouble with the Lance Corporal was lack of field experience. He's been sitting in an office pouring over his intelligence reports for far too long.

Billy was at the rear of the sports centre, where

specialist soldiers were gathered, ready to storm the building if necessary. Bomb Disposal were waiting in the car park and Captain Edwards was still in attendance, constantly on his mobile phone, updating the upper echelons of command on their progress, or rather lack of it as he kept reminding Crane. Kim, in her role as office manager, was holding everything together back at barracks. Feeding him any information he wanted and acting as liaison between the local police and the press office. She had also rung the hospital and left a message for Tina to say that Crane was unavoidably delayed, but in no danger. A little white lie about the danger bit perhaps, but necessary, under the circumstances.

Derek Anderson had stationed local police at the barriers into the garrison, to help explain to local residents that due to an unspecified incident, they would not be allowed access for the foreseeable future. Locals trapped inside had been allowed out, but not until they and their cars had been thoroughly searched and notes taken on each of them. In quieter moments, Crane shuddered at the thought of the lurid headlines to come from the dripping pen of Diane Chambers. A couple of ambulances and a clutch of medics remained, stationed at a safe distance. Most had gone, taking the disabled athletes to hospital, as they were released in dribs and drabs.

As it was now late in the evening, floodlights lit up the car park and illuminated the front of the building. Freed was starkly lit by every light possible in reception and adjacent areas. Crane could see the new lines etched on Freed's face, exhaustion making his eyelids droop. His once slicked black hair was now falling forwards over his forehead and his chin kept dropping to his chest. Dark smudges covered his face, where stubble was breaking through the surface of his skin. Freed had not eaten for hours now, but Crane had smiled when earlier the man had pulled several bottles of water out of the plastic carrier bag near his feet, obviously prepared for the long haul.

Crane felt they were close to the end now. But what the end would be was still anyone's guess.

"There's something a bit off here, sir," Dudley-Jones murmured, not wanting to be overheard by Captain Popal.

Crane sauntered away from the Afghan officer, using lighting a cigarette as an excuse. "What do you mean?" Crane kept his voice low.

"Well, I know I've no experience of hostage situations, but the Afghan doesn't seem to want anything."

"He wants glory for Allah or some such doesn't he?"

"Oh yes, he's spouting loads of rhetoric, but no specific demands. No safe passage out of here, money, food…"

"I don't think suicide bombers do that, do they?"

"Buggered if I know, sir," Dudley-Jones admitted. "But then, if he really was a suicide bomber, wouldn't he have just blown himself away and everyone else with him to start with?"

Crane played with his scar, scratching at his beard as though it itched, which it didn't.

"You know, that's a good point, lad, remind me of it later at the de-briefing, in case I forget."

"If we're alive to have a de-briefing," Dudley-Jones thrust his hands in the pocket of an oversized coat that someone had lent him.

"For God's sake, Lance Corporal, you can't ever

think like that, do you hear me?" Crane reached out and pulled up Dudley-Jones' head by the chin. Staring into his eyes he hissed, "Stay positive, it's the only way. We will make it, and we will get out of this. Understand?" Crane was breathing hard and glaring at the young Lance Corporal.

When Crane let go of him, Dudley-Jones kept his chin high, "Understood, sir," a small smile starting to thaw the icy fear still present in his eyes.

"Right." Crane threw away his cigarette. "Let's finish this."

Captain Popal had also been taking a break. His hands were now wrapped around a mug of hot something or other. Mint tea maybe Crane thought. He didn't think Afghanis drunk coffee, or alcohol, but then again he couldn't remember. He seemed to be blundering around in a fog of tiredness and stress, clear thinking becoming more and more difficult to sustain.

"Shall we continue, Captain?"

Crane, Dudley-Jones and Popal walked back to their negotiating position at the bottom of the steps. Crane noticed the Captain had kept his mug. The call made, all three men listen via radio microphones and earpieces, installed when Captain Popal arrived to help.

The Captain began by reminding Freed that it was now dark. He pointed out that Freed must be tired and cold and wondered if he wanted a drink of the hot mint tea he was holding. By way of response, Freed slowly sat down and crossed his legs, but kept his arms wide and his thumb on the trigger of the mechanism. He slowly nodded his head. Faran began to move up the steps towards the door.

"Captain, what the hell were you doing?" Crane hissed, falling in step behind him. But Faran didn't reply, merely continued speaking to the bomber in a soft sing song voice.

"What the hell is he saying?" Crane demanded of Dudley-Jones.

"Um, something about remember the scriptures, the words written in the Qur'an."

"Keep translating," Crane hissed as Popal continued to mount the steps.

"Keep your eye on the bigger picture. Remember the higher goals. Allah is great. Allah is good. Allah will look after all those who are true believers and keep a place for them." Dudley-Jones followed the stream of words as best he could.

"Crane?" the horror in Captain Edward's voice cracked in his other ear like lightening. "What the hell's going on?" Crane imagined he could hear the lock and load of the sniper's rifles in the background.

"Give us a moment, Captain. I think Popal is going to do it. Looks like Freed is giving up. Hold back for now."

"You better be right about this, Sergeant Major!"

Crane tuned out Edward's voice as best he could. Dudley-Jones was still translating and Popal still speaking in his hypnotic voice. Cold sweat trickled down Crane's back. Even though he was stood behind Captain Popal, he knew that if the suicide vest was detonated now, all four of them stood little chance of surviving either the blast or the shards of glass that would rain down on them. Pushing the thought away and trying to detach his mind, Crane put one foot in front of the other, following Captain Popal up the steps, moving slightly sideways so he could see what was happening, even though he was even more exposed to any blast.

"Hold steady, sir," Crane whispered in his mike to Captain Edwards.

As he looked through the glass doors he saw Freed slowly lower his hand containing the detonator. Crane held his breath. Equally slowly Freed's arm returned to its outstretched position. His hand was empty.

"Hold fire, he's giving up. Hold fire," Crane repeated, hoping his throat microphone picked up his low voice, afraid that any shouting would disturb the delicate situation playing out in front of him. In the background Dudley-Jones continued translating and Captain Popal continued talking in Pashtu.

"He's asking Freed to put his hands on his head, sir," Dudley-Jones said. As Freed complied, Crane started breathing again.

Day 35

Crane was sitting through the interminable de-briefing meeting, trying hard to keep himself from looking at his watch. Everyone had commented on the support services, the role of the Royal Military Police, the assistance of the Aldershot Police, the tricky business of evacuating disabled athletes from the sports centre, communications between all parties and back up from Bomb Disposal and Special Services. Captain Edwards complimented the team on their successful operation, particularly Crane and Dudley-Jones for their roles in the negotiations. After acknowledging the praise, Crane turned to the subject of the suicide bomber himself.

"Do we know what explosive were in his vest?" he asked Kim.

After shuffling paper, she replied, "No report from Bomb Disposal as yet, sir."

"Very well, chase them up."

"Sir." Kim nodded and made a note on her pad.

"Where is he now?" Crane asked Staff Sergeant Jones, meaning Captain Freed.

"Under arrest in the guard room. We haven't interviewed him yet, we're waiting for your decision on how to proceed."

"Good. Billy, Dudley-Jones and I will come over and interrogate him after this meeting." Crane looked at Captain Edwards, "Oh, if that's alright with you, sir?" he asked as an afterthought.

"Very well, Crane, but I think it should be an interview, not an interrogation."

"I beg your pardon?"

"I merely meant that you should remember he is an officer and a member of the Afghan Army."

"That tried to blow up a lot of people." Crane threw his pen on the conference table.

"But he didn't did he, Crane?" Edwards was talking down his nose as usual.

"Um, excuse me, sir?" Dudley-Jones interrupted looking from Captain Edwards to Crane, clearly not sure who to address.

"Yes?" Edwards and Crane said in unison.

"Um, it's just that Sergeant Major Crane asked me to remind him of something at the de-briefing today."

"And that was?" Edwards sounded irritated.

"Um, sir, my question last night. Why didn't Freed blow himself up to start with?"

"What?" Edwards looked at Dudley-Jones and then Crane. "Do you know what he's talking about, Sergeant Major?"

Crane smiled, "Yes, sir. Dudley-Jones made a good point last night, that suicide bombers usually just go ahead and press the button. They don't negotiate or hold hostages."

"Indeed, sir," Dudley-Jones addressed Edwards. "The whole idea of a suicide bomber is firstly surprise and secondly to kill as many people as possible. Saving himself is just not normally on the agenda. So how come Freed didn't do that?"

"Well, I guess that's something you'll have to ask him." Edwards collected his papers. "If that's all, then I'll be off. Dismissed." Everyone stood as Edwards left the office and then looked at Crane to see if they were actually dismissed.

Shaking his head he said "Just a minute, people."

Once the team were settled again Crane continued, "Kim, did you manage to keep the boards up to date last night?" Crane referred to his white boards displayed along the back of the open plan space.

"Yes sir, I've just got the Freed board to finish. I want to make sure I've got all the information gathered from last night."

"Good, make sure you put the latest queries on and the info from Bomb Disposal when it comes in. Oh, and I want the tapes from the negotiations last night. Can you separate out the part from when Captain Popal approached Freed with a hot drink? That's the only bit I want."

"Certainly, sir."

After Kim acknowledged the order Crane turned to Staff Sergeant Jones. "Has Freed said anything?"

"Not a bloody thing. At least not in English anyway. He just sits in his cell, rocking backwards and forwards and mumbling in Pashtu."

"Has he had any contact with the other Afghan officers?"

"No. Requests were made, but we've deliberately ignored them for now."

"Good, let's keep it that way. I want him to feel isolated. That may help us to get him to talk."

"Very well, sir."

"Sir?" Billy joined the conversation.

"Yes, Billy?"

"Should I ask Captain Popal to attend the interview......sorry interrogation?"

"No. We'll rely on Dudley-Jones if Freed refuses to speak English. Remember we know he can, it's whether he will or not that's the problem. Is that alright with you, Lance Corporal?"

"Yes, sir. All this translating is good for keeping my language skills up."

"Glad I can be of help." Crane collected his papers, a small smile playing across his face. He then addressed the team, "Okay, dismissed. Billy and Dudley-Jones, you're with me. Let's go and see Freed."

On their way over to the guard room, Crane asked "Is the sports centre open now, Staff?"

"Yes. The area was swept again last night after Freed gave himself up. Nothing was found, so we gave the BOA the all clear and the Paralympians were back in this morning to continue with their training. At least, the ones that weren't involved in the hostage situation and taken to hospital."

"Oh God, I'd forgotten about them, are they all alright. No harm done?"

"Pretty much, sir, no physical injuries as far as we can tell."

"Good, at least things were beginning to return to normal."

Night 35

The voice filled the empty office. Crane stabbed at a key and shut it off. The lights were subdued in the main office and he only had an angle poise lamp throwing a narrow beam on his desk. He felt as though he was cocooned within the SIB offices, as if in a cave, safe from the shifting shadows outside, that held only menace. As he yet again pressed the play button for the media player on his computer, the shadowy threat gained form and once again invaded his space.

The sing song voice of Captain Faran Popal emitted from the tinny speakers on Crane's laptop. Having trouble hearing properly, Crane plugged in a set of headphones. Immediately the voice became richer and deeper. Hypnotic. Even though Crane couldn't understand the Pashtu words, there was a deeper feeling behind them derived from the softness of tone. It was as though Popal was reaching out to the suicide bomber, using his voice like a warm blanket, wrapping itself around Freed and supporting him. Encouraging him, praising him and then reeling him in. Crane stopped the player and stared into the empty office beyond his door.

Captain Edwards said this was entirely normal. That it was what Captain Popal had intended to do. Persuade the suicide bomber to give himself up without any loss of life, even Freed's own. But Crane wasn't sure. It didn't sit right with him somehow. Pressing the play button once again, Crane listened to Dudley-Jones translating as Popal sang his Pashtu song.

"Keep your eye on the bigger picture. Remember the higher goals."

Crane punched the stop key. Strange words. Why would Captain Popal encourage Freed to think about pictures and goals? What bloody bigger picture? What bloody higher goals? Was Popal sending a message to Freed, or was Crane just clutching at straws? Becoming side tracked by Dudley-Jones and what he perceived to be vital intelligence?

Crane punched play. "Allah is great. Allah is good. Allah will look after all those who are true believers and keep a place for them."

Stopping the player once again, Crane mulled over the last few phrases. At least those he could understand. The usual religious rhetoric about Allah. But then again, the phrase 'true believers' stuck out. Struck a discordant note. As Dudley-Jones intimated, true believers who were suicide bombers, just pressed the button. The whole point was martyrdom. Crane also noted that Freed said nothing throughout the whole ordeal. He simply nodded or shook his head, depending on the question. It was the same in the interview this morning. He said nothing. Spoke not a single solitary word. Crane wondered why, but had no answer. Yet.

Crane rewound the sound bite and started again. With the mint tea. He reached for his own cup, so caught up in the recording that he was surprised when he lifted it to his lips and found it wasn't mint tea but coffee. Stopping the recording he wondered what the hell the significance of the mint tea was. Or was there nothing significant about it, was he just blundering about desperate to find some meaning behind the innocuous words?

After listening to the recording one more time, Crane was no nearer figuring anything out. So he shut down the computer, left the office and walked out to his car.

The night was clear and Crane looked up at a sky filled with stars. It made him feel small. A tiny insignificant dot on the surface of the earth. The earth that must itself look like a tiny dot from any one of those stars. Whilst Crane felt overwhelmed with the vastness of the sky and the galaxy, what it didn't do was make him feel inconsequential. He knew what he was doing was important. He no longer felt like a babysitter. He might be very confused about what was going on, but he trusted his intellect, instincts and his team to help him solve the mysteries. For now the threat was over. He could go home. After visiting Tina in hospital, that was.

Day 36

Praise be to Allah and the Prophet Mohammed for showing me the way. The path. The right and true road to travel down. Praise be to their holy names.

I told you I could do it. I hope you believed me. Well, even if you didn't, if you doubted, then doubt no more. I have had nothing but congratulations from the officers of the Coldstream Guards. Obviously I had had to apologise profusely for my colleague Freed, pretend I felt bad about what had happened. Insinuate how ashamed I was that a fellow Afghan officer could do such a terrible thing. Act as if I am humiliated. That I had no indication he could do something so dreadful. I managed to show incredulity when we discussed how he must have planned the whole thing in secret, with no one any the wiser.

So I am now a trusted member of the team as I told you I would be. I managed to keep my mask in place throughout the negotiations and the ensuing melee. With the help of Allah the great one.

But I must not forget Freed. He played his part well. I will pass on my whispered congratulations to him when I am allowed access. For now your Royal Military

Police won't let me anywhere near him. But I am sure they will relax that constraint in due course. At the end of the day they won't have very much on him. Once the full facts emerge. In the meantime he has his instructions. Say nothing. Speak to no one. Offer no explanation whatsoever. Refuse to speak English. Simply pretend you cannot understand what they say.

The successful negotiation has been noted on my file and I am now destined for greatness. Destined to be a leader of men, in my beloved Afghanistan. But that is not enough for me. I do not crave the praise and acceptance of the British Army. I crave only the praise and acceptance of the Muslim nation that I represent. The glory I can bring to the name of Allah. This is my reason for living.

Soon, I will walk that particular path. And no one can stop me. Not even your redoubtable Sergeant Major Crane.

Night 36

Crane was only able to visit Tina during the early evening visiting hours in the maternity ward. A transient place, where mothers to be were waiting to go into the labour ward as their time approached, or resting after giving birth. The little ones by the side of their mother's bed in their see-through Perspex cots. As good a place as any for an enforced stay in hospital, he supposed, as there was lots of hustle and bustle to watch and new born babies to coo over.

As Crane entered the ward Tina caught sight of him. Her smile held all the warmth and encouragement he needed. Reassurance that she understood it was difficult for him to visit at any other time. No trace of petulance marred her features. He noticed that someone must had helped her wash her hair as it was hanging long and lustrous around her shoulders and she had put on a touch of makeup. Crane tried to remember a small gift each time he came to visit and so placed a mother and baby magazine in her outstretched hands.

"Oh thank you, Tom. Just what I wanted," she enthused. "The newspaper trolley only holds trashy celebrity magazines."

Crane smiled at the praise and mentally thanked Kim for her suggestion and earlier purchase of the magazine.

Leaning to kiss his wife, Crane then settled into a nearby chair, taking off his jacket and tie. He reached down to untie his shoe laces, before remembering where he was. He would love to remove his shoes and slip into a comfy pair of slippers. If only he was at home. He yearned for the stability it brought to his life. Home, with Tina waiting for him. An oasis of calm after the swirling molasses of work. Realising he was starting to view his domestic life through rose tinted glasses, he focused on the here and now. On his wife lying in a hospital bed.

"How were you?" he asked.

"Tom, I feel fine. I don't really feel ill you know. But they won't let me out. I keep asking, but….." Tina played with the edge of the sheet covering her swollen stomach.

"Don't fret about it, love. Just try and enjoy the rest."

"That's what everyone keeps telling me."

"Everyone? Who's everyone?"

"Oh, you know the staff, mum, hospital visitors."

"Hospital visitors? Who are they?" Tom feigned interest, to keep the conversation going, afraid he would fall asleep in the chair.

"Well, the hospital chaplain for one. Although as I'm not seriously ill he didn't really have much to say to me. My soul doesn't need saving before my imminent death does it?" Her laughter played a merry tune.

"No, I guess not." Crane didn't like the turn of the conversation, so quickly moved on. "Who else?"

"Oh a few ladies who come onto the wards in the afternoons. To chat to those who haven't got visitors.

To stop us feeling left out I guess." Tina's head dropped as she played with the magazine on her lap.

"And do you?"

"Do I what?"

"Feel left out?"

Raising her head, Tina looked at him and smiled. "No, I don't." She reached for his hand. "Anyway it gives me a chance to chat about babies to my heart's content. But enough about me - what's the latest from the garrison?"

Crane got to the happy ending that none of the Paralympians had suffered any lasting damage and that Captain Edwards was happy with him and Dudley-Jones's performances, then stopped speaking, slumped in his chair, stretched out his legs and stuffed his hands in his trouser pockets.

"So why don't you look happy?"

Crane lifted his chin from his chest and looked at his wife. "Happy?"

"Yes, you look very pissed off for someone that foiled an attempted suicide bomb and earned the praise of Captain Edwards." Tina tucked her loose hair behind her ears, as if pulling back a net curtain so she could see him better.

Crane put his elbows on the arms of his chair and pulled himself upright. Shaking his head he said, "I don't know. It doesn't feel finished somehow."

"Well it isn't is it? The Paralympians don't leave for another what, five days."

"Four."

"Okay four then. That's probably all it is."

The shrill bell announcing the end of visiting hours also terminated their conversation. Crane clumsily embraced his wife, kissing her as though she was a piece of fine china.

"Go on, get off home," she gently pushed him away. "I'm tired enough to sleep now anyway. So don't worry about me."

But Crane wasn't tired enough to get off home and sleep. Recounting the events of the past few days had brought back his feelings of unease. His mind was too active. He sought sanctuary in his office, with his seven white boards for company. Listening to them, trying to hear their voices and failing. So he decided to go over them one by one.

Crane pulled up a chair in front of the boards and firstly looked at the one documenting the death of Corporal Simms. Accident or murder, it made no difference, the young soldier was still dead. His body discovered within the bowels of the swimming pool complex. Nothing missing, nothing found. The only evidence just a single black hair on his clothes. Forgetting for a moment Captain Edwards's theory that it was an accident, if he took it as murder, Crane mused, the only possible motive is that the soldier saw something or someone he shouldn't have. Crane let his thoughts wander further. Someone or something that was in the wrong place. Didn't belong.

The second board was the murder of Corporal McInnes. He was definitely in the right place but at the wrong time. The military cemetery was on the guard duty roster. But he was alone, when he should have been accompanied by Corporal Cable. This one was clearly murder as his body was dragged behind a pill box. Forensics found blood and torn bits of clothing. Some of them were from McInnis himself, but there was no match to the samples from the unknown suspect. There was also something missing. His gun and live ammunition. Despite extensive searching of the cemetery they had never been found.

Crane moved his chair along to sit in front of the third board. The theft of property from the Aspire Defence stores. Why had he done that board? It wasn't a major investigation. But it was still something that had gone wrong on his watch. Something that happened whilst Team GB were on the garrison. Crane stood and took down the list of missing material. Just cleaning stuff, paper and paint brushes. Where was the list from the landscape gardening contractor? Crane couldn't remember if it had ever come into the office and made a mental note to ask Kim tomorrow.

The fourth board wasn't anything to do with theft or murder. In fact Captain Edwards had argued that it was nothing to do with anything. Apart from Crane's paranoia with the Afghan officers that was. Still, it was Crane's office so he had a board with pictures of the four officers on; their self elected leader Fahran Popal; the quiet one Dehqan Khan; the one who turned out to be a would be suicide bomber Behnam Freed and the one that supposedly lost his way on Ash Ranges, Azar Niaz.

After standing and stretching and discounting the idea of going out for a cigarette, Crane moved his chair along again and sat in front of the fifth board. The Afghan officer who went missing on Ash Ranges. Who was presently in the guard room, saying nothing. Offering no explanation whatsoever for having been found holed up with food and water. A forensic examination of his clothes had proved fruitless. The man was filthy, bringing a large part of the ranges back with him on his clothes.

Crane reluctantly turned his attention to the sixth board, the one he didn't want to face. The murder of Padam Gurung. He wasn't entirely sure why this death had affected him so badly. Considering it, he felt empathy with the old soldier's plight. The difficulties and prejudice he must have encountered whist trying to build a new life in England. What on earth possessed him to come here, Crane wondered? He was angry that the way life in England was being misrepresented to the Gurkhas back in Nepal. Angry with the so called officials, who were no better than thieves, taking money from the old soldiers for visas. He had done some research and found that unscrupulous firms were charging the old men hundreds of pounds for visas that were actually free. How could someone defraud old and vulnerable people like that? Crane shook his head in disgust. Still, turning back to the case, he found once again there was no forensic evidence of any value. It looked like the environment Padam was found in had beaten the science. Rolling around on the ground in a wooded environment had obviously dislodged any evidence. If there was any in the first place.

The final board Crane turned to was the one detailing the attempted suicide bomber. Looking closely, Crane found nothing from Bomb Disposal on the explosives used. He wondered what it was and where Freed got it. He makes another mental note to talk to Kim about it in the morning.

Crane finally succumbed to both tiredness and the need for nicotine, so pushed the chair back under a table and left the office, clicking off the lights as he went. Leaving his boards to sit in the darkness, still waiting for someone to hear their voices.

Night 37

My brothers and I continue with our mission. To take the one true path that Allah has decreed all Muslims should travel down. Niaz and Freed have played their parts well and continue to do so and will be rewarded by Allah when their time comes to stand in judgement before him.

As for Dehqan Kahn and myself, we continue with the struggle. Continue with our mission to strike against those who invade our country and force them to leave. For we Muslims must once again acquire power over the state in our country, so we can establish religious order. This religious order will then stabilise social, economic and political order. Every one of our people shall know that Allah is great. Allah is good.

As I speak, Kahn is working hard on our mission. The blood, sweat and tears he sheds will be illuminated by the brightness of our attack that will shine around the world. Leaving you infidels in no doubt that you must leave our country immediately, or risk invoking the wrath of Allah again.

And so my brothers and I will enter paradise when we die, as a reward for our actions. How do I know that? How can I be so sure? Why it is written in our holy book. Here is the verse, let me read it to you.

Verily, Allah has purchased of the believers
Their lives and their wealth
For the price of Paradise,
To fight in the way of Allah,
To kill and get killed.
It is a promise binding on the truth in the Torah,
The Gospel and the Qur'an.
Qur'an 9:11

I say to you again, we shall fight in the way of Allah, kill and be killed and our reward will be entry into Paradise when the time comes. The fight continues. You will see. It's not over yet.

Day 38

Mired in paperwork, Crane was slowly going through his in-tray. The plethora of reports, memos and notices were beginning to merge into each other and he decided he needed more coffee before he could finish the job. As he stood and stretched, a single piece of paper slid from the rickety pile on his desk and fell to the floor. Stooping to pick it up, Crane saw it was a report from Aspire Defence. Intrigued, he carried it with him through to the main office, where he found Kim in front of the white boards.

"Sir," she said, "I was just wondering if I should take these down now."

Going to stand alongside her, Crane also mused over the boards. "No, I don't think so," he said slowly. "Not just yet anyway."

"Any particular reason?" Kim blushed and quickly said, "If you don't mind me asking, sir?"

Smiling Crane answered, "No I don't mind you asking, Kim." Setting down his coffee mug and the piece of paper he was holding, he perched on the side of a desk. "It's just that I don't think it's over yet."

"What isn't, sir?"

"The threat I suppose. I can't seem to draw a line under it. At least not until the Paralympians have left the garrison."

"In another two days?"

"Yes, Kim, so keep the boards up a while longer would you?"

"Of course, sir."

Crane and Kim were still looking at the boards, both deep in thought, when Billy crashed through the door.

"Boss," he calls. "I've got it!"

"Got it?" Crane looked at Billy, who was dishevelled, with tousled hair, his face shiny with sweat.

"The smell, boss. The one I smelled under the swimming pool the night I was knocked out." Billy was jiggling up and down.

"Alright, Billy, calm down and sit down. Kim, go and get me some coffee would you and a cold drink for Sergeant Williams here."

Once everyone was settled with drinks, Billy explained. "I was passing by New Mons Barracks. The landscapers were working there, laying new turf and stuff. For some reason I stopped the car to see what they were doing. And that's when I smelled it, that strange smell. So I wandered over to one of the contractors to ask what they were doing."

"Which was?"

"Turning fertiliser into the soil to help the grass grow." Billy sat back looking very pleased with himself.

"But why would you have smelled fertilizer in a concrete structure?" Kim wanted to know. "And where would it have come from?"

"Oh shit!" The involuntary exclamation came from Crane. "I think I know" and he reached for the piece of paper he had carried into the office.

A quick skim of the contents confirmed his fears.

"The break in at Aspire Defence stores. This was the report from Ms Stone. Fertilizer was stolen from the landscape contractors who were keeping it there."

He passed the paper to Kim. Luckily neither Sergeant had the courage to ask how he got the piece of paper, nor how long he had had it. Crane remembered the time when Ms Stone arrived at his office unannounced. He was so flustered by her sexual overtures that he had completely forgotten about the paper she'd handed him.

"But there's more, sir," Billy dragged Crane's attention back to the present.

"I was walking through the RMP office after that, when I smelled paint. The barracks is being revamped and there were painters in some of the corridors. It made me realise that what I smelled was a mixture of paint and fertilizer."

"Paint and fertilizer? Are you sure?" It was Kim asking the question, turning round from updating the Aspire Defence theft board.

"Positive, Kim. The only thing I don't know is what it means."

"I think I might."

The voice at the door caused everyone to swivel round. Crane found himself staring at Dudley-Jones.

"What had you got for us?" Crane beckoned the young Lance Corporal into the office. He was holding a piece of paper in his hand.

"An intelligence report, sir. This was a transcript of a mobile phone conversation intercepted last night. I've just received it and thought it was worth bringing straight over." Dudley-Jones held out a single sheet of paper to Crane.

"Right, Lance Corporal. You know the drill." Crane handed Dudley-Jones his empty coffee mug as he moved around and sat at the nearest desk.

INTELLIGENCE REPORT
DATE: 7.08.2012
TIME: 23.30 hours
PREPARED BY: Sgt P Smith
CIRCULATION: Aldershot Intelligence Operative
Below is a transcript of a mobile telephone conversation recorded at 23:00 hours on the 6th August 2012.
PERSON 1: How is our friend?
PERSON 2: Fully recovered now, thank you.
PERSON 1: Good. I was getting concerned as I hadn't heard from you. When will he be able to leave?
PERSON 2: Tomorrow night.
PERSON 1: Excellent, I'm sure it will mean a great deal to him. Thank you for your efforts.
PERSON 2: It has been an honour, sir.
The connection was then broken. The call lasted less than 60 seconds and originated from a mobile phone in Helmand Province, Afghanistan. The receiving mobile phone was in the Aldershot/Farnborough area. At this stage no information is available on either mobile phone number, with regards to the registered user or network provider, although enquiries are ongoing.

The report did make interesting reading, Dudley-Jones isn't wrong there. Crane passed it to Billy, who after scanning through it passed it to Kim. Dudley-Jones returned with the coffee and was immediately quizzed by Crane.

"Right, Lance Corporal, take me though this."

"Yes, sir. Well the first thing to note is that the phone call and conversation was between the same two parties as the one a couple of weeks ago. Our voice analysts have confirmed that they are identical. In fact, some of the actual words are identical, but I'll get to that in a minute."

Dudley-Jones retrieved the report from Kim and put it side by side with the previous one, with the air of someone about to perform a magic trick. Trying hard to keep his face straight, Crane waited while Dudley-Jones paused theatrically.

"The first thing to note, sir, is that the first question was the same – '*how is our friend?*' That's how we realised the two conversations were related. The answer – '*fully recovered now*', makes us think they mean everything is ready. The phrase – '*when will he be able to leave*' we believe is code for the question, when will the incident occur. But the reply is the worrying thing, sir, - '*tomorrow night*'."

Growing impatient after yet another dramatic pause by the young Intelligence Operative, Crane said, "Anything else?"

"Yes, sir, the penultimate line – '*I'm sure it will mean a great deal to him*', is again a verbatim quote from the first conversation and signifies that the organisers are very pleased. The final line – '*it is an honour*' we believe has religious connotations, as though the person talking seems to realise they couldn't openly use religious rhetoric."

"Is that all?"

"Yes, sir. If there are any further conversations, I've arranged to be notified immediately."

"Well, I doubt there'll be any others, at least not until this is over. I think we're all agreed on what we're dealing with aren't we? A bomb, more than likely under the swimming pool."

Crane's gaze swept along this team. Kim looks as calm as ever, but her knuckles were white where she was still clenching the white board pen she was writing with. Billy had gone pale under his freckles and picked up his cold drink to take a large gulp. Dudley-Jones was swaying on his feet and his hand groped blindly for a chair as he sat down.

"Right, it's now 18:00 hours, this is what we'll do. Kim, find out what's happening at the swimming pool this evening, phone it through to me and also alert the Adjutant, DI Anderson and Bomb Disposal. Billy alert Staff Sergeant Jones, arrange for the RMP to lock down the garrison and then meet us at the swimming pool. Dudley-Jones, you're with me, we're off to see Captain Edwards."

Edwards was just leaving for the Officers' Mess and seemed none too pleased by the disruption to his plans.

"This better be good, Crane," he grumbled as he waved them into his office.

"Well, that depends on your point of view, sir."

"What does?"

"Well, sir, I had a very good reason for interrupting you, but I'm afraid you're not going to like it."

And Edwards didn't.

"Let me get this right, Sergeant Major. You believe there is a fertilizer bomb located in the area beneath the swimming pool."

"Yes, sir. Made from the stolen fertilizer and ammunition from Corporal McInnes' weapon."

"Which is going to be detonated tonight?"

"Yes, sir. According to the intelligence report."

"So what's the smell of paint all about?" Edwards rose to pace the small space behind his desk.

"Well, sir, as we've never found the bomb, it must be disguised somehow. Placed there and then somehow painted over. I can't dismiss the fact that Billy smelled both paint and fertilizer."

"And what have you done so far?"

Crane explained his earlier instructions to Kim and Billy.

"Very well, Crane, get over there and sort it out. Try and find this bloody bomb. Dismissed."

Crane and Dudley-Jones rose to leave. They were nearly out of the door when Edwards called, "Oh and, Crane?"

"Sir?"

"You'd better go via the armoury."

Night 38

The temperature under the swimming pool was decidedly chilly, but Crane felt cold sweat sticking his shirt to his back. The large grey space echoed with noises. Water grumbled along pipes as pumps churned it round and round, trapping it in an everlasting cycle; sucked from the pool, along a pipe, through a filter, heated and then back into the swimming pool. The voices of the disabled athletes upstairs in the pool, who were being evacuated, echo strangely. Warped and distorted, fading in and out, with the occasional scream piercing through the melee. Footsteps scraped and scuffled, as though a swarm of rats were down there with him, all wearing hobnailed boots.

Crane's hands were sore, his finger tips close to bleeding from countless passes over the gritty concrete walls of the massive structure. A finger tip search was necessary. They couldn't risk poking the walls, resulting in an unplanned explosion.

Crane was convinced the bomb was in here somewhere. Hidden. Possibly painted over. He wondered if the rest of the team thought him mad - as Captain Edwards had done on many occasions. But still, here they all were, carrying out his instructions, the brave lads from Bomb Disposal and the Royal Military Police. He daren't think that the bomb might explode before they find it. That thought was pushed far back in his mind. Along with his guilty pin and worries about Tina. Will she have the baby while he's entombed down here? Will he make it out alive to see her and his son? Please God let that be the case he silently pleaded. Crane could only hope that the evacuation of the Paralympians was going well and that everyone would get out before the bomb exploded. He was stunned when Kim told him there was a full scale night practice in the swimming pool. In preparation for the real event. So not only were all the swimmers there, but all the other disabled athletes as well, making up the audience.

"Fuck!" Billy's shout could be heard over the clatter of his torch as it hits the floor.

"Billy!" Crane called, "Are you alright?"

"Yes, sir. Over here, sir."

Following the direction of the voice, Crane arrived at Billy's side to find him cradling his right hand, which was bleeding profusely.

"Caught my hand on a nail or something, sir."

"Where?"

"Just here on the palm."

"For God's sake, I meant where on the wall?"

"Oh sorry, sir. Quite high up, about here I think."

Billy passed his torch beam over the offending piece of wall. That no longer seemed to look like a wall, as it was sagging and bagging and threatening to fall down. An undulating grey landscape.

"Well done, Billy, I think you've found it." Crane reached for the wall at the point where Billy cut his hand, his finger tips scrabbling against the wall, finally curling around paper. Taking a deep breath, he pulled. The paper came away easily, ripping through, as though he was pulling away old wallpaper. The tear revealed the top of a sack, with wire visible from a small opening in it. The wire then disappeared back underneath the rest of the paper wall.

"That'll do for now, Billy. Round up the others and get Bomb Disposal. Give them directions to the bomb. Then go outside. I'll wait here for them. Oh, and get that hand seen to."

The speed at which Billy retreated showed how frightened he must be. Crane took several deep breaths, wiping his sore hands along his trousers, trying to dislodge some of the grit embedded in them. He played his torch beam over the paper wall. No wonder they hadn't seen it. Someone had done a good job of hiding the bomb in plain sight. Right under their noses. Probably stacking the sacks flat against the wall all connected together to whatever trigger they were using. Finally, covering it all in grey painted paper. All the equipment the terrorists need stolen from the stores on the garrison.

The clatter behind him heralded the arrival of Bomb Disposal and Crane dutifully followed their shouted order, to get the hell out of there.

As he emerged from the underground hell hole, Crane squinted as the bright lights hurt his eyes. He was in the main foyer of the sports centre, now crammed with athletes, helpers, wheelchairs, frames and walking sticks. RMP lads were gently urging everyone forwards through the wide glass doors that were fully open. All the flood lights had been turned on outside and vehicles were circling the car park, stopping in front of the steps to load passengers, before gliding forwards towards the safety of the wider garrison. As one vehicle slid away, it was immediately replaced by another. And so the evacuation continued. Those who could walk were being shepherded away in a different direction, to keep the narrow access roadway clear for vehicles. A fleet of ambulances waited at a safe distance, to help with any casualties. Alongside them were several fire tenders. Despite his worry, Crane couldn't help feeling a sense of pride at the well organised military operation.

Looking across the car park from his position on the steps, he saw Derek Anderson having a conversation with Billy. After making a quick call on his mobile, Crane hurried over to them.

"Glad you could make it, Derek," Crane said as he stopped in front of Anderson.

"Never one to miss a good party," grinned Anderson. "Billy here tells me you found the bomb."

"Not me, Derek, it was Billy catching his hand on the wall that nailed it."

"Very funny, sir," smiled Billy ruefully, cradling his bad hand as if to protect it.

"Is your hand sorted?"

"Yes, sir, I've had it cleaned and bandaged. They want me to go to hospital for stitches and a tetanus jab, but I said I'd go later. When it's all over."

"Fair play, Billy. So, Derek, everything organised from your end."

"Of course, Crane. The local police are with your RMP on the barriers explaining about the lock down, keeping everyone out and of course, keeping the press at bay. The fire brigade are here and the ambulances. We're all getting rather good at this aren't we? What's this, the second time in two weeks?"

Crane nodded in agreement and took his cigarettes out of his pocket. But his hands shook as he tried to light one, so Anderson gently took the lighter from him and held out the flame with a steady hand. Billy suddenly found the ground behind him very interesting. After taking a few deep drags and calming himself Crane asked, "Billy, have you spoken to Kim?"

"Yes, sir, she's fine. Liaising with the BOA, the Commanding Officer and fielding press calls. Oh and by the way Bomb Disposal reported in. The trigger for the bomb is a mobile phone. They think they can defuse it, but it may take some time."

"Right, it looks like everything's under control, so I'm off."

"Off?" Anderson had spoken, but both men looked equally astounded.

"Yes, I think I know how the bomber gained access underneath the pool, so I'm going to check it out." Crane ground out his cigarette and walked off. He tried to march, but it came out more as a stumble, so he slowed down, trying to settle his ragged breathing, the regular pacing helping to calm him.

Arriving at the side door that served as a maintenance access, Crane tried it and found it unlocked. Again. Guessing that the bomber wouldn't be in the building anymore, but probably used the side door to gain access earlier when he armed the bomb, Crane placed his back against it, looking outwards across the wide swathe of grass. He caught sight of a small thicket, from which a weak light briefly glowed and then dissolved. Wanting another cigarette, but not daring to give away his position, Crane pushed the nicotine craving away and struck out for the thicket.

Day 39

"Good morning, Sergeant Major." The man who owned the voice stepped out of the thicket.

"Is it?" Crane replied. The identity of the man no surprise to Crane, who hadn't been able to get those trigger phrases out of his head, '*keep your eye on the bigger picture, remember the higher goals*'; ever since the fake suicide bomb.

"What?"

"Is it good or is it morning, or both, Captain?"

"Very droll, Crane." Captain Popal pulled his mobile phone out of his pocket and started to turn it over in his hand. In his other hand, he held a gun. Aimed at Crane. "Both, actually. Things are going very well at the moment although somewhat delayed because of your frustrating lock down. But no matter, I managed to get out of New Mons Barracks in the end. Also according to my watch, it's just after midnight, so it must be morning."

"So, what exactly is going well at the moment, sir?" Crane tried not to stumble over the word 'sir'. Not wanting to use the address, but needing to show the Afghan respect. Also, not mentioning the fact that

Crane himself engineered the opportunity for Captain Popal to leave New Mons Barracks, despite the lock down. A quick call made to Staff Sergeant Jones after Crane found the bomb and stumbled into the foyer, had set it up. A fake message to the Afghan officers, giving them permission to leave the barracks.

"I think we both know the answer to that question, Crane."

"In that case, may I ask another question, sir?" Crane continued to be respectful.

"Very well." Captain Popal looked down at the mobile phone in his hand and pressed a button, the light from the display throwing his face into relief.

"Why?"

Popal pressed a second button and then looked up at Crane. "You mean you don't know?"

"Well, obviously I have inkling, but I'd rather hear it from you, sir."

"Why for Islam of course. For the glory of Allah! Surely you can see that."

Popal pushed a third button and Crane tried to remember how many digits there were in a mobile phone number. He couldn't conjure that piece of information up from his tired brain, so he pretended Popal was pressing the buttons to call his own number. Three so far so 077.

"Ah, so that's it," Crane replied.

"Of course it is, you stupid man. What other reason can there be?"

Popal stabbed a fourth button. 0775 recited Crane in his head.

"So, tell me, Captain, how exactly would blowing up a building full of innocent athletes, disabled ones at that, be for the glory of Allah? Some of those athletes are disabled ex …"

As Crane realised one of the reasons behind the attack, it rendered him speechless. Adrenaline coursed through his body, increasing his heart rate and breathing. He wanted to run at the terrorist, knock him to the ground, beat him to a pulp, but knew he couldn't take the risk. Not with Popal's gun still aimed at him. So he stood there, reigning in his anger, his clenched jaw causing the sinews in his neck to stand out like piano wire.

After stabbing another digit, Popal lifted his head.

"Were you going to say ex-forces, Sergeant Major?" Popal scrutinised Crane. "I thought so." Popal smiled his smarmy smile. "We only managed to maim them first time round with the IEDs. This time I'll finish the job. That should send a signal to the high command of your infidel army that we will not tolerate your presence in our country." He jabbed at another number, to make his point and then brandished the phone towards Crane.

Shit. 077516. Crane realised he was running out of both time and numbers. "But I thought we were saving your country from terrorist rule, Captain. Aren't we?"

"You just don't seem to get it do you?" Popal stabbed angrily at his phone. "We don't want you there. We can sort things out ourselves. Bring the people together under the rule of Islam and Sharia law."

Stab.

Crane added another two numbers. 07751634. Three left. The cold night air tugged at his sweat drenched shirt, bringing Crane's body temperature down and causing him to shiver.

"And your army? Will you be able to control them as well?" he asked Popal.

"Why are you people so stupid?" Popal was shouting now. "The new leaders of our army, people like me and my brothers, will succour our soldiers, ensuring they are taught loyalty to Islam and they will become defenders of our country, rising up against the evil marauders - forcing you from our sacred land." Spittle was flying from Popal's lips and he wiped his hand across his mouth before pressing another button.

077516343 Crane recited in his head, pulling his jacket around him, exaggerating his shivering and slipping one hand inside it. His fingers felt his clammy shirt sticking to him and then the cold metal of his gun in its holster under his arm. Crane curled his hand around the butt and left it there as though keeping himself warm.

"A noble cause, Captain. But don't you think killing innocent people will turn the world against you? Wouldn't it be better to foster peace and understanding?"

"Peace and understanding? Are you mad?" Popal once again dropped his head to his phone and stabbed. "What peace and understanding did your army show us when you invaded our country. None. Allah is great. Allah is good. His teachings tell us what to do. To kill the infidels. Banish all non-believers from our lands."

Stab.

Taking a deep breath Crane went through his phone number. 0775163433. One digit left. Shifting slightly to steady his stance, Crane slowly removed his arm from underneath his jacket. The barrel of the gun caught the dim light from the mobile phone's display. Cold unforgiving steel pointing at Captain Popal.

"I'm sorry, sir, but I can't let you do it. I can't let you detonate the bomb."

Popal stared at the weapon in Crane's hand then lowering his head stabbed the last number. Placing his thumb over the green call button, he held out the phone towards Crane and spoke his last words, "You can't stop me."

Crane fired first. A head shot. The phone fell out of Popal's hand and lay in the grass between them as the Afghan crumbled to the floor. The display still brightly lit. Crane lowered his gun, closes his eyes, mumbled "Dear God, no," and waited for the explosion.

Looking at Popal's mobile phone lying on the grass near him, Crane could see the display showing the call had been made. But there was no explosion. Not understanding, Crane pulled his own mobile from his pocket. Billy answered on the first ring.

"Boss, was that you?"

"Who else would it be, Billy?"

"Sorry, sir, we're just worried. We heard a shot and….."

"Yes, well, that was me. I've just shot Captain Popal."

"Just shot him? Why? What happened?"

"Billy, shut up and round up the team. I'm in the small thicket, directly opposite the side door of the sports centre. Oh and, Billy, what about the bomb?"

"Bomb disposal disarmed it just a few minutes ago."

Closing his phone, Crane's legs gave way and he sank to the ground and waited for Billy.

Night 39

Crane had spent the last twenty or so hours on the base, partly because of the lock down and partly because he couldn't leave until he'd completed his reports and been interviewed. He had, after all, shot a man. An officer at that. Who was also a terrorist. A terrorist who, thank God, had failed.

Now all Crane wanted to do was to see Tina and then go home. But Edwards had still not given him permission to leave the base. In fact no one had been given permission. The whole team were still on site. Listening to Edwards drone on in the team debriefing.

"Taking everything into consideration," Captain Edwards said, "you've done a good job, Crane. Although I think it's a shame the Afghan officer is dead, but at least the final one of the four, the quiet one Behnam Khan, is now in custody."

Without his leader, the man had fallen to pieces and told them everything. How he was tasked with the job of building the bomb and then covering it over with paper and painting it grey. He explained how Popal meticulously planned the operations, before unveiling his strategy to his three fellow officers. They in turn were so frightened of him that they had no option but to carry out his orders. After all, each man had family back in Afghanistan. And everyone knew what happened if you didn't obey orders. Your family would be hurt, or worse, disappear forever. Your home would be destroyed. Your life effectively over. So they had no choice. A sort of kill or be killed. Either option horrendous.

Once Kahn started talking, Crane had the ammunition he needed to use against the other two Afghanis still in custody. Freed said his part in the plan had been organised by Popal as well. He was to pretend he had a bomb strapped to him and stay in the foyer of the sports centre, until further orders. The mug of mint tea being the trigger, to let him know the ordeal would soon be over. The phrases Crane worried over were, of course, the signal to give himself up. Popal assured Freed the British Army would had very little to charge him with, once it was discovered the suicide vest was a fake. Dudley-Jones was especially pleased about that confession, his point about suicide bombers pressing the button immediately, having been validated.

As for Niaz, who supposedly got lost on Ash Ranges, he was also singing like the proverbial canary, insisting that Popal killed the old Gurkha, Padam Gurung. Popal told him where to hide and even provided food and drink to keep him going until he was found. Crane didn't had any evidence either way about which man committed the murder, so Captain Edwards wanted to give Niaz the benefit of the doubt. One officer to another. Jesus Christ. The officer's code of honour even extending to the Afghan Army. Another indication to Crane that as his army career progressed, he should stay as an NCO and not take a commission.

If he stayed in the army that was. If Tina came round to his way of thinking.

One last piece of information Crane was particularly pleased about was that Captain Popal told Kahn he had killed both Corporal Simms and Corporal McInnes. Corporal Simms because he had inadvertently seen Popal casing out the under belly of the swimming pool and McInnes killed for his ammunition, which was needed for the bomb. The weapon was incidental.

Edwards at last ended the debriefing. He had finished proudly stalking up and down the office like a peacock, as though he had had something to do with it all. Crane tried hard not to shake his head at the man's arrogance and closed his eyes to shut out the display. As a result, he isn't really listening and was falling asleep when Edwards called his name.

"Sergeant Major!" Edward's abrupt shout jerked Crane awake.

"Sorry, sir, did you say something?" Crane rubbed his eyes, then his beard.

"Yes, Crane, I was trying to get your attention, to tell you I received a call about half an hour ago from the hospital. You are to report to the Maternity Ward immediately. Your wife's in labour."

Crane sat up in his chair. Then realised he could stand. "Yes, sir, thank you, sir," he gabbled.

"Why don't you let Billy drive you, Crane? You look done in. And Billy had the advantage of a few hours sleep on the sofa. So off you go the both of you."

Not wanting to waste time saying anything else, Crane ran for the door, with Billy close behind. Outside the night air revived him and he stopped to light a cigarette, throwing Billy his car keys.

During the short journey, Crane tried to calm down,

but his hands were shaking. After he finished smoking, he made an attempt to tidy himself, but gave up. It didn't really matter what he looked like. He just needed to get there. He couldn't let Tina down and miss the birth. She'd never forgive him. Come to that, he'd never forgive himself. Or the army.

Billy drove fast, but safely and deposited Crane at the door to the maternity wing. Crane told Billy to take his car back to the house in Ash and said he'd get a taxi back home later. Afterwards. After he had spent some time with his wife and son. As soon as the car stopped, Crane was out - running for the entrance.

Day 40

A nurse on duty recognised him and called, "Your wife's in Labour Room 9, Sergeant Major. It's all right, no need to rush. The baby's not here yet."

Crane paused outside the room. He had to be strong now, for Tina's sake. She needed his support and anyway they still had things to sort out. A cry from the inside the room had Crane panicking and he pushed open the door so hard it slammed back against the wall. Tina was lying on the bed, her face distorted with pain. As Crane watched, she grabbed the gas and air mask lying by her side and breathed deeply. Once she'd had enough, she dropped the mask and looked up, a wide smile breaking across her face.

"Oh, Tom, thank God. I was afraid they wouldn't let you leave the garrison."

"It's alright, Tina, I'm here now."

Crane moved to his wife's side, tenderly pushing the damp hair off her face before kissing her. Then he grabbed her hand.

"I've been watching the television," she said. "It's been all over the news channels about the bomb. But of course the reporters weren't allowed onto the garrison.

They were reporting from outside, against one of the barriers. It was awful, but I couldn't stop watching. It was my only way of knowing what was going on, although they weren't saying much of anything really. I just thought that if I kept watching I might see you. Just a glimpse. Anything."

Tears filled her eyes and he squeezed her hand. "But you knew I was fine. I called as soon as I got back to barracks."

"I know, I got your message. But I couldn't really believe it until I'd seen you."

"Jesus, Tina, I'm sorry you had to go through that alone." Crane kissed his wife's hand.

"Oh but I wasn't alone, Tom."

But before she could tell him who'd been keeping her company, a contraction hit.

Once she recovered she continued, "You know I told you about the hospital visitors?" Crane nodded. "Well, one of them was Derek Anderson's wife, Jean."

"And?"

"And she's lovely. We, um, had a few good heart to heart chats."

Crane's stomach did a flip. "About?"

"About being a policeman's wife. It doesn't seem much different to being a SIB investigator's wife."

Crane increased the pressure on his wife's hand. Willing her to say the words he needed to hear. The only way he could communicate with her as he was afraid to speak.

"She helped me understand," Tina continued, "that I had to let you go."

"Let me go?" Crane's voice was like a rusty saw.

"Yes, let you go and do what you had to do. Find a way to live with the worry and loneliness when you're away. She said that maybe I shouldn't be so dismissive of the army way of life. To think about moving back to the garrison and joining the support network of the other wives."

Crane had to clear his throat before he spoke, "Do you think you can do that?"

But he had to wait for his answer, as Tina rode the next contraction, gulping deeply on the gas and air, Crane standing by, helpless.

"Yes, I do," she said once she could speak again. "I'm sorry I was angry when you talked about moving back to the garrison, so I would have a community to be involved in. I was so determined to be independent, but now I realise I don't have to be. There's nothing wrong in asking for help when I need it. So, I'm going to embrace the army, and the military way of life, instead of pushing it away."

"Oh God, Tina, thank you. You don't know how much it means to me to hear you say that." Then sheer relief made Crane laugh, "But it looks like the only pushing you're going to be doing at the moment, is pushing that baby out!"

Continue reading for an excerpt of the next Sgt Major Crane novel in the series, Honour Bound.

Honour Bound

Sgt Major Crane is unwillingly dragged into an Aldershot Police investigation after a young girl is raped and murdered, because witnesses describe the attacker as a young soldier. Can Crane stop the rapist before he strikes again, whilst simultaneously working on his own case - the repeated rape and bullying of a soldier on Aldershot Garrison?

Rape

Rape is not merely violation with a sexual reference, it is much more. It is an assault by intimate physical violence, it is extreme aggressive bullying and an act of oppression. It is a crime where the victims are often found guilty by their peers and carries a lifelong stigma.

Anon

1

At 11pm, Saturday night, Sgt Major Crane was on the streets of Aldershot. Flashing blue lights ripped through the night, bizarrely revolving in time to music throbbing out of the open pub doors. Young men were shouting lewd remarks across the street to clutches of girls helping each other totter home on their impossibly high heels. The local kebab shop was doing a roaring trade in food purchased on a whim and then discarded after the first bite. Greasy wrapping paper spreads like confetti around the overflowing refuse bins.

Crane spotted a body sprawled half in the road and half on the kerb. The girl's dress, if you could call it that, Crane thought, was hitched up around her hips showing flesh spilling out of a tiny thong. A pool of vomit lay close to her face. Crane averted his gaze and nodded to a young woman police officer who went to her aid. She coaxed the girl upright, removing her shoes when it became obvious she couldn't balance on her cheap Jimmy Choo rip offs. After a quick conversation she pointed her in the direction of the traffic lights at the bottom of the road. The girl drifted away, shoes in hand, but no handbag or coat. Crane knew there was no point in calling her a taxi as the drivers won't take those likely to throw up in their car. Crane wondered if she had her house keys, but then decided that as the girl was clearly too far gone to care, why should he? He found it hard to muster sympathy for her plight. After all, as far as he was concerned, it was self inflicted. He shook his head in dismay, at the lack of self respect displayed by the young people around him.

Crane lit a cigarette and wandered over to DI Anderson of the local Aldershot Police. "Jesus, Derek, what a bloody mess."

For once Crane was referring to something other than Anderson's grey wispy hair.

"Tell me about it, Crane. This bloody lot costs us a fortune, what with extra officers on the beat and overtime. Anyway, what are you doing with a cigarette in your hand? I thought you were going to give up when the baby was born?"

"Well, you know how it is. I've cut down a lot though, no smoking at home, that sort of thing."

"What does Tina say about that?"

"Nothing, as long as I don't smoke around the baby. That's her main concern at the moment. The baby." Crane took a long noisy drag on his cigarette.

"Well, it will be. Feeling a bit left out are you?"

Crane didn't answer the question, choosing instead to grind his cigarette out under his shoe. "Right, I'm off now. Are we agreed that the problem here is booze not drugs?"

"Definitely. There are always a few tablets floating around, but nothing serious. Most of the kids just do booze. I don't think they can afford both."

"Okay, I'll report back to Captain Edwards on Monday and hopefully I won't have to do another Saturday night stint here. Bloody idiots, I don't know how you stand it."

Crane nodded his head at the police officers still dealing with the sea of humanity breaking out of the pub doors in waves.

"Oh, right, so you don't get drunk then?" Anderson snorted. "What about all your ceremonial dinners? I hear they disintegrate into wild nights once you're all tanked up."

"Maybe they do, Derek. The difference is, we keep it on the Garrison and the wives dress like women not whores."

Crane turned and marched off in the direction of his car, leaving the destruction behind him, not noticing Anderson's smile.

2

The wailing cut through Crane's dream like a knife, plunging him awake, as though he had been ducked into a freezing cold bath. Instinct took over and within seconds he was out of bed and at his son's side. Picking up the soaking baby from the cot, he held him close, while they both calm down. He was going to had to stop reacting like that, he knew, but well, it was his military training. At the first scream, his instincts take over and he's in the other room before conscious thought kicks in.

"You beat me to it again then," Tina's eyes were glazed with exhaustion and she leaned on the side of the bedroom door, trying to push her greasy dishevelled long black hair off her wan face. The baggy t-shirt she sleeps in, failing to hide the sagging flesh around her waist and stomach, left over from her pregnancy.

"Sorry, I just…sorry." Crane didn't know what else to say to make the situation any better, so settled for, "Look, you sort yourself out and I'll clean him up and bring him through in a minute," falling back on his Army training, making sure everything was in order. At six thirty in the morning he simply couldn't deal with emotional stuff.

Tina nodded and turned to go into the bathroom.

Crane thought she looked too exhausted to even manage a conversion.

As he changed his son's nappy he noticed the once organised nursery was a mess. After they'd decorated the small room, Crane put shelves up over the changing table to hold all the baby paraphernalia, so everything was on hand for Tina. But his system didn't work unless items were put back in their correct place and so instead of being a symphony of order, it had become a discord of disorder. The same was true of the rest of the room. Drawers were half closed with baby clothes peeping from them, the small wardrobe doors were swinging open and in the rubbish bin were too many used disposable nappies in sacks. Glancing at the clock on the wall, he thought he should just have time to tidy up and restock the shelves before he went to work. Now they had moved back onto Aldershot Garrison and rented out the house they owned in Ash, it only took a few minutes for Crane to reach Provost Barracks, where the Branch were based.

Once Daniel was clean and dry, yet still gulping back sobs and trying to stuff his fists into his mouth as though they'd provide the nourishment he needed, Crane carried the baby through to the bedroom. Whilst he was happily feeding, Crane had a quick shower, made coffee and then tidied up the nursery. When he popped his head back into the bedroom mother and son were sleeping. Deciding to leave them well alone, Crane went back downstairs, leaving a note for Tina, before heading out.

Their Army quarter was a fairly new link-detached house, the small estate built to resemble a civvy housing estate, rather than the bleak council estate type of older Garrison properties. Crane had ignored jibes of 'lucky sod' and 'do you had to be in the Branch to get one of those then?' The houses were prized amongst the ranks and Crane's neighbours were of the same standing in the Army – Sergeants and Warrant Officers only. The Army doing their usual trick of keeping each rank separate as much as possible.

Tina was very upset about leaving their lovely old Victorian semi in Ash, but the budget just hadn't added up. Without her salary, they couldn't keep up the mortgage payments, feed and clothe themselves and buy all the necessary baby things. So, as they'd got a good long term rental, they moved back onto the Garrison. Crane hoped Tina would embrace Army life more than she had at the moment. Perhaps she would once the baby was a bit older. As it was, he didn't think she was coping, but that was a problem for another day. For now he had to concentrate on his report to his superior, Captain Edwards, about his findings on Saturday night.

As Crane returned from the meeting later that morning, Sgt Kim Weston, the SIB Office Manager called him over.

"Sir, I've had a call from DI Anderson. He wants you to go over to Aldershot Police Station."

"Any idea why Kim?"

"He asked that you go as soon you were out of your meeting. He has a possible new case, but wouldn't give me any details." Kim's uniform, hair and desk were as pristine as ever and she was reading the message from her ever present notebook. Her long blond hair was scraped back from her face and tied neatly in a bun at the nape of her neck.

"Thanks, Kim, in that case you're with me, Billy."

"Boss," Sgt Billy Williams said, grabbing his suit jacket from the back of his chair, as they went to the car.

The short drive, along Queens Avenue, down Hospital Hill, and finally circumventing Aldershot town up towards the police station, only took about five minutes. But it took just as long once they arrived, for Crane to find a parking space in the overcrowded car park.

As Billy and Crane got out of the car, the cold early October wind rushed through the tunnel of walkways leading to the town centre, tugging at their clothes and hair. Crane's close cropped dark hair didn't move, but Billy's shock of blond hair fell over his forehead. One final huff of wind pushed them through the front door and they arrived, amid a swirl of leaves and debris, in the foyer of Aldershot Police Station. They showed their passes to the bored Desk Sergeant and were allowed through to CID.

"Well, if it isn't the Men in Black," DI Anderson called to Crane and Billy as they reached his office door. Anderson's joke was wearing a bit thin as far as Crane was concerned. It was a reference to the fact that Branch investigators didn't wear Army uniform and so Crane and Billy had swopped one uniform for another. They both wore dark suits and white shirts, normally sporting Regimental ties. The only concession being short sleeved shirts in the summer and long sleeved ones in the winter.

"Ha ha, Derek, very droll," said Crane as he brushed some shrivelled brown leaves from his hair. "So what have you got for us?"

"Not a very nice case, I'm afraid. Come on in, I've got copies of the paperwork for you."

Crane and Billy squeezed into Anderson's office, which looked as though the wind from downstairs had been playing havoc in it. Billy stood by the door as there was only one free chair which Crane took; the other one being buried under piles of files. The waste paper basket sported a decorative ring of crumpled paper. Derek himself looked like he'd had an argument with the icy blast and the blast won. His prematurely grey wispy hair, which was normally wrapped around his bald spot, was standing on end. His jacket was discarded on the floor and his once clean tie was loosely tied around a collar frayed from use. However, many an Aldershot villain, to their detriment, had mistaken his sloppy appearance as a reflection of his work.

"I'm afraid we've got a rather disturbing case of rape and murder, Crane," Anderson explained. "A young girl, Becca Henderson, was attacked on Saturday night. It seems she met a boy in The Goose pub, had her drink spiked and was then taken back to her own flat, where she was raped and murdered." Anderson handed over the file and Crane flipped through it with Billy looking over his shoulder.

"Was a full rape kit examination done?" Crane asked.

"Yes, during the autopsy yesterday. Things are a bit quiet over at Frimley Park Hospital at the moment, so they did it straight away. Forensics went over her flat, but there's nothing of any help so far. Not even a bloody fingerprint. This one was definitely premeditated. He coldly picked her out, picked her up and then drugged her. He had the audacity to tell her friends he would help her get safely back to her flat, but once there he raped then killed her, all without leaving anything behind."

"Well," Crane said, handing the file over his shoulder to Billy, "it's very sad and all that, but look at what the girl was wearing." Crane was referring to the crime scene photographs. "Look at her clothes. They barely covered her body. She may as well have been naked. She might as well have had a red light shining above her head, for God's sake, telling any bloke that fancied a bit, that she was available."

"Jesus, Crane, that's harsh. The girl didn't ask to be raped and killed," Anderson looked aghast.

"I'm not saying she did, Derek, but I was with you out there on Saturday night, if you remember and none of the girls acted as though they had one bit of self restraint. They put themselves into vulnerable situations without a second thought. Anyway, what's it got to do with us? By the sounds of it, it could have been anyone."

"Because one witness, the girl's best friend, reckons the bloke who did it was a squaddie," snapped Anderson.

That shut Crane up and wiped the smirk off Billy's face.

■■■

Honour Bound is now available from Amazon

Meet the Author

I do hope you've enjoyed 40 Days 40 Nights. If so, perhaps you would be kind enough to post a review on Amazon. Reviews really do make all the difference to authors and it is great to get feedback from you, the reader.

If this is the first of my novels you've read, you may be interested in the other Sgt Major Crane books, following Tom Crane and DI Anderson as they take on the worst crimes committed in and around Aldershot Garrison. At the time of writing there are six Sgt Major Crane crime thrillers. In order, they are: Steps to Heaven, 40 Days 40 Nights, Honour Bound, Cordon of Lies, Regenerate and Hijack.

Past Judgment is the first in a new series. It is a spin-off from the Sgt Major Crane novels and features Emma Harrison from Hijack and Sgt Billy Williams of the Special Investigations Branch of the Royal Military Police. At the time of writing the second book, Mortal Judgment has just been released. Look out for more adventures from Billy and Emma in the Judgment series in the near future. All my books are available on Amazon.

You can keep in touch through my website http://www.wendycartmell.webs.com where you can sign up to join my mailing list and in return get a free ebook! Everyone who signs up gets a free copy of Who's Afraid Now (kindle or pdf) a 10,000 word story which is a prequel to Hijack. Let me know which format you'd like and I'll email it to you, as a bonus for signing up. I'm also on Twitter @wendycartmell and can be contacted directly by email at: w_cartmell@hotmail.com

Printed in Great Britain
by Amazon